12/18/15
$7.99
B+T

TARGET ENGAGED

M.L. BUCHMAN

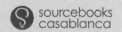

sourcebooks
casablanca

Published by Sourcebooks Casablanca, an imprint of Sourcebooks, Inc.
P.O. Box 4410, Naperville, Illinois 60567-4410
(630) 961-3900
Fax: (630) 961-2168
www.sourcebooks.com

Printed and bound in Canada.
MBP 10 9 8 7 6 5 4 3 2 1

Chapter 1

CARLA ANDERSON ROLLED UP TO THE LOOMING STORM-fence gate on her brother's midnight-blue Kawasaki Ninja 1000 motorcycle. The pounding of the engine against her sore butt emphasized every mile from Fort Carson in Colorado Springs, Colorado, home of the 4th Infantry and hopefully never again the home of Sergeant Carla Anderson. The bike was all she had left of Clay, other than a folded flag, and she was here to honor that.

If this was the correct "here."

A small guard post stood by the gate into a broad, dusty compound. It looked deserted and she didn't see even a camera.

This *was* Fort Bragg, North Carolina. She knew that much. Two hundred and fifty square miles of military installation, not counting the addition of the neighboring Pope Army Airfield.

She'd gotten her Airborne parachute training here and had never even known what was hidden in this remote corner. Bragg was exactly the sort of place where a tiny, elite unit of the U.S. military could disappear—in plain sight.

This back corner of the home of the 82nd Airborne was harder to find than it looked. What she could see of the compound through the fence definitely ranked "worst on base."

The setup was totally whacked.

Standing outside the fence at the guard post she could see a large, squat building across the compound. The gray concrete building was incongruously cheerful with bright pink roses along the front walkway—the only landscaping visible anywhere. More recent buildings—in better condition only because they were newer—ranged off to the right. She could breach the old fence in a dozen different places just in the hundred-yard span she could see before it disappeared into a clump of scrub and low trees drooping in the June heat.

Wholly indefensible.

There was no way that this could be the headquarters of the top combat unit in any country's military.

Unless this really was their home, in which case the indefensible fence—inde-fence-ible?—was a complete sham designed to fool a sucker. She'd stick with the main gate.

She peeled off her helmet and scrubbed at her long brown hair to get some air back into her scalp. Guys always went gaga over her hair, which was a useful distraction at times. She always wore it as long as her successive commanders allowed. Pushing the limits was one of her personal life policies.

She couldn't help herself. When there was a limit, Carla always had to see just how far it could be nudged. Surprisingly far was usually the answer. Her hair had been at earlobe length in Basic. By the time she joined her first forward combat team, it brushed her jaw. Now it was down on her shoulders. It was actually something of a pain in the ass at this length—another couple inches before it could reliably ponytail—but she did like having the longest hair in the entire unit.

Carla called out a loud "Hello!" at the empty compound shimmering in the heat haze.

No response.

Using her boot in case the tall chain-link fence was electrified, she gave it a hard shake, making it rattle loudly in the dead air. Not even any birdsong in the oppressive midday heat.

A rangy man in his late forties or early fifties, his hair half gone to gray, wandered around from behind a small shack as if he just happened to be there by chance. He was dressed like any off-duty soldier: worn khaki pants, a black T-shirt, and scuffed Army boots. He slouched to a stop and tipped his head to study her from behind his Ray-Bans. He needed a haircut and a shave. This was not a soldier out to make a good first impression.

"Don't y'all get hot in that gear?" He nodded to indicate her riding leathers without raking his eyes down her frame, which was both unusual and appreciated.

"Only on warm days," she answered him. It was June in North Carolina. The temperature had crossed ninety hours ago and the air was humid enough to swim in, but complaining never got you anywhere.

"What do you need?"

So much for the pleasantries. "Looking for Delta."

"Never heard of it," the man replied with a negligent shrug. But something about how he did it told her she was in the right place.

"Combat Applications Group?" Delta Force had many names, and they certainly lived to "apply combat" to a situation. No one on the planet did it better.

His next shrug was eloquent.

Delta Lesson Number One: *Folks on the inside of*

the wire didn't call it Delta Force. It was CAG or "The Unit." She got it. Check. Still easier to think of it as Delta though.

She pulled out her orders and held them up. "Received a set of these. Says to show up here today."

"Let me see that."

"Let me through the gate and you can look at it as long as you want."

"Sass!" He made it an accusation.

"Nope. Just don't want them getting damaged or lost maybe by accident." She offered her blandest smile with that.

"They're that important to you, girlie?"

"Yep!"

He cracked what might have been the start of a grin, but it didn't get far on that grim face. Then he opened the gate and she idled the bike forward, scuffing her boots through the dust.

From this side she could see that the chain link was wholly intact. There was a five-meter swath of scorched earth inside the fence line. Through the heat haze, she could see both infrared and laser spy eyes down the length of the wire. And those were only the defenses she could see. So...a very *not* inde-fence-ible fence. Absolutely the right place.

When she went to hold out the orders, he waved them aside.

"Don't you want to see them?" This had to be the right place. She was the first woman in history to walk through The Unit's gates by order. A part of her wanted the man to acknowledge that. Any man. A Marine Corps marching band wouldn't have been out of order.

She wanted to stand again as she had on that very first day, raising her right hand. "I, Carla Anderson, do solemnly swear that I will support and defend the Constitution…"

She shoved that aside. The only man's acknowledgment she'd ever cared about was her big brother's, and he was gone.

The man just turned away and spoke to her over his shoulder as he closed the gate behind her bike. "Go ahead and check in. You're one of the last to arrive. We start in a couple hours"—as if it were a blasted dinner party. "And I already saw those orders when I signed them. Now put them away before someone else sees them and thinks you're still a soldier." He walked away.

She watched the man's retreating back. *He'd* signed her orders?

That was the notoriously hard-ass Colonel Charlie Brighton?

What the hell was the leader of the U.S. Army's Tier One asset doing manning the gate? Duh…assessing new applicants.

This place *was* whacked. Totally!

There were only three Tier One assets in the entire U.S. military. There was Navy's Special Warfare Development Group, DEVGRU, that the public thought was called SEAL Team Six—although it hadn't been named that for thirty years now. There was the Air Force's 24th STS—which pretty much no one on the outside had ever heard of. And there was the 1st Special Forces Operational Detachment—Delta—whose very existence was still denied by the Pentagon despite four decades of operations, several books, and a couple of seriously off-the-mark movies that were still fun to watch because Chuck Norris kicked ass even under the stupidest of circumstances.

Total Tier One women across all three teams? Zero.

About to be? One. Staff Sergeant First Class Carla Anderson.

Where did she need to go to check in? There was no signage. No drill sergeant hovering. No—

Delta Lesson Number Two: *You aren't in the Army anymore, sister.*

No longer a soldier, as the Colonel had said, at least not while on The Unit's side of the fence. On this side they weren't regular Army; they were "other."

If that meant she had to take care of herself, well, that was a lesson she'd learned long ago. Against stereotype, her well-bred, East Coast white-guy dad was the drunk. Her dirt-poor half Tennessee Cherokee, half Colorado settler mom, who'd passed her dusky skin and dark hair on to her daughter, had been a sober and serious woman. She'd also been a casualty of an Afghanistan dust-bowl IED while serving in the National Guard. Carla's big brother Clay now lay beside Mom in Arlington National Cemetery. Dead from a training accident. Except your average training accident didn't include a posthumous rank bump, a medal, and coming home in a sealed box—reportedly with no face.

Clay had flown helicopters in the Army's 160th SOAR with the famous Majors Beale and Henderson. Well, famous in the world of people who'd flown with the Special Operations Aviation Regiment, or their little sisters who'd begged for stories of them whenever big brothers were home on leave. Otherwise, totally invisible.

Clay had clearly died on a black op that she'd never be told a word of, so she didn't bother asking. Which was okay. He knew the risks, just as Mom had. Just as she herself had when she'd signed up the day of Clay's funeral, four years ago. She'd been on the front lines ever since and so far lived to tell about it.

Carla popped Clay's Ninja—which is how she still thought of it, even after riding it for four years—back into first and rolled it slowly up to the building with the pink roses. As good a place to start as any.

"Hey, check out this shit!"

Sergeant First Class Kyle Reeves looked out the window of the mess hall at the guy's call. Sergeant Ralph last-name-already-forgotten was 75th Rangers and too damn proud of it.

Though...damn! Ralphie was onto something.

Kyle would definitely check out *this shit*.

Babe on a hot bike, looking like she knew how to handle it.

Through the window, he inspected her lean length as she clambered off the machine. Army boots. So call her five-eight, a hundred and thirty, and every part that wasn't amazing curves looked like serious muscle. Hair the color of lush, dark caramel brushed her shoulders but moved like the finest silk, her skin permanently the color of the darkest tan. Women in magazines didn't look that hot. Those women always looked anorexic to him anyway, even the pinup babes displayed on Hesco barriers at forward operating bases up in the Hindu Kush, where he'd done too much of the last couple years.

This woman didn't look like that for a second. She looked powerful. And dangerous.

Her tight leathers revealed muscles made of pure soldier.

Ralph Something moseyed out of the mess-hall building where the hundred selectees were hanging out to await the start of the next testing class at sundown.

Well, Kyle sure wasn't going to pass up the opportunity for a closer look. Though seeing Ralph's attitude, Kyle hung back a bit so that he wouldn't be too closely associated with the dickhead.

Ralph had been spoiling for a fight ever since he'd found out he was one of the least experienced guys to show up for Delta Selection. He was from the 75th Ranger Regiment, but his deployments hadn't seen much action. Each of his attempts to brag for status had gotten him absolutely nowhere.

Most of the guys here were 75th Rangers, 82nd Airborne, or Green Beret Special Forces like himself. And most had seen a shitload of action, because that was the nature of the world at the moment. There were a couple SEALs who hadn't made SEAL Team Six and probably weren't going to make Delta, a dude from the Secret Service Hostage Rescue Team who wasn't going to last a day no matter how good a shot he was, and two guys who were regular Army.

The question of the moment though, who was she?

Her biking leathers were high-end, sewn in a jagged lightning-bolt pattern of yellow on smoke gray. It made her look like she was racing at full tilt while standing still. He imagined her hunched over her midnight-blue machine and hustling down the road at her Ninja's top speed — which was north of 150. He definitely had to see that one day.

Kyle blessed the inspiration on his last leave that had made him walk past the small Toyota pickup that had looked so practical and buy the wildfire-red Ducati

Multistrada 1200 instead. Pity his bike was parked around the back of the barracks at the moment. Maybe they could do a little bonding over their rides. Her machine looked absolutely cherry.

Much like its rider.

Ralph walked right up to her with all his arrogant and stupid hanging out for everyone to see. The other soldiers began filtering outside to watch the show.

"Well, girlie, looks like you pulled into the wrong spot. This here is Delta territory."

Kyle thought about stopping Ralph, thought that someone should give the guy a good beating, but Dad had taught him control. He would take Ralph down if he got aggressive, but he really didn't want to be associated with the jerk, even by grabbing him back.

The woman turned to face them, then unzipped the front of her jacket in one of those long, slow movie moves. The sunlight shimmered across her hair as she gave it an "unthinking" toss. Wraparound dark glasses hid her eyes, adding to the mystery.

He could see what there was of Ralph's brain imploding from lack of blood. He felt the effect himself despite standing a half-dozen paces farther back.

She wasn't hot; she sizzled. Her parting leathers revealed an Army green T-shirt and proof that the very nice contours suggested by her outer gear were completely genuine. Her curves weren't big—she had a lean build—but they were as pure woman as her shoulders and legs were pure soldier.

"There's a man who called me 'girlie' earlier." Her voice was smooth and seductive, not low and throaty, but rich and filled with nuance.

She sounded like one of those people who could hypnotize a Cobra, either the snake or the attack helicopter.

"*He's* a bird colonel. He can call me that if he wants. *You* aren't nothing but meat walking on sacred ground and wishing he belonged."

Kyle nodded to himself. The "girlie" got it in one.

"*You*"—she jabbed a finger into Sergeant Ralph Something's chest—"do not get 'girlie' privileges. *We* clear?"

"Oh, sweetheart, I can think of plenty of privileges that you'll want to be giving to—" His hand only made it halfway to stroking her hair.

If Kyle hadn't been Green Beret trained, he wouldn't have seen it because she moved so fast and clean.

"—*me!*" Ralph's voice shot upward on a sharp squeak.

The woman had Ralph's pinkie bent to the edge of dislocation and, before the man could react, had leveraged it behind his back and upward until old Ralph Something was perched on his toes trying to ease the pressure. With her free hand, she shoved against the middle of his back to send him stumbling out of control into the concrete wall of the mess hall with a loud *clonk* when his head hit.

Minimum force, maximum result. The Unit's way.

She eased off on his finger and old Ralph dropped to the dirt like a sack of potatoes. He didn't move much.

"Oops." She turned to face the crowd that had gathered.

She didn't even have to say, "Anyone else?" Her look said plenty.

Kyle began to applaud. He wasn't the only one, but he was in the minority. Most of the guys were doing a wait and see.

A couple looked pissed.

Everyone knew that the Marines' combat training had graduated a few women, but that was just jarheads on the ground.

This was Delta. The Unit was Tier One. A Special Mission Unit. They were supposed to be the one true bastion of male dominance. No one had warned them that a woman was coming in.

Just one woman, Kyle thought. The first one. How exceptional did that make her? Pretty damn was his guess. Even if she didn't last the first day, still pretty damn. And damn pretty. He'd bet on dark eyes behind her wraparound shades. She didn't take them off, so it was a bet he'd have to settle later on.

A couple corpsmen came over and carted Ralph Something away, even though he was already sitting up—just dazed with a bloody cut on his forehead.

The Deltas who'd come out to watch the show from a few buildings down didn't say a word before going back to whatever they'd been doing.

Kyle made a bet with himself that Ralph Something wouldn't be showing up at sundown's first roll call. They'd just lost the first one of the class and the selection process hadn't even begun. Or maybe it just had.

"Where's check-in?" Her voice really was as lush as her hair, and it took Kyle a moment to focus on the actual words.

He pointed at the next building over and received a nod of thanks.

That made watching her walk away in those tight leathers strictly a bonus.

Chapter 2

DAY EIGHT AND NO FORMATION UNTIL 0600 HOURS. Kyle felt like he'd been lazy and slept in. He did a rough head count. From the first day of 104 candidates, they were down by at least twenty-five.

Several hadn't made it through the day-one PT test, which hadn't even been hard. The only unusual part of the physical training test had been the amount of it. Most of these guys had been in advanced branches of the military—Special Forces, Special Ops, 82nd Airborne. How could these guys not have been prepared for a round of hard-core PT?

Sergeant Carla was one of only three regular Army. All three of them were still in. You had to be tough to think you could jump straight from Army to Delta without spending a couple tours in Special Operations or as a Special Forces Green Beret first.

He'd won his first-day bet with himself when he watched the Hostage Rescue Team dude nearly drown halfway through the hundred-meter swim in full clothes and boots toward the end of day one—without even a rifle in his hands. He'd panicked, grabbed for the boat moving along beside him, and voluntarily quit.

This was real, not a game. He should have known that before he walked through the gate. Sympathy level: zero.

The first day had cut six; the first week had cut about

twenty more. Half of those couldn't deal with the brutal physical workouts, and the other half couldn't deal with the rules. He could pick out another twenty he didn't think would survive much longer for that second reason. Sympathy level: same.

Delta Selection rules were oddly too simple for most. Life in other units of the U.S. military was about explicit orders that told you exactly what to wear, how to make your bed, where to be, and what to do.

Delta rules rarely lasted more than three sentences — for an entire day's exercise. Last night's bulletin board had said simply, "0600. No rucks." That meant no brutal hike with a heavy rucksack, at least not to start the day.

A lot of the guys had cheered when they'd seen that. Assessment Phase had been a week of escalating workouts, lots of PT, and lots of heavy-duty hikes. First day had been an 0200 start, a full ruck, and eighteen miles along the roads of Fort Bragg. They'd also been told that there was an unspecified time limit to each hike, so they shouldn't dawdle.

Any drill sergeant worth his salt would have added something more. "…Dawdle like a little old ladies' knitting circle." Or "…like the lame weaklings we expect from the other services."

Not Delta. Just, "Don't dawdle."

Not real helpful.

Unlike Green Beret assessment and training, no instructor was hovering beside you, yelling at you to dig in and keep up. In Delta, if you lagged, a member of the testing cadre slipped up quietly beside you and asked if you wanted to voluntarily drop out. If not, they let you grind it out against a hidden clock that they never revealed. At times he wondered if the training cadre even knew what the time limits were or if only the sergeant major in charge knew the required maximums.

Whatever was coming, Kyle already knew it would be harder than the day before, heavy rucks on their shoulders or not. No cause to cheer or be depressed. Steady. Just like Dad had taught him.

Without preface, the cadre started calling roll as the sun cracked the horizon, and most guys pulled down their sunglasses. As each man was called, he stepped forward. Per standard practice, they were given a swatch of colored cloth with a number to pin to their uniform and then told to climb into truck number such-and-so.

Today his swatch was "Red 4," and that's all any instructor would call him by for the rest of the day. Truck 2 looked no different than the other two. Only three trucks. They were going to be sardined in by the time everyone was called.

He had looked for a pattern to their numbering but found none. That bothered several of the guys; made others a bit paranoid as they were certain it was a reflection on their prior day's success or failure. Kyle saw no pattern, decided it was a mind game, and stopped thinking about it. They clearly didn't need him to know, so he didn't worry about it.

He admitted to being pretty pleased when "Green 3" climbed into Truck 2 as well. The trainees filled the side benches of the truck as they climbed in, and Carla Anderson ended up directly across from him. She had kept to herself, ignored the subtle harassments, and put down the more obnoxious ones. In whatever direction the candidates would be dispersed through the day, he'd account starting out across from her as a good beginning.

It had become clear to him after day two that she could handle herself just fine. A brain-dead grunt had grabbed her ass and found himself head down in a toilet—not the flush kind, the slit-trench latrine kind. The aggressor hadn't been in the barracks that night; she had. No one said a word and everyone left her pretty much alone after that.

Kyle had been pleasantly surprised as Carla continued to survive each day. Woman was damn tough. She might keep to herself, but she gave a hundred percent. As often as not, she'd be on his heels at the end of each hike or exercise. He sure as hell knew where she was at all times, close and moving at full tilt. She pushed him hard and he appreciated the extra motivation.

Also, in this sea of guys, she was a sweet relief to look at, even if the "Don't Touch" sign was glowing bright above her head.

"Check it out," she said and nodded toward the rear of the truck. They were the first words she'd spoken directly to him since asking where to check in.

He turned to look. Damn, he'd been staring at her again. He really had to cut that out. Well, if she wasn't going to complain, maybe he'd just enjoy it while it lasted.

Out on the assembly ground, thirty guys were still standing at roll call when the Sergeant Major closed his clipboard.

The three trucks that the roll-called soldiers had climbed aboard started their engines but didn't move off. They weren't packed in any tighter than usual.

"Men." The Sergeant Major raised his voice.

Kyle could hear him clearly despite the rumbling.

"You have failed to achieve the times necessary on the hikes. We will be sending you back to your units with letters of praise. You are fine soldiers, but regrettably, you aren't what The Unit is looking for. Thank you all. Pack your gear. Transport arrives in fifteen minutes. Dismissed." The Sergeant Major snapped a salute that was returned sloppily by the shell-shocked soldiers left standing in the dirt.

"Shit!" Kyle knew a half dozen of these guys. Three were Green Berets from his own battalion, though none of his own company were here. They were damn fine soldiers.

The trucks dropped into low gear and moved off as the shock continued to ripple through those left behind. Several dropped to sit in the dirt. Others stood and wept openly. Most simply watched the trucks drive away with a look of desperate longing on their face.

"Harsh," Carla observed.

Kyle looked at her. No sign of pity in her face. No sign of fear that it might just as easily have been her left standing in the dirt. A number of the guys on the truck looked aghast at their narrow escape from such a brutal cut, a full third of their forces gone in a single moment.

Sergeant Carla Anderson wasn't worrying about being cut. She was facing what was right in front of her. Like a good soldier, she focused on what came next.

He was starting to learn that whatever it was, she'd hit it full force and be damned good at it. Few soldiers and, up till now, no women, ever truly impressed him.

Kyle gave her a grin across the jouncing bed of the

truck as it slammed into the now-familiar potholes along the road outside Delta's front gate.

"On the bright side, at least they'll be spared an opportunity for you to send more of them swimming in a latrine."

She smiled back. It was a good smile, the first one he'd seen cross her face. It was easy and lit her eyes as well. "At least I didn't break any bones. I guess I *was* being a little mellow. I was in a good mood that day."

He cringed in pretend fear. "Ooo, so scared."

"How little you know."

That was the most words he'd heard her say since her arrival, the guys seated to either side watching her in surprise.

Himself, he was under the sway of that hypnotic voice and wouldn't mind hearing a lot more of it. But it took a more than a pretty face and a bit of training to make Delta. So, show her that there was a deep end of the swimming hole.

"Will we be seeing you at the end…girlie?"

Her returned smile was wicked; wicked enough that he wondered if there might be a latrine swim in his own immediate future. If so, he wasn't going in alone.

"You'll be seeing me only if you're still here, tough guy."

Kyle laughed back. It was a good moment.

And Sergeant Carla Anderson, both the soldier and the woman, impressed the hell out of him.

—⁓—

Carla had set her sights clearly on her target, and he was sitting right across the truck from her. The men who'd

been cut hadn't surprised her at all. They'd always been
the slowest or the worst complainers.

Her target was Special Forces Sergeant First Class
Kyle Reeves. Dark-haired, dark-eyed, far too handsome
for his own good, and he knew it. He added a deep voice
and a shining integrity that threatened to dazzle. Such
perfect control of temper was hiding something, and she
wanted to dig down to find out what really lay beneath.

But most importantly, it had been clear from the first
moment that he was the very best one here. He totally
kicked ass without breaking a metaphorical sweat. Real
sweat in the North Carolina heat…no one was avoiding that, not even with a serious investment portfolio
in antiperspirants.

The best was something that Carla always strove for.
It drew her like a compass too close to a magnet.

Kyle made PT workouts look like a warm-up exercise and had been the only one able to simply walk away
from her on the long hikes. It took everything she had
to chase him down, and still she never quite caught him.
There'd never been a grunt who could out-hike her, not
in training and not in the hell of the Afghanistan dust
bowl, but a full week into testing and she had yet to
catch Sergeant Kyle.

His steady calm was already legendary by the third day.

The others saw it too. At night in the barracks
there'd always be a group around Kyle. Usually the
guys sat around jawing about women or motorcycles;
she was the former, though she resisted telling them
how damn little they knew, and she didn't really care
about the latter, even though she rode one of the fastest
machines here. But when Kyle was part of the group,

the conversation was all maneuvers and tactics, and that fascinated her.

When it became clear that her presence in the circle was too disruptive—assholes that most men were—she'd taken to casually sitting close enough to listen.

Actually, she took some hope. The worst dozen of those assholes weren't in the trucks rolling to some unknown destination. They were still standing in the dirt back at the compound, looking like stunned chickens. They still had their heads, but they'd sure looked like their balls had been cut off and handed to them. She tried not to snigger, even to herself. After all, they were having a shit-bad day.

Kyle, always situationally aware, noticed her listening in the evenings. He made a point of speaking loudly enough for her to hear. Sometimes there'd be bragging sessions about hot drop zones and dug-in ragheads.

But when Kyle spoke, he'd skip the blazing gunfire and the "I was that close to being dead, I swear" routines. Instead, he talked about the enemy's tactics and strategies.

It had taken the U.S. military a long time to learn that the fastest and safest way across a rough neighborhood was not along streets and alleys, but rather through the buildings themselves. Locals cut holes between kitchen walls in adjacent structures, knowing where every passage led, and from which second-story window they could jump safely onto an adjoining first-story roof. They could race through a war-torn city better than a professional lab rat in his favorite maze.

Kyle talked about how to learn those passages, to see the patterns that let locals walk right through the middle of a city block and show up behind your front lines.

Carla knew the terror of those passageways, had run through them never knowing from one passage to the next if she'd find a startled woman grinding flour by hand or a circle of men wound up in some warped religious right-wing fervor and clutching AK-47s like their firstborns.

Kyle talked about how he'd followed and learned. And that was just one of a hundred conversations.

When the trucks lurched to a stop and killed their engines, the trainees jumped down to the ground. They were out at a Fort Bragg–ugly shooting range. Safety berms of mounded dirt were riddled with tons of lead driven four grams at a time at supersonic speeds. There was not a single shade tree. Nothing blocked the dusty wind. It looked like the apocalypse had happened here but there'd been no one to care.

This wasn't some prettied-up officers' range with floating targets, shooting benches, and watered grass. This was dirt, dust, and sun-faded distance markers. Carla preferred the authenticity of it. Nothing between her and the shot.

A Humvee sat there with cases of rifles. Not the disabled and awkwardly heavy M16s they'd been carting along on every hike, but rather the Heckler & Koch HK416 specifically designed for Delta.

She lifted one and it simply felt right in her hands. The weight, balance, even the handgrip. Her hands were smaller and her fingers definitely thinner than almost everyone else's here, but still the weapon fit. In seconds she had the buttstock adjusted to fit comfortably against her shoulder.

Carla caught Kyle looking at her. He did that a lot.

All of the guys did. After all, she was the only female here for them to all pool their idiot staring needs toward. She did her best to ignore all of it. Easily done with most of these dim bulbs because the regard was so not mutual.

But she'd felt that look of pure heat from Kyle since the moment of her arrival when he'd stood ready to take out the 75th Ranger meathead.

It was sweet of him, but wholly unnecessary. She'd learned Carla Lesson Number One ages ago: *You're on your own, girl.*

No question of that even long before the day she'd hit Basic Training. On her first day in the Army, a drill instructor had tried to grope her and ended up eating dirt right in front of a passing major, which hadn't gone over so well. The other drills weren't too pleased about their buddy spending a month in the stockade and losing two grades, but no one else had messed with her, other than making her eight weeks with them a living hell.

Still, it had been thoughtful of Kyle. The applause had been a nice gesture too, though she'd noted it wasn't exactly a popular one.

Now his look was a questioning one—she could read his face so easily. She didn't wait for him to ask.

"I know what to do with one of these, tough guy. Do you?"

He looked down at her hands and how she held the weapon and then back up at her face. "Loser buys the first round of drinks once we're through selection."

"Deal!"

Then the words registered.

Damn! She found herself liking him despite her better judgment. He'd just said that he fully expected her to be one of those still standing at the end of the thirty days of Delta Selection.

Compliments never went to her head because they were always about her being female. "You did that really well…for a woman."

Yet Kyle was looking right past that as if he could actually see *her*. It was pretty damned sexy.

He turned to receive his magazines from the training cadre.

"Five rounds to zero your scope." The Delta trainer handed Kyle a short magazine.

Carla felt that was pretty damn stingy. Ten to fifteen rounds would be more appropriate for an unfamiliar weapon.

The trainer also handed out three long magazines—fully loaded by the way Kyle was holding them. "Ninety rounds for thirty targets. You must hit twenty-eight of the targets to complete Assessment Phase of the selection process and continue on to the Stress Phase."

Kyle glanced her way and winked. Then he slipped two of the magazines into a thigh pouch, which left him holding the zeroing rounds and only one magazine.

Thirty rounds, thirty targets. Mister Show-Off, huh? She'd take that challenge.

He grinned at her when she did the same with her rounds.

A number of guys had been watching them. Some laughed at her in derision, which didn't bother her any. If they wanted to underestimate her, they were welcome to; it gave her the advantage. Some looked thoughtful. About a third of the men took the challenge of tucking away two of their magazines. That bravado so wasn't going to last.

"Green 3" was the first one called forward to zero her weapon.

She took a quick look at the range. There were targets that were posted pretty damn far away from the shooting positions. She normally zeroed at thirty meters. This time she went for fifty.

———

Kyle tried to keep watch. He should be entirely in his own head and worrying about his own shooting, but he couldn't resist assessing the others. At the first distance, at the close-in ten-meter targets, there were still several guys out of the fifty shooters who missed at least one of the five targets and had to expend an extra round.

He'd thought that the men they'd left on the ground back at the Delta compound had thinned the herd, but the day wasn't over yet. Didn't these guys even know how to zero their weapons?

At thirty meters, five more targets and the number of misses increased.

At fifty, they were down to twenty shooters maintaining the one-round-per-target ratio.

After a hundred meters, there were ten. They also added an extra target. Four shooters who'd been counting targets rather than looking at all available objectives safetied and aimed their weapons at the ground signaling they were done. The extra target was marked as a miss. The training cadre never said a word until after each new candidate had come up the line and done his shooting.

Kyle liked shooting. He'd never been one of those guys who got sexually charged up while firing a weapon. There was something very primal about it, but it had never affected him that way. He simply enjoyed the precision and control.

Watching Carla Anderson fire a weapon was a whole different matter. It was a vision that sure as hell fired up his juices.

The guys who'd been teasing her had shut up by now.

They were no longer shooting at paper targets. At this distance, there was a hand-wide circle of steel suspended at the middle of a wooden target. It gave out a bright *plink* sound and a puff of reluctant dust no matter how many times it was struck.

Carla's time as she shifted her fire from target to target was also damned good, especially using an unfamiliar weapon.

When they went from standing to prone positions for the six targets at three hundred meters, he swallowed and had to look away. Even through her Army combat uniform she looked amazing. ACUs were baggy, hid shape. Except when she was lying flat in the dirt and they clung around her buttocks.

She was a fellow soldier and clearly a good one. So what did it say about him that he wanted to tackle her right there on the ground—their fellow soldiers and the training cadre be damned—and see just where it led?

Get the woman out of your head, Kyle! Yeah, like that was going to happen anytime soon. He'd given up on that after the first day of Delta Selection. No amount of his father's martial-arts training about controlling chi and finding his center was helping either.

She'd come into the mess hall after check-in—out of her leathers, wearing camo pants and a black T-shirt. She was now dressed just like every other jock in the room yet looking like none of them. But that wasn't what had gotten him. It was the juxtaposition of the babe on a bike and the total soldier who'd strode into a room of a hundred men with her head high and her stride sure.

If the positions were reversed, Kyle didn't know if he'd have that much nerve.

Face it, dude. You walk into a room of a hundred women, you're gonna be happier than a pig in shit. Okay, he'd grant the truth of that statement, but it didn't make her one bit less impressive.

Especially when she was one of only five still maintaining a single shot per target. The hot winds and inevitable swirling dust devils of the North Carolina heat didn't deter her one bit.

At three hundred, they permanently left behind four shooters who had already run through their ninety rounds. They'd fired at twenty-seven targets; no one ignored the sixth target at this distance, but some didn't have the rounds to hit it. Or they'd used their last shot. With nothing left in the three magazines to shoot at the hardest targets, the three maximum-range ones, they were out. They had to hit twenty-eight. Four guys were starting the final-distance targets with only a single round still left in their chamber.

The training cadre walked them past the five-hundred-meter shooting position out to six hundred. That was the practical limit of the 5.56 x 45 mm NATO round they were firing.

At this distance, Kyle was the second one up. Three targets, three rounds left in his magazine. Twice he waited out hard gusts, but he managed to hit all three on his first try.

A Green Beret named Chad also made thirty for thirty.

A SEAL and a Ranger cursed and had to pull out a second magazine to get all thirty targets, but easily qualified with two nearly full magazines remaining.

Carla was the only one left with a chance at a single round per target.

Six hundred meters was a world different from three hundred. Out here you had to have perfect control of your heartbeat and your breathing and know what to do with both them and the environment.

Two guys spent a whole magazine, thirty rounds, before managing that crucial qualifying twenty-eighth target. Ten more were told that if they wanted to take the next six months or more to improve their shooting skills, they were welcome to reapply to a future selection process, a courtesy not extended to the four guys they'd already carted away from the three-hundred-meter position.

Starting at three hundred meters, the attitude had changed as well. The training cadre wasn't merely sitting back quietly and announcing "hit" or "miss" in deadpan voices. They started telling the shooter what they were doing wrong—shooting on the breath but not the pulse beat or the wrong part of the pulse beat.

"Green 3" was called up last. The day's heat had continued to rise throughout the shooting, especially as shooters took longer and longer between shots out at this range. The sun had shifted from behind to a quarter off the targets, really irritating. The winds across the range were chaotic, gusting as high as fifteen knots, which could knock a round completely sideways as it traveled for a full second to cross the six-tenths of a kilometer to target.

Everyone, even those who had failed, gathered around to watch Carla. She snagged her hair back into a rough ponytail, teased and snarled by the wind. Kyle's hands itched with the desire to comb her hair out between his fingers and find out if it was as soft as it looked.

She settled and waited. A few of the guys were still dense enough to be nudging each other and trading knowing nods. No "girl" could shoot reliably at this distance.

Kyle knew full well that the number one sniper in Russia's history had been Lyudmila Pavlichenko, with over three hundred confirmed German kills during World War II—and that was with a weapon that was so much less than the HK416. These weren't even sniper distances. Those didn't come into their own until they were out past a kilometer.

Someone had told Kyle about a "hotshot bitch" flying with the Night Stalkers who was unbeatable in competition. It didn't sound right. A helicopter was a crappy sniper platform, but that's what the guy had said before going on to describe each of her fine physical attributes: *pint-sized, Asian, and built like a brick shithouse*. As if that was more important than how she did what she did when she outshot him. *Yep! Just brush that bit of bruised ego under the carpet, buddy. You stick with your story*.

Kyle willed the winds to die for Carla, but they didn't appear to be cooperating.

Everyone jolted when she unexpectedly fired. She must have detected a cosmic wormhole through the wind that he'd missed.

There was no bright *plink* sound, but she was already

swinging her weapon to the next target with a calm assuredness before the bullet could possibly arrive.

Then the spotter called out, "Hit." A second called, "Confirm hit," from behind his scope.

The wind had carried the sound away.

—∿∿—

Carla's world had narrowed to an arrow point. There were only weapon, range, and target. There were only her pulse and the beat of the wind. When everything aligned, she nailed the second target and moved on to the third.

Her brother had taught her the basics after she'd almost become mountain lion food on a hike. He'd bought her a used Remington 597 WMR with a scope and a hundred rounds of ammo. The next time, she'd taken a thousand rounds and hiked deep into the Colorado Rockies to practice. Not only did she sleep better after that, but she also ate better out in the wilderness. The .22 Mag rounds killed smaller game up through fox and coyote and scared off most big game.

The Army had taken those skills and honed them with too much experience. She'd never be a true sniper, waiting for days to take a single shot at two kilometers out before sliding away just as quietly, but she knew what to do with the weapon in her hands. The shorter distances had familiarized her with the HK416's quirks, or rather, lack of them. It was a finely honed shooting machine, and she was now as integral with it as her heart was with the winds. Fort Bragg's winds had nothing on the howlers that shot through the deep canyons of the Colorado Rockies.

She took the final shot with reluctance, knowing she'd have to leave this perfect, quiet space when she did.

The bolt rang empty as she spent the last round in the magazine and rested her cheeks against the sun- and powder-warmed weapon. She closed her eyes and waited.

"Hit," her spotter announced.

"Confirm hit," the second one agreed.

Then another sound came at her, battering her senses that had been so wrapped in the quiet.

She rolled over and sat up.

There was Kyle Reeves front and center, applauding.

And, so different from her arrival just a week ago, they were all doing so, every last man jack of them.

A rolling wave of noise.

Applauding her.

The faces blurred. She'd often won praise from her immediate fireteam, but this was a circle of fifty of the best soldiers there were, and they were applauding her.

She didn't know what to do with it.

Overwhelm slapped at her. Carla wanted to curl up until they went away, go back to the peace of her shooting space.

But she couldn't or she'd never live it down.

So instead she unbuttoned her thigh pocket, pulled out the two still-full magazines, and tossed them to Kyle. At least he had to stop applauding to catch them. Once he had them, he tapped the two against the pair he still had buttoned up in his thigh pocket.

Rather than panicking, she sat there like the village idiot, grinning up at the man who looked at her like she was the most amazing thing he'd ever seen.

No, the heat still burned there, deep in those dark eyes.

He looked at her like the most amazing *woman* he'd ever seen…

Carla had to admit it felt pretty damn good.

And that it was totally mutual.

Chapter 3

"Day thirty," Carla muttered to herself as she shouldered her rucksack. "Oh joy." She made sure the ends of her hair weren't pinned under the straps and headed to roll call. Last day of Delta Selection. Though this day was starting at straight-up midnight, it was still the last day.

She'd survived seven days of Assessment, the burn-out series of exercises and hikes. She'd survived the one-week cut, the shooting assessment, and now twenty-two days of the Stress Phase.

"Last day." She grunted forty-nine pounds of ruck back off her shoulders once she reached the assembly point. She dropped the pack in the dirt and offered it an admonitory kick, over a third her body weight. Forty-four pounds—twenty kilos—was the required minimum for this hike. She added the extra two kilos to make sure she was over the minimum at each of the check-in point scales along today's route.

She hated how easily guys like Kyle could just sling on a heavy ruck. Carla could do it, but it took work. It didn't seem fair that they got all the upper-body strength and didn't appreciate it while she'd earned every last muscle fiber the hard way.

The last thirty days of testing had leaned them down. Short on calories because they simply couldn't consume them as fast as they were burning them. Short on sleep and long on physical workouts, especially massively long hikes with heavy loads and difficult orienteering over complex terrain.

The day after the shooting assessment, they'd been loaded into trucks and shipped out to the Uwharrie National Forest for Stress Phase hikes, lots of them.

At least this hike didn't also require the thirty pounds of her LBE. The load-bearing equipment harness was a soldier's personal "essential crap" carrier. In case she ever had to shed the rucksack, her LBE made it so she'd still be fully armed and have water. This hike was rucks only.

She'd grown up hiking the mountains of Colorado, sometimes walking several weeks into the wilderness with only what she could carry; this was no different. Back then, it was either hike or hang out with her drunk dad in Durango—man, that was like eight kinds of suck.

Well, in the Colorado Rockies she didn't usually walk with a heavy M16 in her hands. She typically packed her 597 over her shoulder for hunting and a .357 on her hip in case she stumbled on a bear who needed convincing to change direction. She almost shivered recalling the day she'd learned just how little a black bear cared about a .22 round, even a WMR one. The rifle—which had been her constant protector until the two days she'd spent clinging high in a slender aspen tree—had only pissed off the bear.

A lot of the guys had griped about not being allowed to sling the M16 rather than carry it. Didn't bother her a bit. Having a desire to survive her service in dangerous places, she'd always carried her Army-issue for fast access. That habit had saved her life more than once.

It was also useful for rapping the occasionally

overconfident grunt hard in the balls. If you came up alongside the leg and gave a final twist at the last moment, it got you in under most brands of body armor.

Delta Selection had leaned them down in other ways.

First day they'd taken a photo of the squadron of 104 cocky soldiers. Mostly cocky. No sign of the Neanderthal who'd greeted her and then tried to eat a concrete wall. And her face was sober in that photo.

Carla didn't have any hoo-ha in her head about representing the first women to break yet another gender barrier. She'd stood there during that photo and contemplated what it would take to reach the end of this and still be standing. This hadn't been about anyone else, the way she thought it would be—not even her dead mother or brother. This was about her.

She was learning to be down with that and prepared herself for whatever was coming.

Carla would wager that today's rules would be as simple as usual despite it being day thirty, the last day of testing…unless there was another surprise on the far side of the day.

If there was, she'd do that too. Bring it on.

Only twenty candidates remained here at the end of week four.

Eighty-four were gone. And among the departed wasn't the "little woman" or "girlie" or any of the other names they'd called her. She was still standing despite the betting pools that she knew were strong against her.

Kyle Reeves was still in too, his dark gaze ready to devour her at the least invitation—which she still hadn't issued, despite the temptation.

The dude was different. In some ways he was almost

as whacked as the Delta compound…which she'd
become quite used to by now. He looked more handsome with time, which seemed impossible considering
where he'd started out. It certainly didn't hurt that his
hair was forest-dark brown and clearly meant for a
woman to run her fingers through. Or that his whiskey-
warm eyes could see right down into her soul.

If she'd had one.

She was only too aware of that part of her lying
buried with her mom and brother in Arlington Cemetery.
Someday she'd wind up beside them, but not yet. She
was going to honor them with every heartbeat and every
breath she had.

Kyle was also the king grunt here. He was the only
one who consistently beat her times on the hikes—
every, single goddamned hike. That the bastard also beat
everyone else's times didn't make her feel any better
about him doing that to her.

A wave of unofficial hand-to-hand, mano-a-mano,
wrestling competitiveness had swept through the group
in week three, which was spent around campfires deep
in the Uwharrie. Kyle put them all down. Though Chad
the Green Beret was stronger, one of the few who was,
Kyle was faster.

She'd sat as an unchallenged spectator. At first she'd
considered going in and teaching them a thing or two.
Then she'd figured that she'd ultimately end up down
in the dirt with Sergeant Kyle Reeves, and she wasn't
ready for that…yet.

That in itself was an odd thought. In two ways. One,
that she was holding off on taking a sexual partner who
tempted her. And two, that she hoped he'd be just as

eager. Normally she didn't care about the latter one way or the other as long as he said yes.

The final and totally impossible thing that was wacko about Sergeant Kyle Reeves was that he appeared to be content with the world around him. At ease in every situation, which she found even more engaging than that first heated look.

Oh, she'd caught him watching her plenty since that first day. No big surprise, as she was the only chick here.

But ever since the shooting assessment, there'd been something more. Gal with a gun gave him a hard-on? Fine. He wound her own fantasies up every time she couldn't beat him.

Well, turnabout was fair play. If there was anyone she was going to best on this last day of the Delta Force Selection Stress Phase, he was it. She was done fooling around.

She wasn't a woman hoping tremulously with quivering lip to be let into The Unit. She was gonna kick ass, excelling right past their number one soldier or run herself into the ground trying.

Now, on day thirty, she wasn't sure it was possible, because Kyle was just that damn good. But it was the last day and she'd give it her all.

Yeah. Good goal for the day. *Reeves, your tight soldier ass is mine!* She wondered if there was a department of the Army where she should file her claim—they had a department for everything else under the sun. The name would be something obscure that you'd never associate with what it was: Department of Acquisition of Rear Echelons.

DARE, girl! Dare to be great and kick his ass.

Sergeant Major Maxwell, the head instructor of the Delta training cadre, called them to order. He had always made the rules of what was expected absolutely clear, if you only listened and didn't try to interpret. There wasn't any deeper level. They told you what they wanted you to know—no more and no less.

"Final day," he announced once they'd formed up in a ragged line. Delta wasn't big on formality, and there weren't enough of them left to call for forming in ranks. "Time for the Forty-Miler."

It deserved capital letters. There'd been rumors of it, even on the outside. It was the only thing in Delta that wasn't done in metric. Almost everything else in the U.S. military had converted over to aid interoperability and joint-operations communication with other national forces. Even Liberia and Burma were flipping, which left U.S. civilians as the only ones still using English units.

But the "Forty-Miler" was tradition even as Carla's brain automatically converted it to sixty-five kilometers. Sixty-five klicks with a full ruck. *Definitely time to pony up, girl.* This wasn't going to be any cakewalk along some fire road like the early days of Delta Selection. She was going to be chasing Kyle's ass over rough territory.

"Twenty kilos, forty miles, folks," in yet another of the brilliantly screwed-up double-unit standards that thrived in so many corners of the U.S. military. "You have your map and compass. No roads or trails except when approaching or departing an RV."

The training cadre always set up rendezvous points where they could drive in a truck to haul away those who voluntarily quit.

"As usual, there is an unspecified time limit to this

exercise, so you don't want to be strolling. I will mention that the terrain is no more pleasant than usual."

They'd spent the last twenty days crisscrossing the Uwharrie National Forest, which nestled in the foothills of the Appalachian Mountains thirty klicks northwest of Fort Bragg. She now knew it would be brutal without being told. If there was a single piece of non-ugly terrain in the entire forest, they hadn't found it. The twenty days of Stress Phase that they'd spent here had intimately introduced them to the very worst elements of these rugged hills.

His wry comment earned a weak laugh and several groans from the group. A selection-process hike meant swamps and mountains and brambles and... Didn't matter. One day. She could do one more day.

Night.

It was zero-dark-zero now, which meant the first six hours of the hike would be in darkness. No way to scout the route visually; this would start as a pure map-and-compass job from the start..

Kyle shot her a cocky salute.

She gave him the finger and a grin. He absolutely knew that she'd be coming after him this time.

He wasn't a big man, just an inch over her own five-eight; no soldier still remaining was big. Delta didn't select for towering and broad-chested—though Kyle had the broad-chested part down cold. They selected for tough and more tenacious than a Tasmanian devil.

That was the part she had down cold.

Over the last month, there had been a lot of reactions to her. After feeding that guy the outhouse, the physical crap (pun intended) had stopped.

She never thought she'd be thankful for those last two years of high school spent working nights and weekends as a bouncer in her cousin's strip club—a job she'd initially gotten because of how much time her father spent there. She'd learned most of her early manhandling skills fending off Dad's "pals" and dragging his drunk ass home. It had paid off innumerable times in the military. Who knew.

The more typical reactions to her only continued through the first week. They were split between those trying to harass her and those trying to curry some sort of favor. The first group, she was pleased to see, went away because they didn't survive that heavy first cut at the end of week one.

The guys who were trying to curry favor through unexpected niceties learned: first, that it made no impression on her, and second, they were soon too tired and sore to think about anything other than themselves.

In regular Army, the guys were always offering to press her uniforms, teaching her how to use a heat gun to expand her boot's leather to take the polish better, or hiding chocolates and mash notes in her bunk. Scanty lace undergarments were also a common gift. The next time she saw them, she would thank them, return the note or the underwear—though she ate the chocolate—then walk away. Didn't matter if it was in front of the guy's buddies, a drill sergeant, or a bird colonel. Confused the shit out of most of them and made it stop pretty quickly.

Sergeant Kyle Reeves had done none of that. He'd simply been steady. She felt the heat every time his eyes lingered, but otherwise he treated her no differently than any other candidate. Perhaps friendlier, but he was one of those naturally friendly guys who seemed to know everyone's life story within minutes of meeting them. Not something she'd ever been good at, not even close.

"Also per usual," the Sergeant Major continued, "you may not speak to or assist another candidate unless they are critically injured and unable to help themselves."

That was the rule that had weeded out over twenty candidates in the second week. They didn't know how to be self-reliant, how to function outside the structure of a military team.

Delta Lesson Number Kajillion Four: *You gotta be able to do it alone against all odds*.

"Remember, create a small fire in an open area if you're hopelessly lost and voluntarily withdrawing. Do not use your radio unless it is a matter of imminent death and we need to get a medevac extract team to you. You're good to go."

Delta Lesson Number Kajillion Four and a Half: *You gotta do it exactly by their rules*. You just wanna quit and you use the radio, then no nice-nice letter when they kicked your ass back down to the regular units.

That was the problem with Delta rules. The trainers were Delta themselves. They never got upset and they never explained. They tell you to go for a brutal hike, you go. They tell you to go sit under a tree with your ruck, you go and sit under a tree with your ruck. They tell you to go take yet another psychological question-naire, you take it—and they did that a lot. Weirdly, it wasn't about blind obedience, though that's how Carla had taken it at first. Instead, it was about doing what was needed without hesitation—right now.

Only once in the last month did the day's orders

have anything to do with hygiene—a daily harangue in regular Army. They'd had a half day off, just one, after the shooting assessment. They'd been advised to clean up before going into town. That was it. She'd gotten a pizza and a soda and then spent the rest of her half day asleep, knowing they were far from done. Three guys had dropped because the next day's march hadn't mixed well with a crashing hangover. Good, she didn't want any grunts with the play-hard, fight-hard mind-set beside her during trouble anyway.

"Have a good 'un." Sergeant Major Maxwell offered the standard Delta end-of-instructions. They each said it with an easy Southern accent, whether they were Yankee, Texan, or inner-city LA. She'd asked one of the training cadre about that after he'd cleared her to continue through an RV in the middle stage of a brutal hike that crisscrossed a mountain six different ways in a star pattern like a bad Jewish joke. Seems the saying traced back to the sergeant major who'd helped form the unit.

"Have a good 'un."

And with just that much ceremony, they were ready. They were released at three-minute intervals. They had five RV points to hit on the hike, but how they got there was up to them. Shortest possible route was forty miles. Longest route? Depended on how lost you got.

Kyle's number was called first out. Figured.

"Kiss ass," she called out to him as he hauled on his ruck and headed out.

"Whatever works…girlie." Then he was gone before she could nail his cute ass to the trail.

Later, she promised his retreating form.

"Blue Five." The number she wore today was nineteenth of twenty off the line.

Fifty-seven minutes cooling her heels. She should have taken a nap.

Carla hated it, but that was just something you learned to do. Cooling your heels was definitely *Army* Lesson Number One.

—◊◊◊—

Kyle Reeves followed his first heading easily. The opening six kilometers of tonight's hike was along a "trail"— which in Delta-speak meant something a Humvee could force its way down if you were being chased by a rabid horde of zombified Chinese.

He was allowed to follow the trail, if possible, but he couldn't get within fifteen meters of it. Fifteen meters into the thick Carolina brush, six klicks in a straight line. After the first week of brutal road hikes and then three more of orienteering, this leg was a piece of cake.

He'd faced a lot of grueling workouts; Green Berets were good at that. His dad had been one too. A tae kwon do, kung fu, and weapons sensei who didn't hesitate for a second to knock you down if your defenses were weak, not if you were his son and not if you were a teenage girl. He wasn't brutal—he'd never hurt you more than a hard block and a tumble, maybe leave a black-and-blue mark or two—but he wore you down until you learned.

Mom had a full-time office gig, so after school, the bus dropped Kyle at his dad's dojo. There he got a snack, did his homework, and then hit the mats right through until the evening classes were done. Didn't matter what the class was, he was in it. Advanced weapons at the age of six, white-belt introduction for first graders when he was fifteen and wearing black himself.

Saturdays were in the dojo until two, then as often as not, they were out the back door and headed up into the fishing streams of Washington State. Mostly car camping, with tent and campfire. Those were the times he loved the most. He, Mom, and Dad standing in a glacier-fed stream together and pretty much doing nothing.

The hard discipline of Delta was so familiar to him, between martial arts and Green Berets, that it seemed to make sense when he bothered to think about it.

It was almost a shock when he reached his first marker of the hike, a sharp bend in a narrow but fast stream. He crossed it, getting wet to the thighs in the strangely warm water. He'd never get used to that— mountain streams were supposed to be so cold that just thinking about them made your balls shrivel.

No training cadre member was waiting at the RV. For a moment he wondered if he was in the wrong place. They were always there to make sure you were on track and coherent enough to keep reading your map. Also to dispense their constant offers to quit.

Not tonight. Tonight he and the others were on their own, though a trainer probably sat nearby watching him through night-vision gear even now. Might as well be alone, which was fine with him. No way to spot a Delta operator who didn't want to be seen, though he'd bet on the snarled clump of bushes about ten paces out.

He took a moment to drink water and check his map and compass. He refilled his canteen from the stream, dropped in purification tablets, and hung it back on his harness. It would get plenty of shaking as he walked.

The next leg was three kilometers...if you were an eagle. Being merely human, it was a four-kilometer-long, brutal-looking ridge ascent then descent on a nearly direct line—or an eight-kilometer walk around. Only the RVs mattered—you couldn't miss those. How you got there was up to you.

He'd been moving well so far, but he wouldn't be able to count on that at the other end of sixty-five kilometers. The shorter route would be faster, just riskier. He was used to risk.

He resettled his ruck, checked his watch.

Fifty-six minutes. He was already sore, sweaty, and barely a tenth of the way done, at least in distance. Looking at the map, that first section was definitely going to be his fastest stretch of the night. Well, he wasn't covering ground standing still. But just for the hell of it, he kept his eye on his watch, letting his body rest another forty-five seconds.

There.

Fifty-seven minutes.

He strode out at exactly the same moment Carla Anderson would be taking her first step. He liked the feel of that, as if they were walking along together though they were six kilometers apart.

Keep blowing wind up your own backside, Reeves.

They weren't walking together, as nice as that sounded, but apart. She'd be coming for his ass on this hike. Well, that only made it all the better. He dug in. She'd have to run to catch him, even with those amazingly long legs of hers.

That woman did something to him. Well, she did something to every one of the guys. The way she looked, it was impossible not to. But the other guys mostly left off at the sexual fantasies.

In addition to her poster-soldier-of-the-month looks, Kyle also liked her no-nonsense attitude. Guys would spend evenings in the mess hall or around the campfire if they were out in the wilderness, reliving the brutal day or the stupid psych test or griping about only getting a half-day shooting course.

Didn't they get that this wasn't training? This was selection testing. Delta only let them shoot a half day because that was all it took to make sure you could at least handle and use a weapon without killing yourself or the guy beside you. They'd train you in their own way once you were through and into the Operator Training Course. That was the next prize, getting into OTC, but most guys didn't seem to be looking much past today and maybe tomorrow.

Carla Anderson did. She didn't waste time with griping or complaining; she just got it done. One of only three to shoot thirty out of thirty—it just didn't get any better.

Though it was hard to imagine her as a regular-forces soldier. There was a core feistiness that he bet ran right over anyone in her way, which must have been ugly.

However, to his best guess, that made her perfect Delta material. *Go walk thirty klicks across impossible terrain with marginally sufficient information.* She'd be the second one into the RV—hot on his heels despite his gender advantages.

Now he was walking with her—though *not* with her—in the dark of the Uwharrie. He fought his way up the ridge, steeper than it looked by the map's contour

lines. More than once he unintentionally kicked a rock
loose and listened to it bound down the hillside. He
hoped no one was directly below, the sharp clack and
clatter of each rebound the only sound other than his
own harsh breathing.

He made a bet with himself; Carla would also choose
this shorter route over the ridge. He wanted to stop here, wait
for her, make love on the hillside beneath the starlit sky.

Yeah, and he'd ended up with boot prints right over
his back as she raced toward the goal.

What is your goal, Carla?

Funny how little they'd actually talked. Some teasing, some Army—he was starting to suspect she'd seen
a lot of action despite being a female in the regular
forces—but nothing more.

He crested the top of the ridge in forty-five minutes
and thanked the sudden breakout of moonlight from the
high clouds, which was the only thing that stopped him
from starting the descent much more abruptly than he'd
planned; it was a knife-edge ridge. It would be fifteen
more minutes until her footsteps started crossing over
his back at the bend in the stream.

He liked being that much ahead but could feel the
pressure of her closing in. He chose his route down
from the ridge and pushed ahead hard. No one had ever
caught him yet.

And he had his pride. No one was going to.

Especially not a woman who kept tempting his
thoughts off his route.

He skittered down a scree slope of broken bits of
mountain, moving in a diagonal crossing pattern to
minimize the chance of starting a rock avalanche.

Was that intentional, Carla's constant distraction of him?

No. The woman didn't flaunt herself a bit, other than frying Ralph's brain on that first day. Maybe that was the problem. Perhaps his own brain had been partially toasted in the backlash though he'd been an innocent bystander— his eyes drinking her in like a cool slash of water.

Kyle had seen enough women "working it" in the Green Beret bars to know—women hunting a Special Forces husband knew how to take command of the room.

If anything, Carla understated herself, which was one of her attractions. *Take it or leave it, buddy. What you see is what you get.*

And he wanted to take it. Bad.

So much so that he almost did a header off a short cliff near the base of the scree slope. He snagged a tree at the last moment and slowed his descent enough to make a clean transition to the lower slope.

Barely.

Damn her!

"Get out of my head, woman!" he barked at the night, knowing it wasn't going to happen.

For one thing, if he was so angry at her, why was he smiling like an idiot eight kilometers into a brutal hike?

Time for a new mind-set.

"Bring it!" he told the night. "Just try to catch me, girlie!"

He laughed and broke into a slow trot despite the heavy ruck as he circled to avoid a steep canyon, well worth the extra two kilometers.

By the time she hit the bend in the stream, Carla had passed eight of the eighteen ahead of her. There were those who believed in conserving energy at the start, but *come on, dudes!*

She'd driven herself over the first ground and made good time. At the stream she didn't even slow down except to scoop full an empty canteen as she crossed; the cadre observer back in the bushes had to dodge out of her way before she ran him down.

She'd stop after two hours for three minutes max. She'd studied the first three map sections before starting, had chosen and memorized her route.

Carla took a bearing and kept to the shortest travel line. Three kilometers right over the peak to the next RV. She'd hiked the Continental Divide Trail—far less known than its Appalachian or Pacific Crest brethren—during her last two summers of high school. It required six months of walking over the highest peaks of the country, from the Crazy Cook Monument in the deep desert of New Mexico to Glacier National Park in Montana: three months south from Colorado, and three months north to the Canadian border.

These Appalachian mountains made her feel like she was merely warming up, no more than that. She had to admit, even if she wouldn't say it aloud, that the Forty-Miler with full ruck and an M16 did add to the challenge.

When Carla crested the peak, Sergeant Major Maxwell was standing there.

"Sergeant Major."

"Blue Five." Not a single instructor had yet used her name or anyone else's outside of morning roll call.

"Figured you'd be the one batshit crazy enough to follow this route." .

"Yes, sir." Carla was itching to keep moving, but you didn't brush off a sergeant major. And she liked that the head of testing had decided to place himself in position to wait especially for her.

"So, you're done? No shame in it. You've destroyed pretty much every betting pool so far. You can walk away proud of what you've done. We'll give you a top letter back to your regular unit. Even recommend you to SOF."

Carla didn't know whether to shout at him or laugh in his face. A hundred times she'd been asked that question in the last thirty days, and she'd told them a hundred times no.

Though a recommendation to Special Operations Forces was damn high praise, especially coming from The Unit. But she didn't want to be the first female Ranger or the first female Special Forces Green Beret or anything else. She was going to be Delta.

It took an effort, but she managed to keep her voice steady. "Think I'll keep walking for a bit, Sergeant Major."

"Show me that your flashlight works and show me where you are on your map."

She hadn't used her flashlight yet, preferring the moonlight, and she was standing on the peak of the mountain. She did both without comment, and he nodded and stepped aside with, "Have a good 'un."

Carla made it about three steps past him when a sudden thought struck her. Turning back, she studied Maxwell's face in the moonlight.

"*Pretty much* every betting pool?"

"Pretty much."

"Your money still in there, Sergeant Major?"

"Oh, I put my money down on the first day. Haven't seen any reason to place a bet since."

"Didn't answer the question, Sarge."

"Don't intend to, Blue Five. Have a good 'un." And with that he melted into the night as if he'd never been there and she was alone on the mountaintop. Fifty-six kilometers to go.

———

Kyle stood at what he hoped to God was the last intersection. Sixty-five klicks over rough terrain with a twenty-kilo ruck. Eighteen hours.

Was that right? Or was it a twenty-mile hike and an eighteen-kilo ruck? He knew he'd started at midnight. He knew what the time was on his watch, but he was so hammered that he was having trouble connecting the two. Eighteen hundred hours minus midnight was… still eighteen.

It was nearing sunset.

The blistering heat of the day had sapped his strength along with his wits, no matter how much water with electrolytes and how many energy bars he'd consumed. The straps of the ruck had cut into his shoulders until his hands were numb and he could barely open a water bottle. He had to look down at his hands every now and then to make sure he was still carrying his rifle. Once he hadn't been, but he'd found where it went fast enough. It had landed on his throbbing feet and hurt like unholy hell despite the boot.

His feet were long past agony as he forced them into

the last turn and began climbing up the stiff hill to the final RV; thank god it was the final one. He crested a low rise and could see the trucks of the check-in point waiting just a few hundred meters ahead, like manna from heaven.

"I can do a few hundred meters." He dug deep and began forcing his body to honor his words. It helped that he could see one of the training cadre standing atop the rise looking down at him.

He'd made it about a dozen steps toward the man when there was a heavy crashing sound in the thick brush off to his right.

Kyle had not walked all this way to be surprised and mauled by a bear. He turned and blinked hard to restore his focus. No live ammo, just this shit-heavy M16. Too far downslope still for the cadre to make it to him in time.

Then he heard a sharp curse, followed by the appearance of a woman who looked much the worse for wear. Her hair was snarled with branches and leaves. Dried mud smeared up half her body as if she'd dived into a swamp to do the sidestroke. There were scratches on her face that had dribbled blood and dried crusty brown. She stumbled onto the open trail in obvious shock at her abrupt release from the tenacious clutches of the wilderness.

He probably looked much the same.

"Hey, Kyle." Her smile was a grim acknowledgment of forty miles of pain and strain.

"Hey, Carla." He'd never seen such a beautiful sight as this woman of the wild. No one had passed him through the night and the scorching day. That she'd made up fifty-seven minutes on him should shock the shit out of him—he hadn't exactly been loafing along— but it really didn't. Damn she was tough.

"Race you." Her voice was hoarse with exhaustion.

"Sure," he grunted out.

They turned shoulder to shoulder, a few steps apart so that the cadre could see they were in no way assisting one another, and staggered up the trail, every step stinging his feet like hell, but each one also a little lighter for having her beside him.

At the RV, the cadre separated them.

His sergeant led him over to a truck. "Show me where you are on your map."

I'm standing right here, idiot. Had to be the right place because Carla was here too. Of course, that kind of defined the right place no matter what a stupid map said.

What the hell was he thinking?

He fumbled out the folder paper and pointed. No, that was his starting point on this sheet. He moved his finger along the route he'd taken and found the end point as much by luck as coherence.

"Night is falling. Change out your batteries and show me that your flashlight works."

Shit! Shit! Shit! This wasn't the end of it. No way did he have another step in him. No, this was the end. They were just messing with him. Weren't they?

He managed to fumble open the light. It hurt like grabbing live voltage to make his hands work.

Kyle ignored the whole "you can quit anytime" spiel while he struggled with the fresh batteries, which took him several minutes. Somehow he managed it.

"Read these instructions."

He couldn't even see the instructions. Eight numbers. Map coordinates. It wasn't over.

It took Kyle a full minute to parse the numbers and more time to make the right notation on his own map. Had to hurry or Carla would get a lead on him. Catching him was one thing; passing him was not acceptable.

Eleven more kilometers. Right back over the worst terrain in the entire Uwharrie Forest. No way in hell.

The cadre member checked his notation on his map, nodded, then stepped aside. "Have a good 'un."

Carla stared at her cadre in disbelief.

Have a good 'un?

Eleven kilometers over butt-ugly terrain and he was saying, "Have a good 'un"?

It took everything she had to re-shoulder her ruck.

Then it took everything she had to make that first step.

And her whole being again to take the next.

When the cadre called out for her to stop, she ignored him.

She'd do this one fucking step at a time if she had to. Kyle Reeves was never going to beat her again.

A couple of the trainers came up to block her progress; she bulled her way between them. Unable to stop, she actually ran head-on into one of them. It was like walking into a brick wall.

Sergeant Major Maxwell.

He placed a hand on each of her shoulders and kept her there until she looked up into his face.

"You're finished. Stress Phase testing is over for you."

"Finished? No. I'm not quitting." And then the words

sunk in. "Finished" is what they'd said each of the thirty days when she'd completed the day's exercise. "Finished?" It came out plaintive, more than she'd like but she couldn't fix it.

A grin crossed his craggy face, such a shocking expression across his stoically neutral expression that she wondered if his face was going to break.

If it did, would she be able to bend down to pick up the pieces? More importantly, if she bent down, would she be able to stand again?

"You just won my bet for me, Carla." It was the first time he'd ever said her name.

Once it sunk in that she was truly done with the hike, she wanted to laugh, to cry, to somehow mark the moment.

When the Sergeant Major shook her hand, it was enough.

In moments, someone had taken her ruck and the M16. Another guided her off to the side, down a trail out of sight of the truck. There was a campfire.

Kyle Reeves was sitting there, lying back against a dirt bank, looking pretty goddamn pleased with himself.

They eased her down beside him, pulled off her boots, propped her feet up on her rucksack, and gave her a cup of hot spiced wine well laced with brandy.

Oh God, she was in heaven.

They were smiling now. Congratulating her. Shaking her hand.

Carla had felt this good before, she must have. But she sure couldn't think of when.

She didn't even mind when the unit's doc came over and caused shooting pains as he poked at her feet before declaring them sound. The various agonies of the ordeal were a long way from subsiding, but she no longer cared. She'd passed Stress Phase.

"Well, done, tough guy." She bumped her shoulder against Kyle's.

"Well, done, girlie." He bumped her back with one of his killer smiles thrown in as a bonus that warmed her inside as much as the cider.

They clinked steaming mugs.

A man who could smile at her like that after what they'd both just been through and achieved, he could get away with calling her that. At least this one more time.

They talked lazily back and forth for over an hour before the next candidate was escorted to the fire, mostly about the men behind them. Chad Hawkins, followed minutes later by his good buddy Duane Jenkins, collapsed nearby. Both were grinning like idiots. All too comfortable to move, she offered them "air" high fives, which were happily returned.

Carla was the only one of the three grunts from regular Army to make it this far. One had been unable to hit the twenty-eighth target but was invited back for a later testing, and the other had shattered a hip when he got lost and accidentally walked off a waterfall.

They talked about some of the others who had been left by the wayside as Richie and Andrew made it in. Of course, Kyle knew far more of them than she did. The more they talked, the more impressed she became with herself. She'd done good to have outlasted a lot of these guys.

As her body slowly recovered, she became aware that her and Kyle's shoulders were just brushing. Had been for a while.

She had underestimated him.

Sergeant bloody Kyle Reeves was also a sneaky SOB. He'd slipped right past her outermost perimeter shield.

He wasn't just some beautiful, tough, friendly, totally superior grunt. Finding an excuse to lean against her—a contact that was becoming more and more electrifying the longer she didn't move away—was a totally under-handed maneuver that she hadn't thought him capable of. A whole new side to him. What else was there to discover beneath that tough-guy exterior?

It made her like him just that much more.

By the time they were carried to the trucks—neither her nor Kyle's insistence that they could walk had proven to be accurate—there were only twelve of them around that fire. How many others finished the "official" hike but didn't have the will to take that next step, they'd never know.

—⁓—

Psych evals were psych evals.

Kyle had always said to hell with the headshrinkers. You answered honest and you were done. Trying to second-guess their twisty brains wasn't worth the effort.

Whereas scoring each other had flat-out sucked.

"Would you want to serve with this soldier?" "Would you trust this soldier to have your back if you were in…" Dozens of questions that had to be answered for each of the other eleven finalists.

He hated shit like that and tried not to think about what the guys seated around him were marking down.

"Make a list, in order, of which of your fellow can-didates you would want to serve with. Number one?"

Carla Anderson.

He didn't even think before he wrote down the answer and then blinked at it in surprise. Was that as a soldier or was it personal? Was it because she was the toughest one here after himself—a fact that she'd proven again and again? Or was it because he'd seriously considered kissing the shit out of her and taking whatever the consequences as they'd lounged side by side around the fire last night with their feet perched up on their rucks and their shoulders warm against each other?

The first time Kyle hadn't beaten her time on a hike was the Forty-Miler. She'd taken the disadvantage of starting fifty-seven minutes behind him and turned it into the extra motivation to catch him. He'd been so sure no one could. It had motivated her to burn up that trail in just over seventeen hours to his eighteen. He could seriously respect just how fast she'd been moving.

She'd definitely snagged his attention…his and his body's. But bottom line, it didn't matter.

If she did nothing but fight beside him, he'd find a way to be content, or at least accept it.

Then he thought about the other side of that coin. What if there was more?

Taking down Carla Anderson as man and woman, that could definitely give a man happy thoughts. Or, he had to smile to himself, being taken down *by* Carla Anderson, which was probably her preferred scenario. Nope, he wouldn't be filing a complaint either way.

—∿∿∿—

Carla wondered what the hell Kyle Reeves was smiling about. Psych evals were a royal pain in the ass and she absolutely despised them.

She could never figure out what the crazier-than-she-was psycho-chiatrists were really after. And grading each other was the absolute shits!

She turned the page: *If Delta Selection was up to you, which soldiers would you select, in order*.

Goddamn it! It just kept getting worse.

Well, Kyle was an easy shoo-in for the first spot.

She could seriously respect that he'd held on for the tie at the rate she'd been moving. He was also like a kind of Mr. Perfect Soldier Guy.

What *was* behind that cool facade of nice guy and gorgeous man?

She'd thought Delta Selection had peeled back all of their layers. Right up until Kyle had managed to lean against her without her even noticing.

Somehow, despite the process, he'd hidden away deep—like some stealth weapon—his underhanded maneuver of first physical contact. Had he done the same during the shooting assessment or any of a hundred opportunities since, it wouldn't mean as much. But he hadn't.

Instead, he'd held off so long that even now, sitting at a desk in the concrete-and-blah eval room, that simple contact sizzled through her body. She'd passed out thinking of him and woken doing the same. *Unfair, cheater, cheater pumpkin-eater, low-down… Slick move, dude*.

How far ahead had he planned that moment? All the way back when he'd first challenged her to make it to the end? Now that she thought of that, she knew it was true, or might as well be. It was as if some part of his twisty mind had turned on at the shooting range and begun planning how to sidle up to her without her defenses noticing. Worse, it had worked!

She never did things like that. She could be sneaky, underhanded, downright nasty in the moment. But apparently Kyle's brain could work on a much longer timeline. Probably part of why she'd only led a fireteam of Army grunts and he'd commanded an operational detachment of Green Berets.

What other layers did he have that Delta hadn't exposed?

Her own tough-bitch side had come out more than once. Okay, it was more of a core than a side of her, but it had come out. If there was more to Kyle, she couldn't see it.

She knew for sure that she received more than her fair share of his attention. It was true for a number of the guys, but Kyle didn't make a thing of it.

He wanted more than her friendship—she'd known that since the first sizzling look on day one that she could still feel. She'd kept her shades on that first day to gain some distance from that initial flash of heat.

But it had taken the asshole an entire week before he spoke directly to her, and that was only after she spoke first in the back of the truck while he stared at her face. He didn't even have the decency to stare at her breasts so that she could dismiss him out of hand. Jerk.

He had played a low-key waiting game. It was very risky, but she had to admit he'd played it well—it had one hundred percent worked.

She was to the point that if she didn't tear his clothes off real goddamn soon, she was going to lose it.

Now that they'd finished Stress Phase testing, there

was a desire to find herself a serious release and Kyle was her number one candidate for that as well as for Delta.

However, there was one more big obstacle.

They were still candidates for another two days, not yet trainees. After this dumbass psych eval, they still had to face the last step of the selection process tomorrow: the Commanders Board Review.

Then they each would either be in or out.

If only one of them made it, the cliff between them would be too vast and no way was she signing up for a pity fuck in either direction.

If they were both out, she wouldn't mind a little friendly commiseration with a man who would really understand before they were shipped back to their respective units.

One of the biggest dangers of trying for the elite units was *not* making the cut. And in Delta, there was typically a ninety-five percent failure rate. When you were kicked back to your unit, you were forever labeled "not good enough," no matter what Delta's glowing letter said. The fact that the others of your old cadre stood even less of a chance didn't matter. They could still pretend that they could pass if they wanted to, but not you—your butt had been booted back down.

If they were both in?

Well, that was a whole different matter. In that case, she'd say that a celebration was definitely in order. Wonder how much that would surprise him.

She'd bet not one bit. He would have built plans around possible contingent scenarios. It was hard to surprise Kyle Reeves, but she sure looked forward to trying.

Carla turned back to the eval, hoping no one noticed

her smile. Soldier number two of eleven that she'd want to serve with?

Duane Jenkins. Guy was an absolute rock. You just knew you could always rely on Duane to have your back. That, and right when it couldn't get any worse but was about to anyway, he'd find some joke and make it a bit better.

Number three…

Chapter 4

KYLE COULD SEE IT IN THEIR FACES AS THEY CAME OUT of the Commanders Review Board.

He watched Chad Hawkins come out walking tall. He looked like a corn-fed kid from Iowa, but inside was the archetypal hardened soldier: tough, powerful, and serious about it. He was practically skipping like a ten-year-old boy as he came down the steps.

Chad high-fived several of the guys. When he got to Kyle, he turned it into a hard handclasp and a solid one-armed hug and thud on the back. "Kick ass, bro," which was odd, as the man had barely spoken to him over the last month.

"Thanks, man."

Andrew came out looking like he'd been ass-kicked and then mauled by a pit bull. The Delta cadre escorted him away before his wave of depression could affect the others, but Kyle still felt it. Andrew had survived Delta Selection. A Green Beret like Kyle and Chad with a damn fine rep, he'd been one of the twelve in the fire circle at the end of the Forty-Miler. He'd made jokes about how anything after this had to be easy.

Not so much, by the look of him.

There were several passes and two more hammered-down failures—one who stalked away from the cadre escort with an "I don't need this shit!"—before Kyle's turn came up. Only Carla and three others were left. She offered him a smile. It was tight, almost pained, but it was a smile nonetheless. He did his best to return it and stepped through the door.

The room where the fate of men's careers was decided should have been more impressive. It had beige cinder-block walls, a white linoleum floor, and bright fluorescent lighting. A single chair sat in front of a couple of folding tables. The only decoration was an American flag in a stand.

Behind the tables sat Colonel Brighton and his assistant, Major Clayton. Sergeant Major Maxwell was to Clayton's right, along with two others from the training cadre. And to the Colonel's left sat a man Kyle didn't recognize. They were all dressed in boots, ACU pants, and black T-shirts, not a whole lot to go on for an ID.

The stranger had collar-long brown hair and dark eyes. No one Kyle had ever met looked like this guy. It was almost as if one moment he was the only one in the room with Kyle and it was between the two of them alone—the next moment it was as if he wasn't there at all.

The Colonel waved him into the single chair before the table with little ceremony.

Kyle's butt hadn't quite hit the metal seat when Sergeant Major Maxwell snapped out the first question.

"So, you want to be in The Unit just to impress that bitch outside and get into her pants. Makes you a waste of our time because we're not letting a wench into The Unit. We aren't that fucking stupid. Is that the only reason you're here?"

And that snarl was the friendliest question of the next hour.

———*m*———

"We already called your unit commander and warned him we were dumping your sorry ass back on him. He didn't sound any kind of pleased."

Carla faced the Board and did her best to take a steadying breath, but the Board wasn't big on pauses. Even though the comment wasn't a question, she couldn't stop the answer.

"Then I'll climb to the top of another unit. But you want me in this one."

"Why is that?" Those were the first words the stranger had spoken throughout the entire interview. His voice was soft, yet it silenced the room.

This was her idea of the ultimate Delta operator. He was thirties, maybe even forties—hard to tell. But there was no mistaking his impossible level of fitness or that he clearly saw more in a single movement than most men saw in an entire interview. He…felt different. Like Kyle, but honed down to the essence of Delta through long and hard service.

As they'd harangued her about underlying motivations based on her mother's and Clay's deaths—which, in truth, had started her down the Delta path but were no longer relevant—she'd thought a lot about Clay's stories of what he'd done while flying for SOAR and the people he'd met.

He'd bragged a lot on Beale and Henderson, but a couple times he'd talked about the shadow warriors he'd met, and ultimately, that's why she was here in Delta. The tone of awe in Clay's voice had snagged his little sister's imagination. He spoke of one in particular.

So, she took a guess, though she didn't think it was a wild one.

"Because, Colonel Gibson…"

The man didn't blink, though several of the others reacted. It was exactly as she'd expect from the number one soldier of the number one combat unit in existence. Nothing would surprise him.

"…Delta or CAG or The Unit is about soldiers who are determined to get it done no matter what. It doesn't matter what you call it, it matters what gets done. 'Alone and Unafraid' they say about Delta. But we are—"

"We?" he snapped out.

"We," she shot back, "because you are going to let me in. *We* are more than that. We are that sharp tip of the spear, so fine that you can't see it except occasionally by how the light glints there, which"—she kind of liked how the analogy played out—"is probably why we do so many operations at night."

"Pretty damn cocky there, Anderson." The Sergeant Major scowled at her.

"Yes, sir." She didn't see any point in denying who she was. "This isn't Rangers or Green Beret. This is The Unit."

"What about Kyle Reeves?" Colonel Brighton's voice was a growl. "You marked him number one on your list of who'd you choose to serve with. Why did you do that? Because you want to fuck him?"

Kyle hadn't come back out the front door. She didn't know if he was in or out, and this was the first time they'd mentioned him.

"I put him at the top of my list because he is the best soldier I've ever met."

Brighton narrowed his eyes at her for avoiding the question, so she offered him her best smile.

"Of course a girl would be stupid if she didn't want the best of everything, Delta or otherwise. And, Colonel Brighton..."

He arched an eyebrow at her pause.

"...I ain't stupid."

That got her an unexpected laugh from him. Who knew the man could even do that?

Sergeant Major Maxwell's smile was as big as when she'd dug in at the end of the Forty-Miler.

But it was Colonel Gibson she was watching. His quiet nod confirmed Clay's stories of how it felt to serve with the very best and finally do something right.

───※───

Carla stepped out the back door of the Commander's Review Board's room as they called in the final candidate. She hoped Richie would make it. He'd earned fourth spot on her own list. Richie Goldman was wiry thin, Jewish, and bloody brilliant. Add in enough Delta determination to survive selection and she'd gladly serve alongside him. If he made it, she'd be five for her top five...if Kyle had made it.

This side of the building's yard was empty except for one soldier sitting on the dirt with his back against the concrete wall, covered by the sliver of shadow that the building's eave offered against the blazing midday sun.

Kyle Reeves looked up at her and she could see it. He too had been accepted. And on seeing her demeanor, a huge smile washed across his face.

Her next plan of action was improper in about a

thousand ways, which didn't make her hesitate even half a step.

Carla knelt over his lap before he could even attempt to rise. Wrapping her arms around his neck, she leaned in and kissed Kyle Reeves hard on the mouth.

Her momentum made him hit the back of his head against the concrete wall, but he didn't even react to it. He had one hand jammed up into her hair and another one scooped down around her butt, holding her tightly against him. She'd known he was strong; she hadn't known he was so powerful that his embrace made it tough to breathe, but she didn't care.

His kiss was rough as hell. The need echoed back and forth between them until it burned like live fire. This wasn't about tenderness, greeting, or exploration.

This was about thirty days of choking worry about the selection process and an equal portion of bottled-up lust mixed together and compressed down until the combination exploded into a single instant of raw heat.

It didn't matter if he'd maneuvered her into wanting him or the other way around. She'd never wanted any man more.

The kiss built until the power of it finally blew them back apart, almost as hard as they'd come together. She tipped back off his lap and landed her own butt in the dirt facing him.

"You made it!" Kyle gasped out.

Damn, he was impressive.

No way could she form words around the way her heart was pounding, and her breath ran short.

She nodded.

He held up a hand and she high-fived it hard.

The first woman in history through Delta Selection.

How goddamn awesome was that!

She dove back into his arms and scorch-level blew somewhere past incendiary before they tumbled apart once more, panting hard as if they'd just come off a battle royal.

Oh God, this was going to be so much fun.

Chapter 5

"My name is Colonel Michael Gibson. Your group has the third highest passing rate in the history of Delta. Congratulations. Follow me."

Apparently that and a group photo made up their graduation ceremony — 104 soldiers down to seven.

Kyle had tried another kiss after they'd both gotten up off the dirt, but it hadn't worked. Turnabout being fair, he'd driven her back against the wall and feasted greedily. He'd taken and she'd given, groaning with animal need as he grabbed her perfect handful of a breast and her leg wrapped around his waist.

But it was too forceful, too sparky, and he could only tolerate it so long. They ended up like two gladiators held at bay by some emperor's command — a pace apart and panting hard.

"Maybe it would be better if we don't try that again until we're alone somewhere." But he was sure as hell going to make certain that was real damn soon.

She reached out a hand, but jerked it back after she'd left a searing palm print on his chest with just the lightest touch.

"Yeah." Her nod of agreement tumbled her hair over her face. "Good idea."

He risked brushing aside her hair and tucking it behind her ear. The warrior looked at him from her one uncovered eye. Yep, they'd definitely be doing battle soon.

They'd circled around to the front of the building, carefully a few feet apart—mostly because they couldn't get any closer without losing it—and received the others' congratulations. Chad and Duane, Max and Harry.

Once Richie made it through and had been thoroughly thumped on the back, the seven of them had followed the Colonel across the compound toward a set of concrete block buildings they hadn't approached before.

The final seven.

Kyle couldn't believe it. The other five who'd sat around the final campfire but not survived Review Board had been damn fine soldiers, tough as hell to have survived Stress Phase.

But when he saw who had made it, Delta Selection somehow made sense. These were not normal soldiers around him, nor merely exceptional ones. Not anymore, because those had been weeded out.

These were Delta, as different from the average Special Forces Green Beret as Navy from Army. You could even see it in how they walked. They weren't trooping along behind this colonel, or even watching him particularly. These soldiers were independent, out-of-the-box thinkers who were chatting with and congratulating each other, already well on their way to being a close-knit team.

Except one.

Carla alone walked near the Colonel.

Colonel? Kyle hadn't learned who the man was during the Commander's Review Board, but he'd found that the man's quiet questions were always the deepest and hardest to answer. This guy had the look of coming fresh in from the field. Who even knew there was another colonel in Delta besides the commanding officer? And still on active deployment at his rank? That made the man special in a dozen different ways.

Kyle hadn't given much thought to The Unit beyond joining it. He liked to set a goal and achieve it before assessing the situation and setting the next one.

He'd been in Delta less than an hour and the new goal was clear. Every man in that review board had looked to this Colonel Gibson, not to Brighton, the unit commander. He was the ultimate Delta warrior. Quiet rather than arrogant. Focused.

Most wouldn't see him as anything exceptional, but Kyle's father would appreciate this man. Everything he did—speaking, moving, being still—came from a pure center of attention that radiated outward.

It might take Kyle five years or fifteen, but he wanted people to look at him that way, to command respect simply by being present. He wanted to become Delta's number one warrior.

Kyle moved up close behind the Colonel and Carla to overhear as the Colonel led them toward the largest building on the compound—one they hadn't entered before. Kyle shifted his position in the group as nonchalantly as he could. Only Carla appeared to notice his move, but she ignored him. He'd wager the Colonel noticed as well.

"My brother spoke very highly of you, sir." She kept her voice low and Kyle almost missed it.

"A good man and an exceptional pilot. Emily Beale flew with only the very best."

It was Kyle's first clue that Carla Anderson had a past, and that was a surprise. Everybody did, of course.

There were grunts who talked about theirs—a few who wouldn't shut up about it—and others who didn't so much, and you learned to accept that.

Carla had always been one of the ones who didn't—not at all.

It had added to her mystery, as if she'd been manifested on Earth out of pure soldier cloth. She'd talk about the Army and her time in the dust bowl of Southwest Asia, but that was it. She'd started with Team Lioness, embedded in forward search teams to frisk Muslim women without violating their religious belief that no man other than their husband could touch them. The problem with forward search-and-recon was how often it turned into forward firefight. She'd performed so well in battle that they'd switched her over to a pure combat unit.

Yet here she was, talking to a Delta colonel about people Kyle had never heard of. And the colonel knew exactly who she was.

Because they were in the lead, the two of them reached the building's double doors first, and they each held one wide for the others to enter ahead of them.

Kyle managed to drift back to being last man through the doors to remain close to the two of them. He overheard the Colonel speaking to Carla once more.

"It may be scant comfort, but it was a blindside takedown in the dead of night. There was nothing your brother could have or should have done differently. I did make sure that the shooter's life lasted only seconds longer than his."

Carla's voice didn't find its way out until they were inside the building and gathered in the high, dim concrete hallway with six doors spaced down its length.

"Thank you, sir."

The Colonel merely nodded and led them toward the first door on the right.

Kyle wished circumstances were different and he could hold her for a moment. Not because of all of the heat that even thinking about her sent coursing through his body, but just to give her a moment of stability. Wasn't gonna happen here, so he held the door for her and she entered the room blank-faced.

She gave him a nod of thanks, but he didn't think that she recognized him at the moment.

—···—

Carla stumbled to a halt.

This was not what she'd expected. No classroom of desks. No training mats or weapons store. Beyond the heavy steel entry door off the hallway, she and the other trainees now stood in your average American living room.

There were couches, chairs, a desk, and a kitchen at the far end. Even end tables with knickknacks and bookshelves with books. There were also a half-dozen dummies. Two were sitting on couches, three on stands like clothing-store mannequins, and the last leaning against a kitchen counter. They were dressed in a variety of clothes, and they were all armed.

"Look at this room," Colonel Gibson ordered in that deceptively quiet voice of his. "Study it. Think of it as a problem. How would you attack this room and take out the six bad guys"—he waved his hand at the armed dummies—"without hurting any of the civilians in it?"

There weren't any civilian dummies, but there were chairs, sofas, plenty of places they might be.

The seven of them prowled the room. There were no windows, so the only point of entry was the door, and it was heavy steel. They discussed lines of fire and angles of attack. She liked that she didn't feel too far behind on tactics, despite being the only one who wasn't Special Forces or Special Operations trained.

One thing they agreed on—it would be a total bear to take this room, and the collateral damage in the form of dead hostages was going to be high.

"Now…" The Colonel called for their attention once more. Even as he spoke, the trainees were still scanning the living room, creating strategies.

Carla would have to think later as to how she felt about Colonel Gibson. The man who had killed her brother's killer. She'd never thought to find out anything about her brother's death. Yet on her first day here, she'd met this senior officer who had been there in the field with Clay as he died. Delta had been there and still called it unavoidable. Was it truly, or was there a failure of The Unit's abilities to protect and react to—

"Rearrange this room to make it more difficult." The Colonel interrupted her thoughts. "Make it so that every line of attack you have just thought of would fail. Make it so that the collateral loss of life would be near a hundred percent, no matter what strategy the attacking rescue force might use. Then have a seat as a hostage and we'll discuss it."

So, they were the hostages. That clarified the scenario, made it easier to change it from bad to awful.

They shifted a couch and put a bad guy crouching behind the arm with his rifle leveled to cover both the couch's occupants and the only door. They placed two more mannequins behind a table that they flipped onto its edge to act as a shooting barrier. They worked around the room until it truly was a nightmare scenario.

The seven of them sat. Carla ended up on the couch. She shifted the villain's rifle slightly so that it wasn't pointed right at her, but it was still unnerving.

Kyle flipped the dead bolt on the steel entry door and then chose an armchair that masked a shooter behind him. It was in the corner of the room opposite the door, so there was almost no way to spot the hidden shooter.

She was just turning to see if she could find yet another way to make it harder when the world exploded.

The lights went out.

A massive explosion blew the door off the hinges.

A flash-bang filled the room with a blinding light, and she threw up an arm to protect her eyes.

Silenced gunfire spit around her. She heard a bullet whine so close to her ear that the *krak* of its supersonic flight hurt. The gust of another moved her hair. The heat of muzzle flash washed across her skin.

The lights came back on.

Three seconds.

Four max.

The bad-guy dummy crouched behind the couch arm was now sprawled on the floor with two holes in its forehead.

Four men were moving through the room with night-vision goggles shoved up on their foreheads, stripping the bad guys of their weapons. Each dummy received a third bullet in the head from a silenced revolver as they went.

Ten seconds, it was done. The room was clear and not a hostage was touched.

"I think," Colonel Gibson said drily from where he stood at ease in the middle of the room, "that concludes the discussion. Please feel free to inspect the results."

The seven of them rose from their chairs, some steadier than others. She looked up at the corners of the room's ceiling, but could identify no spy cameras. A glance at the Colonel, and he shook his head. So, no prior intel and they'd somehow done this with live ammo passing inches from her head—despite her being in motion to protect her eyes—without one of the "hostages" bearing a single scratch.

She went out into the hall and found the electrical panel with the simulated charge placed to blow it, though all they'd really done was turn off the breakers.

The door had not been treated so gently. It was definitely blown, but not blown to shit or it would have sent shrapnel into the room. They'd cut the hinges and the locks with small charges and then jerked the door aside with a heavy rope attached to the door handle on one side and a set of powerful suction cups on the other. It wasn't rope, but rather heavy bungee line. So the door had flown out of the way the instant the hinges were shattered. It made entry a half second faster.

These guys were all about half-second advantages. Damn cool.

Every bad guy, including the one crouched out of sight behind Kyle's armchair in a corner of the room, was down with the three bullet holes. Not a single stray shot pockmarked a wall. Four attackers, six dead terrorists, eighteen shots total—less than a single standard magazine for just one of the HK416s that the Delta operators were carrying.

"How the hell…?" the class was starting to ask.

Carla shared a quick look with Kyle. "How" is what they were here to learn.

"How soon?" is what she wanted to know.

At least now she truly understood.

If Delta Colonel Michael Gibson said that her brother's death was wholly unavoidable, she was going to believe him.

"You get tomorrow off. We suggest you sleep. Training begins the day after at 0600, and you can see that you'd better be sharp." Colonel Gibson and the four Delta shooters started to leave the room.

He stopped at the door and waited until the shooters were clear.

"These four men"—he turned back to face the room—"they're the sum total of the previous class. Just like your class, there were seven of them at the start of OTC out of a hundred and twenty applicants." Then he was gone.

The Operator Training Course was six months long. Three hadn't made it, but now she had the answer to how soon she could do this.

"Six months!" she mouthed to Kyle.

"Can't wait," he mouthed back.

Chapter 6

OTC WAS NOT AT THE TOP OF KYLE'S "CAN'T WAIT" list. And despite the Colonel's suggestion, sleep was about the farthest thing from his mind.

He showered, pulled on his civvies and a leather jacket, and walked out to his Ducati. He hadn't been on it in thirty days.

Parked beside his machine was a midnight-blue Kawasaki Ninja. Leaning back against it was Delta Trainee Carla Anderson in those same long, lightning-bolt-yellow and smoke-gray leathers he'd seen her in on the first day.

"*Damn!*" Not the best greeting, but it was just knocked out of him. She was about the most amazing sight he'd ever seen.

She grinned and waited him out while he recovered.

"I was thinking of going for a ride before dinner." He went for the casual glance up at the sun still a few hours above the horizon, though it was hard looking away from her for even a moment.

"There a good pizza place in Beaufort," she offered lazily.

"A hundred and sixty miles. Take us an hour and a half tops." Kyle's bike was just as fast as hers.

"Uh-huh."

"Awfully close to the Marines down there." Camp Lejeune wasn't the issue; keeping his hands off her for that long was.

"Yeah, Marine cooties are a problem." Her voice remained casual and lazy, and wrapped around him with all the certainty of a cowboy's lasso. "I know another spot. I'll lead, you follow." She didn't give him a chance to argue, just pulled on her helmet and climbed on her bike.

He pulled on his helmet and swung onto his own motorcycle.

"That's assuming you can keep up with me on your pansy-ass lipstick-red machine. Don't get lost, tough guy."

"I'll be right on your tail, girlie. And it's *wildfire*-red."

"Uh-huh." She grinned and fired off her machine.

They idled out of the Delta gate along with the other five trainees, two on bikes, a Camaro and a Vette, and Richie's older model Toyota Prius. They were really going to have to talk to him—the man was going to be an embarrassment. Most of them turned for the South Gate, headed to Fayetteville. Chad was seeing a girl in Raeford, so they lost him at the Longstreet Gate. Carla led Kyle across the width of Bragg to the Manchester Gate, out past Pope Army Airfield. No one else was headed out that way.

She opened the throttle before the gate's stick was even half raised. She had to duck to clear it. If he'd hesitated even half a second, she'd have been gone.

One thing Kyle had learned from this afternoon's demonstration of the room clearing: never hesitate.

On that very first day, he'd wanted to see Carla Anderson flying down the road in her lightning leathers, but he'd never imagined it like this.

She hung low over her machine, laying into the corners. His view from close behind was spectacular; that part was much as he'd imagined. It was the heat he hadn't accounted for. July in the North Carolina lowlands was brutal, but he didn't give a damn. It was the heat he had for this woman that was all out of proportion.

If there were cops in Carthage, they didn't stand a chance. To Carla, a red light was an excuse to explore the back roads, only at highway velocities. The open highway itself was more akin to a race course, a race that there was no way in hell he would be losing.

It was only when they flew out of Carthage and were cracking 130 that he saw the sign for their possible destination flash by.

No way!

A dozen miles and five minutes later, the answer was "Yes, way."

They crossed into the Uwharrie National Forest going about thirty times faster than the last time they'd been here.

Now that he knew where they were headed, he could have hiked there over the rough country, but he had no idea how to get there by road.

Carla did. A wild part of her brain had tracked the truck's route that had hauled them back from the Forty-Miler.

The woman was incredible.

Carla took the dirt fast. Might have been able to dust Kyle if she'd really tried, but somehow she doubted it. You couldn't dust the likes of Kyle Reeves unless he let you. She was counting on him not letting her and wasn't disappointed.

She caught air coming over the rise where they'd met at the end of the Forty-Miler, and Kyle was flying right beside her. They hit the final RV exactly in sync, as close together as when they'd hiked it just seventy-two hours before, but this time they were going over sixty across the grassy clearing in the trees.

After crossing the RV, she throttled back and let the bike ease down and coast along the narrow trail to where the final campfire had been.

"Hope you brought the spiced wine," she called out as she shut down her machine and peeled her helmet off. His machine thudded to silence close behind her.

When he didn't reply, she turned to face him.

Kyle Reeves, five-foot-nine of hard-bodied soldier, slammed into her. From standing apart, they went to full-body contact, lip-lock, and full-on grope faster than she could blink.

She unzipped his leather jacket and shoved it off his shoulders. It trapped his arms at the elbows. While he struggled to free himself, she had his T-shirt up so that she could get to his chest. Oh, damn, but the man had an amazing chest. After the workouts of the last month she shouldn't be surprised, but...damn!

Carla broke their frantic kiss so that she could step back and see his chest. Yep! It looked exactly as good as it felt.

Kyle finally freed one arm and shed the jacket and the shirt.

She let him come at her, caught him as they slammed back together. Her need to get skin to skin was fire-hot, but that was a discovery he'd have to make on his own.

His teeth raked her breast through the leathers. If he

left bite marks on the leather, it would be his last act on Earth no matter how incredible it felt.

Then came the moment she'd been waiting for.

Kyle pulled down the front zipper on her leathers and froze. His dark brown eyes went nearly black as he looked down at the exposed narrow V of skin that started at her neck and reached down to her solar plexus with no other material to block the view.

For an instant, he looked her in the eyes, and then, like the good soldier he was, returned his attention to the primary target zone. So slowly that she could feel each zipper tooth release right down inside her, he ran it the rest of the way down.

He may have whispered a prayer of thanks when he peeled the leathers back off her bare shoulders and down to her waist. He stared down at her chest for a long moment in silence.

Carla expected him to grab, to devour, to take. That's why she hadn't worn a stitch of clothing under the leathers. She'd been aching for a month for this man to simply take her. Instead, he brushed fingers along the side of her breast so gently it sent shivers up her body.

She didn't want gentle; she wanted heat, but she couldn't do anything. Couldn't move. Couldn't breathe. Couldn't think as he bent down to take her in his mouth. The heat she wanted slammed into her like a physical blow.

The sound started low. For half a moment she wondered if another bike or a bear was coming to their corner of the woods. Then she identified the source. It was rising from the depths of Kyle's throat.

Without warning, he stripped off the rest of her

leathers with a violence that tested the strength limits
of the material and tossed them aside. He scooped one
arm around her shoulder and the other between her legs
with a hand clamped on her butt and lifted her like she
weighed less than a rifle.

He knocked half of the wind out of her as he slammed
her down to lie atop her own clothes. His mindless growl
grew louder as he fought off his pants and dug protection out of a pocket.

There was nothing delicate in how he took her or
in how she welcomed him when he landed on her.
He entered her in one clean shot, all the way in until
they couldn't get any closer. The heat she'd wanted
was nothing compared to the roaring fire that erupted
between them.

She locked her arms around his neck and her legs
around his hips, and held on for the best ride of her life.
He wasn't some do-it-and-done guy. He'd proven his
stamina on the trail and he proved it now.

It wasn't a question of driving each other upward.
They started at the top and shattered themselves into the
beyond from there.

If she were the sort of woman who clawed, she'd
have shredded his back. Instead, she simply held on as
the ball of heat exploded and rolled through her in massive waves of raw power.

She wasn't often on the bottom, submissive wasn't
her style, but she was past caring, past control. He
pawed her breast and shifted down to drag it once more
into his mouth without breaking the amazing rhythm of
him pounding into her.

Men satisfied her; she enjoyed them.

Kyle must not be a man then, because he sure didn't stay within the bounds of those mundane descriptors. Her body writhed of its own accord. The more he did to her, the more it writhed. Her breath came shorter and shorter, until her hard gasps were exploding out of her with each stroke of his driving rhythm.

She'd never been vocal but couldn't stop the cry that ripped from her throat as her body came apart in tidal waves of glory.

Kyle clamped her hands in his and pinned them above her shoulders, but it wasn't entrapment. It was merely a way to hold on to each other as he drove his mouth against hers and drank down her next cry of sweet agony.

She arched up to meet him. To meet his heat. Because everywhere they touched, Kyle was pure heat…except deep inside her where he was raw fire.

At his release, the waves inside her were reborn, flashing to life and rebounding across her body. All she could do was ride them until they subsided to gentle washes, then echoes…and finally silence.

Kyle lay heavy in her arms, his heart still thudding against her chest, his breath still rough and close by her ear.

He shook it off enough to prop himself up and look down at her. "I didn't hurt you, did I? I've never needed anyone the way I needed you."

"Kyle, I hereby issue you a permanent pass to hurt me just like that anytime you want. That was delicious."

"Delicious?" A smile quirked his lips, so she kissed them and discovered that her own were quite sore.

"Mmm," she managed, a hum of contentment—all that was in her.

"You want delicious? That's different." And he kissed her lips, nuzzled her neck, caressed her hip.

"No. Kyle. I—" Any further protests died as he began working his way along her body. She could do no more than lie back against the bank—the very bank where they had stretched out side by side when they finished the hike—and watch the trees and the darkening sky as he took her aloft once more.

Delicious didn't begin to describe it.

—⁓—

Kyle had known Carla was a smart woman. She'd proven it again by stuffing energy bars and a bedroll into her pack.

Kyle's head had been too clouded with lust to grab more than a water bottle.

He figured tomorrow they'd find a restaurant and a hotel room. Or maybe a hotel room with delivery pizza. Right now, she was snuggled up against his shoulder, her soft hair spilling across his chest and one of those impossibly long legs thrown over his hips. He wasn't sure how such long legs fit on a woman her height, but they looked just fine.

Impossibly, despite everything they'd done to each other this evening, the mere thought of her was arousing him again. He didn't want to wake her. After all, she deserved her rest as well.

But the need was building, not diminishing.

And Carla didn't strike him as a woman who complained much.

She mumbled something unintelligible when he brushed his fingers over her.

She seemed only half-awake as he rolled her on top and she straddled him, her hands braced on his chest, her head hanging down. Her face remained masked the fall of her hair—the ends of which tickled his chest.

Her body came fully to life as she arched back in the moonlight that painted forest shadows against her dusky skin, and she moaned like glory when he drove upward into her and sent her flying once more.

He'd never had a woman like her before. Of course, no woman had ever been Delta before either.

Chapter 7

CARLA TROTTED SILENTLY DOWN THE DARKENED HALL-way. The four other trainees were clustered around her as they moved.

They'd lost Harry and Max in the last six months of the Operator Training Course. Harry decided he just couldn't hack the mental side. Delta wasn't for your average Joe, not even when you were exceptional enough to qualify. They learned everything from how to attack a helicopter to how to fly one. Comm gear, rifles, medicine, languages…the list grew rather than shrank as they started redesigning it themselves to address their own strengths and weaknesses.

They were expected to pick up at least one new language on top of the training time.

Carla already had Spanish and parts of Russian, so she'd gone for Mandarin. Kyle already spoke Mandarin, chunks of French, and gutter Spanish; he'd opted for Russian. Their lovemaking, when they could steal a moment, had become a strange mash-up of polyglot exercises. It was easy to be sexy in Spanish or sly in Mandarin, but for seriously raunchy, Russian kicked ass.

Max had dropped out with a torn knee courtesy of a bad nighttime parachute jump into the high Rockies—though he'd successfully completed the five-day mountain-survival exercise wearing a splint and swore he'd be back in the next class. Delta had given him a pass on Delta Selection; he'd go straight into OTC with the next group.

They approached their target. The door in the hallway had no exterior hinges, no obvious dead-bolt lock, just a flat sheet of metal. Training cadre never duplicated a single exercise, always creating something new.

Duane had shown a real skill with blowing shit up and was now their chief breacher. His smile was bright in his tanned face as he started prepping the door. Richie and Chad were rigging a haulback to snatch the door out of the way as soon as Duane had it blown. The trainers had put a sign on the far wall that said, "This wall isn't here. Don't use it."

Fine. They appropriated a handy forklift to act as the counterbalance. If it got dinged up by the flying steel door, that was training's issue, not theirs.

Carla spotted a shadow high on the wall. She stepped back to squint up at it, lost in the darkness beyond the hanging light fixtures. She flashed a signal to Kyle, pointing upward.

He looked up over his shoulder, assessing what she'd found. In answer to her question, he dropped his back against the wall and cupped his hands. The man was really good at risk assessment and instant decisions, way faster than she was.

Three running steps, a foot planted in his palms, and in a moment she was standing on his shoulders, his hands bracing her ankles. He held her there easily on those strong shoulders of his.

His grip was as solid and assured as when he was driving her body to new extremes of release—she hoped that he never tired of that particular avenue of exploration as he'd proven to be awe-inspiringly creative—or holding her while they slept. What man actually held you in his sleep? Kyle Reeves. That she'd grown to like it, that was the really weird part.

Focus!

A quick glance through the vent she'd spotted proved her right.

She slid an electric screwdriver out of her thigh pocket and in moments had the grill removed from the heating duct. She set it atop a nearby light fixture and leveraged herself into the ventilation system.

One minute and two turns later she was looking down into the shoot room through a ceiling ventilation-intake grate. Once again, Colonel Gibson was doing the spiel to the crop of new trainees who had just survived the selection process. Her team hadn't seen him more than once or twice since their own graduation.

Not daring to make a noise—not even a whispered radio report—she pulled out a cell phone, snapped four images, and texted them to the rest of the crew. She loved going low-tech.

Stay high or drop in? She decided on high, mostly. No need to explain; her team would be looking for her.

Her cell texted back, "Three."

Carla counted in her head, *Two. One.*

And the door blew.

Under cover of the blast, she flipped the ceiling grate vent cover aside and quickly slid forward headfirst until her hips hit the edge of the vent before jamming her feet to the sides of the duct to brace herself.

Hanging upside down, dangling halfway down from

the center of the ceiling, she closed her eyes for an instant to avoid being blinded by the flash-bang.

Then firing from her position like an inverted swivel-gun turret, she took out three of the terrorists with double-taps to the head. By the time she finished, the four guys were in through the door and had taken down the five other terrorists—eight dummies in the room this time, two dressed as housewives, but still armed.

Even as she did a drop-and-roll into the room—long before the "hostage" trainees had a chance to recover enough to see how she entered—she saw the smile flicker across Colonel Gibson's lips. Impossibly, he'd known she was there above him, damn the man. Someday she'd surprise him.

Right. That was about as likely as surprising Kyle Reeves. Just wasn't gonna happen… Wouldn't keep her from trying though.

She reached up with her rifle to knock the vent back into place. To the trainees, it would appear that she'd been teleported magically into the center of the room. In a way she had. When she'd had her first turn sitting on the couch, she'd sat there thinking she knew shit. Now Carla had the sneaking suspicion that maybe, at long last, she finally did know some shit. At least a little.

They finished the weapons strip and "security" shots before turning toward the door. Six trainees had made it through the selection process this time and were just starting to tune in to what had happened around them. Five guys and another woman.

Saddle up, girl. It's gonna be fun. Of course, there's only one Kyle Reeves, and she had him. So, the woman was going to have less fun than Carla, just for that fact alone.

Carla didn't speak to her, of course, or even acknowledge her existence, but the woman's blue eyes were certainly tracking her. Carla could feel the want, the deep-rooted need to conquer this. It was a look that Carla had seen in the mirror every single day, which she figured gave the woman good odds of making it.

Out in the hall, they repacked their gear while the trainees did their inspect and wonder. After his pronouncement about OTC graduates, Colonel Gibson left the trainees behind while he led Carla's five-person team to the airplane mock-up.

Over the last six months, they'd run through the six doorways off this hallway hundreds of times each, though it felt like more. At first, moving step by step with lights on and firing Simunitions that did little more than sting and leave a red-colored dot. Then in pairs, finally as a full team. One terrorist, two, five. Then the same progression but with live ammo. Living room, airplane, ship's bridge, tunnel-and-cave system…they'd done them until the scenarios had oddly all become the same.

The environment controlled what was possible, but not what was required. Each scenario became simply another integrated layer of possible actions, practiced until the varying terrain could be addressed without thought and thus the targets could receive her full attention.

The colonel led them to the far end of the concrete hallway, where they could still hear the echoes of the surprised murmurs of the recent graduates. Last door on the right led them into the nose of a 747. The front hundred feet of an old 747-100 had been put here. They climbed the stairway to the first class lounge.

Duane dug water bottles out of the steward's station

and began tossing them around. They all dropped into a group of deep leather airplane seats facing one another.

———

Kyle rolled the water bottle across his forehead. The action phase was measured in seconds and the overall operation itself in mere minutes, but that didn't make it one bit less of a workout. He knocked back half the bottle and inspected his team.

He wasn't the leader, not really. They were five individuals who were exceptionally good at working together. Drop in another operator or take two away, which they often did during training, and it didn't matter. Delta was flexibility. Not *about* flexibility, rather something they simply *were*. Yet he'd be sorry if this team split up. Not just he and Carla—which was a horrifying possibility that they'd only been able to tolerate discussing once—but this whole team just plain hummed.

Chad was their hammer. His blond good looks and cherubic smile hid a Detroit street fighter who'd clawed his way out of the gangs and would have your back until hell froze over. He was pretty much as sharp as Kyle on tactics. Kyle often used him to lead the other group when they split the team; Chad always knew what to do with them. They tried tagging him with "Farm Boy" for his Midwestern Scandinavian looks, but it hadn't stuck until the day Kyle had watched him during a rapid-fire practice and tagged him "The Reaper."

In contrast, his best buddy, Duane, came from a privileged Atlanta background. He was milder, funny, but no less dangerous when cornered. Carla had called him rock solid once, and he'd been called "The Rock" ever since because it fit him so well. Duane was a really straight-ahead thinker, but he really got it done once you had him aimed in the right direction.

Richie was their boy genius. He was Kyle's age, but it was as if he was walking the planet for the first time. He overanalyzed the shit out of everything, served up exactly the information you needed, and then threw himself full tilt into any situation. His shortcoming was that he often overthought things, but knowing that, he let himself be guided into action easily when needed. He was a huge James Bond fan, so that tag of "Q" had been inevitable.

There'd been an early tendency to put Carla on a pedestal, but she'd slammed down the kibosh on that. Kyle had managed to compartmentalize and only worship her in the bedroom. The rest of the time he simply respected the hell out of her.

Over the months, the team had eventually looked to him.

He didn't really take command, but he could see from an overview level what was needed and lay it out for them. By the time OTC was over, he could do it with three words and a couple gestures. He knew exactly how best to deploy the team's strengths. He'd often assign someone to their weakest skill to get practice in it; they never questioned him about that. It was a giddy feeling, being able to shape such an elite force to the mission at hand.

Richie had tried to tag him with "Bond." Chad had shot for "Superman," based on Kyle's last name, which Duane had immediately rejected with a suggestion of "Clark Kent" because "ain't Kyle so purty and nice?"

Carla was the one who finally tagged him with the

simple "Mister Kyle," as if he were in the *Avengers* TV show and she was his pretty and dangerous sidekick. She'd rejected "Ms. Peel" by knocking Chad back on his ass when he suggested it. Instead, his prone epithet of "Wild Woman" had been what stuck, because she could unleash "wild" big-time when that's what was needed.

For all her attitude, Carla never questioned Kyle either. She was simply a fantastically creative weapon that he could aim and fire with no question of her ability to deliver every time. In planning, in operations...and in bed.

They'd been sleeping together for half a year—sharing a place just off base when they were here at Fort Bragg—and oddly, he knew her less well than most women he'd slept with.

She had proven herself as capable as Kyle or any of the guys. Any lack in upper body strength was more than compensated for with sheer tenacity. And in bed she always packed a sexual fire that burned him up in the very best ways.

He studied her sidelong, but nothing stood out, other than being an exceptionally beautiful woman. But despite giving selflessly to the team and to him personally, it was almost as if she wasn't there.

Then she turned and caught his inspection, and he knew he was being an idiot. Her frank look showed a woman who was one hundred percent present and accounted for. It must be the jags of coming off the live shoot that were confusing him.

Yet he'd had such thoughts before. Or he was losing his mind. Always a possibility.

They were done with the Operator Training Course.

There would be plenty of specialty training, on top of the never-ending general training of Delta. But none of them knew what came next.

And they certainly looked out of place here, every one of them.

The airplane's first class shoot room was somewhat the worse for wear, but the maintenance guys were pretty good at putting it back together each time the trainees tore it apart. So here they sat in a room that could have been comfortably cruising at thirty thousand feet, dressed in tight-fitting black and wearing enough live ammo to take down a dozen shoot rooms. They sat as comfortably in vests loaded with magazines and with HK416 suppressor-equipped, night-vision-scoped rifles across their laps as real first class fliers did with their whiskey miniatures and tablet computers.

"You're only the second one ever to notice the vent system." Colonel Gibson opened the conversation.

Carla hesitated and then nodded. "And you were the first. I was wondering how you guessed I was there. As we walked the hallway, I found myself wondering how smoke is cleared out of the rooms without any windows."

"I spotted the vents clearing the smoke during the initial demonstration. Happened to have blinked my eyes closed and turned away when the flash-bang went off. Spent six months waiting for a chance to use that fact."

She stuck her tongue out at the Colonel, who laughed softly. Colonel Gibson didn't look as if he was someone who did that very often.

Kyle could see the others exchanging looks. He

agreed with them. "Wild Woman" was the most out-of-the-box thinker they had. None of them had thought about how the room itself functioned.

"As you are no doubt aware," Gibson resumed, "the operational tempo at Delta has never been higher. After twenty years of mostly being called to the point of launch and then receiving mission aborts, The Unit has been on continuous deployment for over a decade. For the last four years we have often run four or five operations a night in one theater or another. Over six thousand al-Qaeda, Taliban, and al-Shabaab high-level assets are no longer on the line because of Delta and DEVGRU."

There were low whistles around the room. Kyle had heard rumors of that; it was one of the reasons he'd joined. But to hear it confirmed was another thing entirely.

The Colonel nodded. "The large-scale military served their role, but the Tier One assets are why those three are mostly off the map. New groups are cropping up, of course, and we'll be the ones sent in to deal with them as well."

Kyle looked about the room. This was the team he'd want to be with when they went in.

"Typically it starts with a single piece of intel that leads to an engagement with unfriendly forces, which leads to immediate new intel and continues in a rapid cascade of target opportunities. We can frequently roll up entire cells leading right to a high-value target in a single night. While that would be a normal first assignment for a new team, which is split up and integrated with other operatives in the field, this team has not been selected for that type of operation."

"Excuse me, sir." Kyle sat forward. "Did you say 'not'?"

"That's correct, Sergeant Reeves. This team has performed exceptionally and will be held together as a unit for the time being. You have"—he checked his watch—"twenty-three minutes to gather any items from the quartermaster that you wish to add to your full kit. Showers are recommended as well. A vehicle will be in the compound to take you to Pope Field for immediate departure."

Kyle checked his watch and spun the outer dial to twenty-two minutes from now, then he waited.

Nothing.

Carla and then, one by one, the rest of the team smiled.

Classic Delta. No instructions you didn't need, like where the hell they were going. Which also meant they should be prepared for anything.

"Will you be leading us, sir?"

Colonel Gibson looked at him steadily for a long moment before answering, "You're inside The Unit now."

Right.

Yet another readjustment to his thinking. If they needed a leader, they wouldn't be here. Every one of them had been a squad or section leader in their old units, and that was before OTC. They weren't qualified to command a company or a battalion, but they'd certainly know how to have those commanders lead them to best advantage in a situation.

They rose to their feet and were about to file out when Kyle stopped and turned. The others drifted to a halt to see what he was up to.

He shifted to smart attention and then formally saluted the Colonel. "Have a good 'un, sir." As if the Colonel were the one being dismissed back to training.

His whole team snapped to and mirrored his salute.
"Roger that, Sergeant." Colonel Gibson saluted back.
It didn't get Kyle a laugh, as Carla had, but it did get him
a pretty good smile. Made Kyle feel like he was ready.

Chapter 8

CARLA WAS SO NOT READY FOR THIS.

HALO jumps were fine. Jumping out of a speeding jetliner at thirty-five thousand feet was almost as much of a rush as having sex with Kyle. Well, no, it wasn't that good, but it could sure make a girl feel happy in a lot of ways.

Her problem was that she hadn't slept in over thirty-six hours and they were headed into their first live op on no notice. Well, technically on twenty-three minutes notice, which didn't help a whole lot.

Carla had been unable to sleep the night before their OTC graduation exercise; she'd been too wound up about it. At least that's what she thought it had been. The more she'd lain there inside the curl of Kyle's sleeping arms, the less she believed her first assessment.

Was she worried about the exercise itself? No. They'd practiced a hundred variations on the living room scenario. Delta had started them off with learning to shoot while walking, then at a target behind them while they walked. Then an elevated target, then an elevated target behind them while they were running. Despite being a thousandth the size, Delta fired more training rounds than the entire Marine Corps, and she had the calluses between her thumb and forefinger to prove it.

Was she worried about disappointing Kyle or the team? Wasn't gonna happen.

Was she worried about disappointing the Delta leaders who had let her in? No.

She had slid from Kyle's arms, leaving her pillow in her place for him to wrap himself around, and gone to sit in a chair by the bedroom window streaming with moonlight and look out at their crap view of the apartment's parking lot where their motorcycles sat side by side.

She'd wanted to wake Kyle and slip down the road in the moonlight. Go back into the Uwharrie to their idyll in the wilderness...which had been so rudely interrupted by a thunderstorm that had sent them scrambling to a motel, laughing like lunatics all the way.

Carla wanted to run away from...nothing! It wasn't her style. She faced every problem head-on. So she'd ignored the moonlight and focused back on the night before OTC graduation.

Had she been worried about what would happen to the team after graduating from OTC?

Desperately.

Crap! There it had been.

In the past, Carla had shifted fireteams as easily as changing her billet; it just wasn't that big a deal. But Delta had forced her to new levels in team integration, and she'd hate to lose any of these jokers.

And Kyle. She'd really, really hate to lose Kyle. She never got attached; it just didn't happen. Having Mom gone when Carla was fourteen and Clay gone when she hit eighteen had taught her the danger of that.

But if she and Kyle were separated, she'd just...

She shouldn't be attached, but she was...and hated it. And at the same time loved it. *Damn it!* She wasn't making any sense to herself. She'd barely managed to suppress the scream of frustration that would have had Kyle leaping from the bed and grabbing for a weapon before he was fully conscious.

By sunrise she'd found no answer, not by the start of the final exercise.

Afterward, Carla had frozen up solid waiting for the hammer fall; everyone pretending to be so casual as they sat there in the simulated aircraft waiting for their first orders.

Then she'd looked at Kyle and wondered if she'd ever see him again.

Memorize his face! Memorize this moment! So casual, so excellent, sitting in an aircraft's first class lounge, armed against the world's evil. She stored that image deep and hated her weakness. She didn't need anyone, but she needed Kyle as badly as she needed air to breathe.

Then Colonel Gibson had said they'd continue to fight together and the world had come back to life like a hard slap.

She was so happy that she'd wanted to jump up, scream, do a dance. Instead, she'd mimicked Kyle's salute, adding all the respect she could into it, and followed her team out the door.

They'd flown commercial to LAX, and they were now squatting in the cramped tail section of a 757 and she was no closer to understanding why she was so happy.

The CIA had come up with a plane that had a jump gate buried in her tail. They'd done a last-minute substitution for a Delta airlines flight with a jet labeled "Air Leasing—Delta." She'd bet the paint job would be scrubbed and gone in hours. Meanwhile, regular passengers rode on her, stewards did their steward thing, and five Delta operators crouched beneath them, waiting in a small separately pressurized space in the tail and reviewing the mission profile.

At three minutes to jump: they pulled on their breathers, which held ten minutes of air, and checked each other's gear.

At two minutes: the lights went red, the pressure began dropping, and everyone began holding their noses to pop their ears.

At one minute: the CIA pilot opened the pressure door and they were exposed to the air at altitude—too thin to breathe and cold enough to create instant frostbite at minus sixty centigrade, an average South Pole midnight. They were about to add another hundred degrees of windchill factor, so Carla triple-checked that there was no exposed skin.

At zero: they stepped into space and were slapped with a hammer blow. The plane had slowed to four hundred miles per hour from its normal five fifty, but it was still like being kicked by a *Jack the Giant Killer*–sized boot. The trick was not to spit out your air supply during the kick. The other option was to pass out as you fell. You'd regain consciousness when you hit thicker air, but it was not a fun ride.

Once she'd decelerated below two hundred miles per hour and could breathe again, she switched on her night-vision goggles and did a slow somersault. The plane was an apple-green trace of heat already fading into the distance. The rest of the team flew along with her.

HAHO was more fun, a High-Altitude jump followed by a High Opening of your chute. With the right winds, it was easy to fly twenty, even thirty miles to a chosen landing. The problem with HAHO was that in countries possessing better radar systems, if someone was being sharp, they could see you coming and might send a fighter jet to investigate. Then you'd be dangling there under your parachute like so much target practice.

In situations like this, the solution became HALO— High-Altitude jump and Low-Opening parachute. Basically jump and don't pull the cord until the moment before you cratered in. You plummeted through the sky fast and small, and even if someone noticed you, you were long gone.

All well and good.

The only drawback this time was that it was 2200 local time—pitch bloody black—and what lay below them were the particularly rugged Sierra de Portuguesa mountains of northern Venezuela. Every bit of which was blanketed by the dense trees of Yacambú National Park. A lot of them twenty stories tall. About the worst jump conditions there were… She supposed she should be thankful their first operation wasn't in a hurricane or a whiteout blizzard.

Chad was the best jumper, so he took the flight lead. The blond, round-faced tech sergeant always sported an easy smile. He could have been mistaken for a big, simpleton fourteen-year-old unless you looked carefully at his bright blue eyes. There was absolutely nothing easygoing about his eyes.

So they formed up and aligned on Chad. Carla ended up fourth in the flight, with Kyle bringing up the rear. They fell at near terminal velocity of two hundred miles per hour from seven miles up. Two full minutes of roaring free fall. Nothing on the ground to see where they were. Caracas was a long way to the north and there were no lights in the national park. All she could do was keep her head pointed straight down, fall, and think.

Couldn't she have gotten her thinking done during the long flight to LAX to catch the flight to Rio de Janeiro? *Nooo*. She'd been seated beside Richie, who was dense enough to be a Dallas Cowboys fan despite growing up in New York. The man had been in serious need of a reeducation. Denver Broncos ruled without question. Neither of them had slept, nor convinced the other they were an idiot, but it had made the time pass while they were sitting on a civilian flight and couldn't discuss anything important.

Then at LAX, a CIA spook had handed them a mission file on a USB for their tablet computers. Once they'd uploaded it, he'd locked them into the cargo bay of the CIA 757. She wound up sitting shoulder to shoulder with Kyle Reeves. There was so little room that there was no way to not be—leaving not a chance of sleep, considering how his mere presence raised her pulse rate.

Part of her thought really clearly around him. Like the vent in the training shoot room. She only had to indicate that there was something of interest high up in the darkness, and he'd practically done telepathy on her, offering perfect positioning and assistance to boost her up. They took each other to a higher level in combat.

When they had sex, her thinking was both clearer and foggier. He was far and away the best lover she'd ever had. She could never predict what was going on behind those dark brown eyes. Sometimes a friendly wrestle was just that—sweaty sheets and groans and happy smiles. Other times what had started as a quiet dinner left her prostrate under the dining room table, wondering if she'd ever move again. And that thing with the chocolate sauce… Damn!

She wanted to look over her shoulder at Kyle as they plummeted through the third mile down, but if she did, she would catch the wind, side-tumble, and break the formation.

Then there were the moments like now, when there was a little distance between them—even if it was only the fifty meters of free fall, about a half second apart— and he was as confusing as hell.

They were more than fuck buddies. She'd finally figured that out on her own during the long, sleepless night. But she didn't want a lover. Hell, she didn't even want a boyfriend, especially not now. So, how had she acquired one in the middle of Delta Selection and the Operator Training Course?

The whole boyfriend thing never worked well for her anyway. She'd lived with guys before; one back in high school had made it almost six months. But none of them had been serious. They'd just been convenient and compatible. When Jeremy got the terminal hots for some fiddle-playing singer chick and wanted to go on the road with her, Carla had kissed him good-bye and wished him luck, though she'd passed on his sweet offer of a farewell tumble. That's what a girl did, wasn't it?

In the Army, she'd kept her relationships short, hot, and almost exclusively civilian.

So what the hell was up with fricking Sergeant Kyle Reeves? He fought like a god and made love like a demon, and she wanted both more than she'd ever wanted anything other than Delta or to see her big brother walk through the door again.

They were entering the last mile, so she shifted from her head-down "bullet" position into a skydiver's belly-down spread. That slowed her from two hundred miles per hour down to one twenty; fifteen seconds to chute deployment.

Couldn't she just have that: happy sex and nothing more?

She saw those sly looks of his. He'd talk about his mom and dad or a chick he'd dated for two years of high school—no normal person did that—and she'd see that look creeping into his eyes to peer out at her. He never said anything, he was a smart man, but she could see it there. Some psychotic desire for more.

She liked living with him. He was an easy guy to live with, right down to the position of the toilet seat, about which she didn't really give a damn. It was convenient too. They got a place of their own rather than on base, saved money together, and there was no one looking over her shoulder when she felt the sudden urge to jump him in the shower.

Damn, she was no closer to solving her relationship with Kyle Reeves at a thousand feet than she'd been at thirty-five thousand or before the graduation exercise.

Chad flashed his infrared strobe three times and popped his chute on the third. The black ram chutes blossomed below her: Chad, Duane, Richie, her own slamming her in the crotch, and Kyle above her, though he was now hidden by her own canopy.

They stacked up, each slipping forward and down

barely in front of the one below until Kyle's feet were just above her hands and his riser lines lay against the leading edge of her chute. Her feet were just above Richie's hands. Chad's chute was the lowest and hence farthest back—like the base of a stack of blocks about to topple forward.

Chad steered them in and, just like they'd practiced, they thumped down into the forty-meter clearing in the jungle, each landing a half second and five meters apart.

She gave Chad a high five as they gathered and buried their chutes in the soft, loamy earth of the jungle floor. A small flask of acid that ate nylon, much like Kyle liquidated a package of chocolate-chip cookies, ensured that there'd be nothing much left to identify but a clump of metal buckles if anyone chanced to dig them up.

They unslung their rifles and spent a moment huddled together to verify that their GPS trackers were working and showed their location. The nearest trail was two kilometers to their east, but they were going north. Fifteen kilometers from their target. Eight hours of darkness remaining.

The jungle was thick with smells and sounds she didn't recognize. The uncertain chirps of birds that might have included parrots settling after the disturbance of the team's abrupt arrival. In moments, the unique flutter of zipping bats returned as they hunted back and forth across the clearing, occasionally silhouetted by the bright stars visible directly overhead. All around them, nothing but the blackness of towering trees marked the thick jungle.

No "Hoo-ah!" No command to move out. A shared nod, a swallow of water, an energy bar, and she took the lead. She was best at deep and rough country; Kyle was best in towns and cities. You'd think the guy had been born a second-story cat burglar the way he moved through a building, not some kid who used to fish with his mom and dad in Washington State.

Fifteen kilometers, and they'd need some time once they were at their target. So, now she needed to focus. Carla shoved "lover Kyle" out of her brain. When that didn't work so well, she mentally patted him on the head and nudged him into a back corner pocket. Damn him!

She smelled the air and listened. There was a rich loaminess so different from Colorado Rocky Mountain high (thank you, John Denver, for making that sound stupid in perpetuity) country. That meant stuff had rotted: fallen trees that could collapse under your weight, trail holes washed out between arched roots.

The wildlife night sounds, silenced by their landing, continued to build. Small bugs making large noises. Somewhere a bullfrog setting up a bass rhythm section. Soon it was active enough that if they stayed soft in their passage, it might continue. Also, once they were in position, the animals' silence would make a good alarm system for roving bad-guy guards so it was worth paying attention to.

Then she pictured the terrain she'd studied for much of their flight down from LAX, twisted her mental compass to match the real one on her wrist, and set out at a fast stride with the others falling in close behind her. Three hours if it went well, four if it didn't.

—◆—

The jungle practically flew by. One thing Kyle had learned about Carla: she took pity on no man. He counted on her for that. She moved at an unvarying five kilometers an hour no matter what hell the terrain unleashed. He'd followed her through canyons, waterfalls, and dense jungle foliage—all on this hike alone—and still didn't know how she did it. The same way she'd made up fifty-seven minutes on the Forty-Miler.

The same way she made love. Kyle had counted himself very fortunate in women, until he'd made love to Carla. His lovers were generally more passive, letting the man take control. Some participated more actively than others, but there was a softness and gentleness about them he'd always enjoyed.

That so wasn't Carla.

She was a constant revelation in a hundred ways. She inspired him to constantly find new and creative ways to sate them both; except they'd both proven that satiation was but a brief moment between the storms for them.

They'd avoided the shoot rooms, as there was no way to tell if the monitor cameras were on or not. Neither of them was interested in putting on a show for others. But taking her inside an M2 Bradley after a day spent learning to drive and fire the tank had certainly been memorable. As she remained strapped in the driver's seat, taking them back to the base from the shooting range, he'd fed on her until the rumbling engines had masked her cries. Twenty thousand feet of free fall had proven quite how much you could do in two minutes despite a jumpsuit and a full parachute harness—the unexpected catching air and the resulting tumble only adding to the fun.

Carla shared her body and joined in the initiation of sexual play unlike any lover he'd ever had before. Kyle sometimes found himself wishing that they could slow down and just talk a bit, be together. But when they did, every conversation slid into the current stage of the OTC coursework or devolved rapidly into a glorious wrestling match that he would never refuse.

The woman did everything full tilt, whether they were going down on each other until they both nearly wept with the pleasure of it or covering fifteen klicks of impossible terrain through a dense Venezuelan jungle.

Even now, headed into their first mission deep in the heart of a "friendly" country, he wanted her. Wanted to bury himself in her and never come back. She was a drug he would overdose on if he could and count himself a happy man.

But there was a reserve, a remoteness inside her that he'd yet to breach. Sometimes he could imagine her as wife, mother to their children, the two of them as happy together in later life as his parents. At others, it was hard to imagine her as more than the soldier by his side.

Until he could solve that conundrum, he'd keep his mouth shut. At times he wanted to shake the answer out of her, but if he tried, he knew that those shields of Delta steel would come slamming into place. For a man who daily walked the edge of risk on the thin line between life and death, Carla's occasionally blistering temper represented a line he didn't dare cross just yet. But if he didn't solve it soon, he'd grab the bull by the horns and take the risk. That or he might go stark raving mad.

At 0100 hours, exactly three hours from parachuting into the Venezuelan jungle and after only two three-minute breaks, the team flopped into position atop the cliff's edge to look down at their target. In near unison, they pulled water bottles and traded smiles. "Water doesn't do you any damn good unless it's in your body." Only heard that a thousand times.

The hacienda of General Carlos Vasquez sprawled down the hillside. It was a classic mix for a South American drug lord—part opulent home, part military fortification. The tiny village of Cubiro lay in the narrow notch of a valley five kilometers away.

Vasquez had a towering rock-wall defense perimeter on two sides like a medieval fortress topped with concertina wire. Any attacker from the valley would also be hampered by the one-lane road at the bottom of a sharp slash of creek bed. The third side was protected by a fifty-meter climb from a very fast river with tiers of barbed wire anchored in the top ten meters.

The fourth side, directly below, presented them with eighty meters of near-vertical cliff. It soared upward behind the hacienda, which gave their team a perfect position to sit, look down, and study.

The compound itself was alternating sections of pitch dark and floodlit pathways. Mistake one, all of the floodlights pointed down, lighting the compound. They also masked the entire cliff in darkness, because it had been perceived as impenetrable and secure.

That's what had convinced Kyle that this was their best approach when he'd been studying the CIA's briefing package.

Smaller structures huddled all around the inside of the towering stone walls. Sheds, garages, somewhere were barracks for guards. The center of the compound was dominated by an opulent two-story structure that might have looked fine along the boulevard of a wealthy Miami community.

"You been a very bad man, General. We here to spank you. *Sí, mis amigos*?" Carla whispered in a cartoonishly broad Spanish accent. She made it sound as if she were a *matrona*, not someone who had just trotted over fifteen kilometers of jungle-covered mountains.

Kyle laughed as he studied the compound through the night scope on his rifle. The woman had a direct line to his funny bone.

"*Sí, señorita*." They answered in unison, except for Richie. As their most fluent Spanish speaker, he decided to answer in German. "*Ja, mein Fräulein*."

General Vasquez had been a very bad man. In his governmental role, he'd taken U.S. drug-war money and used it to buy himself a major stake in the drug-smuggling business. A trio of government Huey 212 helicopters—that Colombia had purchased through large Foreign Military Sales loans that would never be repaid—had taken to servicing his Venezuelan stake. That was going to end tonight.

"Lookee what's parked to the east," Chad whispered softly.

There was one of the helicopters in question.

Kyle swung his PSG1 sniper rifle to check the view. Out of his other eye, he could see Carla tracking exactly the same way, as if they were mounted on the same turret. He'd never been so in sync with another fighter, not in the Army, Green Berets, or Delta. It was almost symbiotic how perfectly they matched each other in the field. Whereas their lovemaking was anything but. That was a constant world of exploration and discovery, of carnal delights often barely raised above primal—

Later, he promised his libido and sighted down the scope at the bird. Twin M240 machine guns. They either had to use or deal with those. The chopper itself was very tempting, but it would certainly get attention from the whole compound—and not in a good way.

Ha! Yes. It certainly would.

They spent fifteen full minutes inspecting the compound's layout and then pulled back a hundred meters into the trees and started planning. Delta was about improvisation and flexibility. It was about being so unexpected that not only would the bad guys never know what hit them, but they wouldn't be able to figure it out afterward either.

It took him two minutes to lay out his plan and twenty minutes for the team to buff and polish it. Twenty more to prep for it.

They set the bulk of their gear back in the jungle. Kyle had Duane rig a surprise that would utterly destroy it along with whoever poked at it the wrong way. For this operation they were going to be moving fast and light.

In many ways.

Carla moved into the shadows of the jungle to shed her bra and undo her khaki shirt far enough that no man would ever think to look at the danger in her expression until it was far too late. Hell, Kyle could barely think seeing her like that: double holster slung around perfect hips, two bandoliers of spare magazines, and the two rifles across her back, muzzles sticking up over her shoulders like Japanese swords. She undid her ponytail and let her hair swing loose across her face.

The other three were at the cliff edge preparing their gear.

Kyle took full advantage of the opportunity. He grabbed her by the bandoliers of ammo, spun her about, and slammed her back against a tree so big that the entire team wouldn't be able to reach around the trunk.

He pinned her there with one gloved hand inside her open blouse and cupped her butt hard with the other. He drove his mouth against hers and plundered.

She fisted one hand in his hair to drag him in harder and then grabbed him through his khakis, rubbing her palm against him in rhythm with the attack of his kiss. It lasted one second, maybe two, five... How the hell was he supposed to know? He just knew that she left him hard as a rock and ready to take on the world.

"First Delta mission, Mister Kyle. Don't fuck it up," she mumbled against his lips.

"I won't if you won't, Wild Woman. And I'll be saving that particular verb for you, for later."

Her grin was feral when she slid out from between his body and the tree. She didn't even bother to straighten her shirt before they joined the others.

Chapter 9

KYLE HUNG IN THE DARKNESS ABOVE THE GENERAL'S hacienda near the tail end of a hundred meters of black, nine-millimeter climbing line. His feet were braced against the cliff wall just a meter above where the floodlights shone down into the compound. He would be invisible here to anyone looking up from below, or even well to the side. The baddies should have had defensive lights that shone up the cliff, but clearly they weren't paranoid enough.

Should have been; Delta was coming.

He locked his descender to hold him in place and slid his PSG1 sniper rifle free. Through the scope, he could see that Carla hung in a position similar to his own on the far side of the compound, with Richie close by. Duane was midway between them and higher up the cliff. Chad was their high reserve, still at the cliff top eighty meters above.

Everyone except Carla had pulled up the black bandanna they wore about their necks. The bandannas had been in the kit provided by the CIA. On the front of them were printed the lower half of a white skull with fangs and a pair of spread eagle wings down by the throat. It was the symbol of the lethal Los Antrax, the elite kill squad of the Sinaloa Mexican drug cartel reportedly run by Claudia Ochoa Felix, the Empress of Antrax.

Sinaloa hadn't been in Venezuela as far as anyone

knew, but the woman was hot in the news as the Kim Kardashian of the Mexican cartels. She had very similar looks to her Hollywood counterpart and also boasted a massive social media presence. She kept a very high lifestyle, a constant circle of armed guards, and a custom-made hot-pink AK-47 that she was reputedly exception-ally skilled with. Even mere rumors of her hitting a site deep in Venezuela would certainly stir things up.

The fact that intelligence pointed to the much quieter and less visible sisters Luisa Marie and Marisol Torres as being the actual Empresses of Sinaloa and Antrax didn't matter for Delta's purposes; the news and hype is what they were leveraging. And the Empress of Antrax was a lethal force, no matter which woman actually held the reins.

The CIA was leaving the three women alone because one of the greatest interruptions to the flow of drugs through Mexico had been the drug war between the Mexican cartels themselves. The Delta team was here to see if they could spread that type of confusion into Venezuela. If the cartels were busy killing each other, they'd be spending less time killing Americans with their drugs.

Kyle checked his watch and eyed the patrols. They still had five minutes before 0200. It was risky to hang here, but since General Vasquez was military, they were count-ing on a fairly standard changing of the guard at two.

As they'd anticipated, he ran a tight ship. Right at the hour, a half-dozen armed soldiers came out of a room near the front gate. They were still yawning and scratch-ing, which meant that was the barracks.

Carla slid to the ground, down into the darkest corner

of the compound, and then came out moving fast. Her
hair was tousled, which hadn't been Kyle's doing (or
maybe it had—it was difficult to remember details
like that when she was in his arms), and her shirt was
still mostly undone, which he'd certainly enjoyed. Her
black bandanna hung rumpled at her throat. She looked
exactly as if she'd just crawled out of someone's bed.

She strode right into the middle of the compound as
if she belonged. A lot of the guards stopped to admire
her passage across the flagstone courtyard but, as he'd
guessed, not a single hand reached for a weapon. Her
hips swayed and her hair masked her face, almost forcing the men's attention downward. That she wore all
those weapons only added to the wet-dream fantasy she
was drawing for them.

She was inside the walls, so she must belong.

Right?

So not, guys.

Carla timed her walk exactly per his plan.

He watched her stride to the barracks entry on the
far side of the hacienda at exactly the same moment
that the six now-wide-awake soldiers reached the men
they were replacing. Instead of six men manning the
broad arc of the hacienda's perimeter walls, there were
now twelve.

And all twelve were eyeing the hot babe walking
through the middle of their compound at two in the
morning, not watching for an attack over the walls or
even checking on each other.

A dozen ducks perched in a neat row and facing away
from the rest of the team.

Kyle and the other three Delta began dropping the

teams from the rear as the guards gawked. Two shots to the head each. He took out the left hand of the closest pair, while Duane took the right. Richie and Chad "The Reaper" began laying them down in neat rows from the other end of "duck row." Even from the top of the cliff, these were short-range shots for their sniper rifles. Since everyone was looking toward Carla's approach to the front gate barracks, those still alive didn't see what was occurring behind them along the walls until it was too late.

The last pair of guards closest by the front gate had time to turn and startle at their dead companions before they too dropped to the ground with a pair of bullets where their brains used to be.

The quiet spit of Delta's suppressed weapons hadn't woken anyone. Everyone changed out magazines even though they weren't empty.

While they were shooting, Carla had entered the barracks. The next few seconds were going to affect their next steps.

There was a long silence, at least ten heartbeats. Had Carla faced overwhelming odds, she'd have solved it with a grenade. Instead, she stepped out of the barracks doorway, dropped a magazine out of both of her silenced Glock 17 handguns, and reloaded them with fresh magazines from her bandolier.

The guards weren't the only ones having wet-dream fantasies about this warrior woman. She was like a sucker punch to Kyle's hormones every time he saw her. And when she did something like that…even Hollywood never had it so good, because Sergeant Carla Anderson was the real deal.

Kyle and Richie slid to the ground, heading toward

the main building that intel had identified as the
General's most likely personal residence. It was a grand,
two-story affair close to the cliff at the center of the
compound. Duane kicked off the cliff face and timed
his fast descent down the last of the rope to land on a
second-story balcony.

At that moment, the compound's lights went out.
Carla must have stumbled on the generator that they'd
been unable to locate from above. Darkness only
improved their advantage.

Kyle pulled down his NVGs and studied the one side
of the building they hadn't been able to observe from
above. Heavy front door, enough so that it might be
fortified and guarded. But there were low windows to
the sides.

There was a shout from the far side of the compound,
but it didn't last long. Chad took care of it from on high.

It was a warm night and Kyle had observed during
their high reconnaissance that one of the windows was
open. He dove through it and rolled to his feet in a living
room with a layout so similar to the shoot room they'd
just cleared twenty-four hours earlier that it was actually
disorienting for a moment.

The man sleeping beside the door and cradling an Uzi
never woke as Kyle ended his dreams. Richie came in
from clearing the other side of the first floor.

Even in the green tones of the night vision, the opu-
lence of the room was fantastic. Marble floors covered
with thick rugs that now padded their footsteps. Large
comfortable chairs, a dining table fit for feeding twenty.
A huge marble fireplace that had to be strictly for show
in this tropical country. Chandeliers of gold and crystal.

Art on the walls that his night gear couldn't resolve, but he'd wager was equally astonishing.

An old lady came out of a back doorway, wrapping a scarf over her head as she did so. She gasped but didn't scream, so he whispered to her softly, "*Silencio, señora.*" Showing she was a smart woman, she nodded several times and then moved backward through the door she'd entered from.

He followed.

It was a long and narrow kitchen. Whatever money the General had invested elsewhere, he hadn't bothered here. It was a rough and rude space with only the soft hum of a modern refrigerator breaking a scene that could have easily served during the time of the conquistadors.

The woman returned to a mattress in the corner and sat on it, doing her best to mask three sleeping children, the oldest a girl in her early teens. No man, no weapons. Kyle held his finger to his lips, which she'd see by the light of the single night-light. Her nod confirmed her lack of desire to have any part in what was about to happen.

She would also give a useful report about the man with the white skull mask, so it was even advantageous to let her go.

Returning to the living room, Kyle followed close behind Richie, who was already well up the stairs.

Six doors, six bedrooms. The first two were empty. The next had a rifle propped just inside the door and an older man in the bed with a very young girl—as young as the one sleeping behind the cautious cook. From the briefing materials they'd studied during the flight from LAX to the drop zone, he recognized the man as Major Gonzales, the General's chief assistant. He was a vicious assassin who had helped the General control whole sectors of the military through intimidation and hostage-taking among officials' families. The man woke to a gag entering his mouth and zip ties snapping around his wrists.

The girl whimpered but didn't cry out.

Richie jerked the man from the bed to the floor and then bound his ankles.

Kyle scanned the room for other weapons and caught the girl sliding her hand under the pillow. The move was too surreptitious. Kyle didn't think…didn't have time to… didn't need to. His training kicked in and he shot her twice between her small breasts and once between the eyes. Her body's final flinch pulled a long-barreled, stainless-steel Smith & Wesson 686 revolver into plain view.

Shit!

He knocked the weapon clear of her dead hand, then kicked Major Gonzales in the kidneys on his way back to the hall, receiving a very satisfying grunt despite the gag.

Duane entered through the balcony door and held up two fingers. A pair of hidden guards outside, no longer a problem.

As the three of them were moving back into the hall, Kyle heard the first whine of the helicopter starting up and then the climbing cry of the engines.

Carla was still on the move, and that would draw all attention her way.

Two more empty rooms and then the door at the end of the hall. Locked, of course. And probably not in a way that could be simply kicked in. He flagged Duane forward.

When Kyle saw the size of the breaching charge Duane was setting up, he knew the door was even worse than he'd thought. General Carlos Vasquez was a man who didn't sleep comfortably at night.

Kyle tapped Duane's shoulder and signaled that he and Richie were going in from the outside. They went back down the hall and entered rooms to either side. In moments, he was out on the balcony that encircled the upper story. He'd chosen the side closer to the chopper.

He couldn't see Carla, but he could hear her exhorting the pilots to action.

"*El Jefe!*" she kept screaming at them. "The Chief!" She would look as if she'd just come from his bedroom with urgent orders for the General's men to get the helicopter.

As he arrived to one side of the long line of French doors and windows that lined the balcony for the whole length of the master suite, a spate of loud gunfire sounded from inside, shattering the glass. With his panicked shots, the General had just given them his exact location.

A loud *krump* sounded as Duane blew the door.

He and Richie rolled in and tackled the General from behind as he turned toward Duane's destruction.

They had him facedown on the floor as a line of gunfire raked over their heads. A woman stood in the center of the mattress, firing an AK-47. She was shooting above their heads into the darkness, but would realize and correct her mistake in a moment.

Duane shot the woman where she stood, clothed only in the light of her weapon's backfire. Her face matched the photo of the General's wife.

General Vasquez cried out in deep pain from where he'd been pinned to the deep-pile carpet as she crumpled slowly onto the mattress. The fight went out of him in that moment.

They dragged the General down the hall and gathered up the Major as they went. Kyle quickly rifled through the small office off the master bedroom and came out with a backpack of matériel. Richie was doing the same in the Major's room where the dead girl still sprawled on the bloody mattress, her mouth open in a small O of surprise.

Kyle forced himself to focus and gathered up a laptop, a messy inbox, and a couple dozen file folders that Richie had unearthed.

Then Richie tugged on a picture above the desk. It didn't move. He ran his gloved hands around the frame, then under the edge of the desk where he must have hit a switch. The picture swung away from the wall above the desk. There was a safe behind it.

Kyle slapped his shoulder and made the American Sign Language gesture for the letter *Q*.

Richie grinned and waved Duane over to blow the safe, which took him only seconds.

Money. Big wads of it. Bloody waste of time.

Kyle scooped the money out onto the desk. The safe had a hollow panel in the bottom. Two USB memory sticks. He jammed them in a shirt pocket and started to walk away from the million or so in cash. What the hell. He tossed a couple bundles of hundreds into a thigh pocket in case they needed any big bribes to get out of the country, but left the bulk of it.

Someone would sort through the intel later; that wasn't part of their assignment. They dragged the two men downstairs as the helicopter came to a hover above the master suite, right where it could drop a ladder down onto the balcony.

His team exited the house through the kitchen where he was glad to discover that the matron and her kids were nowhere to be seen. He hoped that the girl in Major Asshole's bed hadn't also been one of hers.

Carla met them at the back door, her Mexican drug cartel bandanna now covering her lower face, just as Chad shot an RPG into the helicopter from above. The rocket-propelled grenade struck the top of the cockpit, crashing through the windshield before it blew. The pilots and gunners were dead in that instant. The helicopter hovered for several long seconds as if nothing had happened, then plummeted all at once down onto the roof of the master suite.

Rotor blades screeched across clay roof tile as they shredded, then the roof collapsed and the Huey 212 disappeared from view.

Damn thing didn't have the decency to explode.

Then Kyle saw the sharp arc of Chad's second RPG plunging down from the top of the cliff. He and Carla grabbed the General by the arm, Duane and Richie had the Major, and they sprinted along the cliff away from the main house.

This time the house shattered. The jet fuel in the helicopter went off like a bomb and sent a pillar of fire into the sky that did a partial mushroom-cloud thing, bathing the entire hacienda in a garish red-yellow light and a wave of heat. Kyle hunched with his back to the explosion as chunks of brick and stone rained down from the sky, though none of the heavy stuff reached them.

At the cliff base, a doubled line was waiting for them. They tied the General and Major to one side, while Richie and Duane began climbing the other. The line

was run through a pulley at the top of the cliff. The two
climbing Delta operators counterweighted the General
and the Major so that the four of them ascended the cliff
at the same rate. If the bad guys with their hands bound
took a couple of dings as they bounced and scraped over
the cliff face, tough.

Kyle crouched where pavement met cliff and took a
moment to survey the results of the last seven minutes.
Carla squatted close beside him, her weapon raised and
ready, but there didn't appear to be any need.

No guards were alive atop the perimeter walls. The
only people moving were rushing out the small door in
the front gate, not even trying for the vehicles. Which
was wise because Carla would have booby-trapped anything that could move.

There was a massive *krump!* on the far side of the
compound, followed by a cascade of auxiliary explosions and the whine of rounds cooking off, more squeals
and bangs than a July Fourth on the Seattle waterfront.

The people at the front gate pushed and shoved more
frantically to escape.

"I must have accidentally dropped something in the
General's weapons' store. Bill me." Carla spoke the first
words of the entire operation and made him laugh.

Then he remembered the two shots he'd placed
between barely pubescent breasts and sobered. That
was an image he wasn't going to forget anytime soon.
He'd half feared she was going to pull a doll out from
beneath that pillow as he shot her. He wanted to go
kick the Major again, but he was already halfway
up the cliff and would be in his own world of hurt
soon enough.

The main house was a shattered wreck. This would look like a drug hit, a particularly violent one. The shattered helicopter, now at the center of a roaring inferno that had once been a plush mansion, would hide the fact that the General had not died there along with his soldiers. What would happen to him would be up to the CIA, not some half-mad hopefully soon-to-be ex-President of Venezuela who was clearly also on the take—obvious for how he'd been defending the General against extradition.

Somewhere along the way, Carla had re-buttoned her blouse. Now no one but the Carla soldier knelt beside him.

Kyle found it disorienting. She had this switch somewhere deep inside that she could throw on a whim. He could focus on a mission just fine, but that didn't stop him from being a man who could not get enough of the woman beside him.

Yet at moments like this, there was no woman. There was almost no Carla Anderson the person. She was pure soldier. He had put her at the top of his own list of who he would most like to fight beside. She'd just proven that was the correct choice, but she wasn't the most predictable person.

He was starting to wonder if the correct choice was the wise one.

———

Carla could feel Kyle thinking as they crouched together at the base of the cliff in the shattered remains of General Carlos Vasquez's hacienda. And she could feel him thinking about her, despite or perhaps because of what they'd just done.

His plan had gone off like clockwork. There'd been a dozen variations on the theme as they went, but he'd nailed it—right down to the helicopter destroying any evidence of the General's continued existence. How could Kyle see so much ahead of time? It was like his brain wasn't trapped by the clock. Give her a task and she could kick ass, but not view and execute whole operations at once. And he'd done it without issuing a single order or making a single demand.

The only demands Kyle Reeves made were on the limits of her body and her brain. That fiery, testosterone-laden grope and kiss at the top of the cliff had certainly rung her bells. Her adrenal glands had fired up on all cylinders and continued to build under the pressure of the action phase of the operation.

As she'd sashayed across the compound, confounding the guards who were about to die, all she'd been aware of was Kyle's raking inspection through his sniper scope. Standing in the barracks entry and killing eleven more men had definitely lessened that awareness.

But not removed it completely.

There'd been this thread of connection throughout the action. She knew where the whole team was—that was Delta training. But she could *feel* where Kyle was.

She didn't want this connection with any man, not even one as exceptional as Sergeant Kyle Reeves. Not that she wasn't enjoying it; she just didn't want it.

A glance aloft showed the rest of the team was nearing the top of the cliff. No one left in the compound was showing the slightest interest in the activities going on seventy meters above in the dark of the night.

Kyle tapped her shoulder, and with a nod, they

moved together to a pair of ropes. At the last second she peeled off her bandanna and let it flutter to the ground where it would be discovered by anyone investigating the wreckage. *The U.S. military had never been here. It was strictly a drug war hit, folks. Nothing more.*

Lashing on her ascenders and double-checking Kyle's harness while he checked hers, she felt her awareness of him continue to climb.

Get a grip on your hormones, girl. But it wasn't only her hormones that were the problem. She liked this man as well, and that didn't sit comfortably.

Both safely on their ropes, they headed aloft. She climbed ten meters, then turned and unslung her rifle to watch for bad guys—the ones not smart enough to be sprinting for the horizon—while Kyle climbed past her to twenty meters and then shifted to guard position while she climbed past him.

Their passage to the top of the cliff was uneventful.

They recovered the lines and unrigged the booby traps on the packs they'd left behind. She cut the ankle ties on the two men they'd captured. They were going to be moving some distance, and it would be easier if their team didn't have to carry the prisoners.

She heard Chad say quietly to the two bound men, "You can walk, or we can carry you. But if you don't use your legs, we'll cut them off to save the useless weight. *Comprende?*" He didn't wait for their answers. Chad could be scary as shit behind that boyish face; she actually believed he'd do it.

Carla checked her watch, fifteen seconds shy of 0220. Under twenty minutes total contact time on the site from top of cliff to top of cliff.

Right on Kyle's schedule, which didn't surprise her for a second.

Trusting that, she had set up a surprise of her own.

She called the others over to the cliff edge to look down one last time. The fires were still going; not a soul moved in the compound.

She held out her hand where the others could see it lit by the flames below and folded her fingers to count down: *five, four, three, two…*

Her timing was off a little. On *one* a ripple of explosions cascaded across the compound. Every vehicle exploded in a shred of metal and a ball of flame.

"I've been taking lessons from Duane. There was a surprising amount of C4 and a bunch of very cute triggers in the General's toy collection."

Then the massive gate exploded, and the heavy archway over it, like an old fort's, collapsed in on itself.

"Carla's Lesson of the Day: *Never do anything by halves.*"

They slapped high fives all around.

Duane grabbed her shoulder and gave it a hard shake of congratulations. "The teacher is so proud, Wild Woman."

She punched his "Rock"-hard arm in thanks, and they began their walk back into Yacambú Park.

The General cooperated, though he was out of shape and it slowed them down, but Kyle was unwilling to remove the gag to give him more air. The Major needed the occasional rifle butt to the kidneys to remind him who was in charge, which Kyle meted out with atypical severity. Knowing they'd have at least one hostage, Carla planned a slower, easier hike out.

Five kilometers and ninety minutes later they arrived

at a different section of the park, at the head of a large waterfall that stair-stepped downward in cascades for several stories. It was ten meters wide and simply gorgeous. Each tier was so square that it looked hand carved. She'd bet at another time—that wasn't 0400 in the middle of an exfiltration—it would be a beautiful and idyllic getaway.

An image of her yanking down Kyle's shorts as they splashed about in the lower pool rocketed through her nervous system, and Carla filed it away for future reference.

They put lifting harnesses on their two captives and rebound their feet. Carla could see the Major eyeing the jump down into the lower pool. It was just marginally possible, if he weren't bound.

She moved close to whisper in his ear. "Try it, *Señor Mayor*. Take the dive. Please. I'll gladly put two rounds up your ass before you hit the water. Bet I can get both to go *swish*, right in the old butthole."

"And I'll shoot off your fucking balls while she's at it," Kyle snarled right in the man's face. Then, even though the Major was taller than Kyle and overweight as well, Kyle lifted the guy by the throat with one hand and slammed him onto the ground hard enough to knock all the air out of him.

Carla had never heard such a sound from Kyle or seen him so angry. There was a livid fury there that the Major recognized as mortally dangerous. He stopped eyeing possible getaways and lay there gasping for air through his gag.

She led Kyle aside. "What was that about?"

He shook his head.

"Don't shake me off, Kyle. Others, okay, but not

me." Now where the hell inside her had that come from? Since when did she care?

He walked away from her, and she felt like she was the one who'd just gotten a rifle butt in the kidneys.

Well, she was only sleeping with him, she wasn't his keeper. His choice.

Still…it hurt.

———∿∿∿———

No goddamn way was Kyle going to take that nasty image from the Major's bedroom and give it to Carla.

He checked his watch. Fifteen minutes ahead of schedule, so no need to signal their arrival.

Chad and Duane put fresh batteries in their night-vision goggles and moved into the trees to set up a perimeter. The Major and General had made so much noise that the silence of the jungle about them had been complete. Even now, they were crunching branches and grunting at each other through their gags.

Apparently tired of their fussing, Carla nudged the General from sitting to his side. When he rolled onto his stomach, she sat down on him and aimed her rifle lazily at the Major's crotch. That seemed to calm them both down.

A parrot squawked questioningly from the trees.

Richie swung down his backpack, pulled out the satchel of intel they'd dragged out of the hacienda's offices, and began sorting through it.

Yeah, they might as well.

Kyle squatted beside him, clicked on a small flash-light, and began scanning the folders.

He hoped someone cared about the content of these

files, because he sure didn't. Long sheets of payments to coded entries, a couple of old appointment books... assorted crap. Nothing that looked immediately actionable, which was all he really cared about. If he found something that said, "Drug shipment tonight leaving from..." But he didn't, so he could leave it all to the analysts.

Richie didn't have any better luck.

The laptops both had passwords.

Kyle turned to force their prisoners to key them in, but Richie stopped him.

"Nope. They could have a second code that destroys everything on the drive. I could crack it, but I don't have the tools with me. Leave it for the CIA."

First Kyle had heard of that trick, but he wasn't Q.

They dumped it all back in the bags.

He checked his watch: one minute to exfil.

That would be good. Get in the air and get the hell out of this country. Maybe then he could figure out what the hell was going on in his head. He was such a mess right now because of that young girl that if he'd tried to explain anything to Carla when she'd pushed, he'd probably have wound up leaning into her shoulder for support or some such stupid-ass move.

That would actually be stupid in a whole lot of ways. Not the least was that he'd bet that Carla would have less of an idea of what to do with that than he did when a woman wept on him.

Get it done. Get out of here.

Eleven seconds before scheduled pickup was the first moment he heard the helicopters. They came out of nowhere, fast, and one slid to a hover thirty meters up, barely clear of the treetops. A line snaked down three seconds early as the other bird set up a circling patrol. The U.S. Army's 160th Special Operations Aviation Regiment was banging it out like usual. He'd only ridden with them a couple of times as a Green Beret, but they were always there within a thirty-second window.

He went down the line checking that each person was snapped in. The SPIES rope—Special Patrol Insertion-Extraction System—included a series of embedded D-rings separated by a few meters each.

He moved to the last ring in the line, hesitating just a moment at Carla's second-to-last position to brush a hand of thanks over her shoulder for not pushing. She looked at him like she was some kind of pissed or hurt, hard to read in night-vision green. Not the time to ask.

At the last position he snapped the D-ring onto the lift point of his vest's harness and held both arms out to his sides with his thumbs up. The others were doing the same, except for the two with bound hands.

A spotter high above them noted they were all ready and took them aloft.

Even before they cleared the trees, SOAR was reeling them up and moving out—fast. Kyle, in lowermost position, kept pulling up his feet as they approached treetops at over 150 miles per hour. The more they reeled the group in, the more his bare clearance over the trees remained unchanged. As the SOAR pilot bobbed and dodged above the terrain, they were also descending by exactly the amount he was being reeled in. It was freaky how good these guys were. With each slow spin, he had a clear view of the smaller Little Bird attack helicopter flying rear guard.

He was last aboard as they swooped down into the countryside of the coastal lowlands.

The outside of the helo had looked strange as he came aboard and he'd been unable to identify the chopper by sound, which was odd; he'd had a lot of training in that. Carla helped pull him in as the helicopter actually climbed to clear a pile of hay in a field and then descended once more.

From the inside, he could see it was a Black Hawk. Kyle could fly a Black Hawk, but only if he was desperate. SOAR made the machines dance and sing.

A final glance out the open cargo-bay door; he watched a house go by at eye level, a one-story house. He looked back inside quickly as the helo bobbed upward, then back down—probably avoiding a gopher hole mound at this altitude.

"These guys are cool," he shouted to Carla as one of the crew chiefs snapped a safety line to the D-ring on his chest and then demonstrated with a yank that it was well attached to the helicopter's frame before she released him from the SPIES harness.

Then the crew chief leaned in and shouted loud enough for him to hear over the pounding of the rotors and the wind rushing by the open cargo bay door: "We're especially cool because we're...not-guys."

Well, if that didn't beat all.

⁓⁓⁓

A Black Hawk flown by "not-guys."

Carla decided that was beyond especially cool.

A SOAR Black Hawk flown by women. There was only one of those that she knew of. Clay had flown with these women and couldn't stop talking about them. And here they were.

Carla sat with her back against the cargo netting and contemplated just how small a community Special Operations Forces really was. Delta operators numbered in the low hundreds, and SOAR wasn't much bigger. There just weren't that many soldiers at this level. She'd always felt awkward about how Kyle seemed to know the background of almost every candidate in Delta Selection.

"Served with him in Bolivia." "Spends a lot of lead, but real steady in a firefight." "We did Airborne together. He squealed like a little girl on his first jump."

But she was starting to see how it happened. Because her brother had died flying with SOAR, she actually knew *about* them even if she didn't know them.

Kyle was close beside her. Shoulders bumping lightly with the helicopter's rollicking flight just as if they were at the very end of the Forty-Miler around the fire. So, whatever had been bugging him on the ground must not have anything to do with her. She almost asked him, "What the hell?" but then thought better of it.

Focus on the mission, that's what mattered. Their relationship—damn, there was too heavy a word to tote around for everyday use—would take care of itself.

The General and the Major were tied back-to-back in the middle of the helicopter's cargo bay and attached to a couple of tie-down points. The other three Deltas were doing exactly the same thing she and Kyle were, restocking their ammo from their packs.

The female crew chief who'd latched them in had the name Davis on her gear. So this was Connie Davis. She offered them a box of cartridges.

"No thanks. We hand load our own rounds."

"So does she." Connie pointed at the other crew chief. "At least for match shooting."

"She do a lot of that?" Kyle asked.

"Yes, she has been President's Hundred four years running. Twice number one." No sound of pride in her crewmate, just simple fact stated as such. The woman drifted away. The President's Hundred was the premier shooting competition of the year.

Carla turned to Kyle. "You know who that is?"

"No. I had no idea a woman had ever placed number one, though I remember an unlikely story about a serious babe of a shooter."

"The one just talking to us is considered the number one mechanic in all of SOAR, and the other one just has to be Kee Stevenson. Top five sniper in the U.S. military four years running. And I've heard that they're both serious babes."

"Top five only 'cause Delta never shoots in that competition."

"Right, tough guy. And you're welcome to outshoot Kee Stevenson anytime you want."

"How do you know this, Anderson? It's like with that colonel. You seem to know everybody."

She kept her mouth shut.

"Damn! Sorry." Kyle kept his voice down. "I'm even dumber than Richie."

Which wasn't saying much, considering that Richie was the genius of the crowd. Though he could be pretty inept at times, especially around her when they were off duty. He really didn't have a clue about women. He got tangled up trying to memorize everything when she was trying to give him social skills, as if women could be approached using a rote list of techniques. Telling Richie to be himself totally snarled him up, so she saved that for when she just wanted to watch the show.

"Your brother, right?" Kyle said softly.

She'd rather bite off her tongue than try to speak. It wouldn't come out well, not at all. This was the kind of thing Clay had done, flying into foreign countries at night with no one a bit the wiser. Until it went to shit and he ended up in a sealed box in a hole in the ground.

Kyle was waiting on her, so she managed a nod. It had been her big brother.

He left a respectful pause before continuing.

"So, these women are hot shit?" Somehow, Kyle knew she needed the subject change and he made it funny, bless him.

It helped her get control back. She nodded again and then whispered, "It was his stories of these women that made me go for Delta. That and Colonel Gibson. The perfect soldier. It's so what a man should be."

Kyle grunted as if she'd just kicked him.

"You really are a dumbass, Reeves."

"Why's that? Because I don't like the woman I'm sleeping with lusting after a colonel? He's way older than you, you know."

She smiled at him. "Because you don't see that you're the younger version of him. You're that damn good."

Their flight abruptly leveled out and steadied. They must finally have been over the water and headed for whatever craft was awaiting them offshore.

"Am I good?" Kyle asked, clearly going for the joke rather than letting the compliment in. Typical. "Or am I, you know, goood?" There was no doubting his second meaning, not with that low, seductive voice of his.

Well, she wasn't going to stroke his ego that much.

"You'll do." She almost added "for now," but a part of her bit it off. A part of her that she was becoming very suspicious of.

He acted like he'd been shot in the chest. Clamping his hands over his heart, he gasped out, "The wound. 'Tis mortal." Then he collapsed to the deck and spasmed once or twice.

The other three guys just looked over at him and shook their heads.

She hated when he got all cute like that.

Guys weren't supposed to charm the shit out of her.

Chapter 10

IF SOMEONE MADE KYLE CHOOSE BETWEEN THE DELTA
Selection psychological evaluation and a CIA debriefing,
he'd be hard pressed to decide which was more irritating.

There were always two analysts in the small steel
room they'd stuck him in within minutes of boarding
the Littoral Combat Ship USS *Freedom*. Though not
always the same two. As if they were kaleidoscopi-
cally interchangeable.

He'd tell them his actions on the mission, such as he
sprinted from the cliff to the hacienda.

One would ask for clarification.

He'd been focused on live and mobile targets, of
which he hadn't seen anyone closer than fifty meters.

The other one would start to argue that Kyle hadn't
said that to begin with and then proceed to totally mis-
construe his words.

*Don't you mean fifteen meters? Because fifty meters
is a long way, way bigger than fifteen.*

This would escalate as if he wasn't even in the room,
until half the time he didn't know where reality had
actually been, and then they'd ask him to repeat what
he'd done.

Kyle could see the method to their madness —
ferreting out only the consistently repeatable facts — but
he didn't like it one bit more for understanding the tactic.
And then somewhere in hour three, while describing the

money in Major Gonzalez's safe for the fourth time, he finally remembered the two USB drives he'd slipped into a shirt pocket.

They went ballistic. It was another hour, dragging him back through the whole operation step by individual step, to make sure he hadn't forgotten anything else.

When he finally remembered all of the cash tucked in a different pocket, he kept his mouth shut just to avoid going through it for another hour. He'd turn it in when he didn't have to punch out a CIA agent to do so.

By the time they were done with him and let him escape into the hall, he couldn't remember his own name. The debrief had lasted as long as the operation, from HALO jump to SPIES extraction, and been far more exhausting.

He'd graduated from OTC thirty-six hours ago in a different country on a different continent. He'd participated in a highly successful operation. Major Gonzalez was way high on the CIA's kill list, and they'd brought him out as well. And he was so wiped, whipped, and—

His Spider-Man senses went off and slapped him most of the way back to consciousness.

Not ten feet down the hall, Carla staggered out of a doorway that looked suspiciously like the one he'd just escaped. Why they were released at the same moment, he didn't have a clue, but he wouldn't be turning back to ask those jokers. It would probably cost him another hour, and he'd never get the answer anyway.

She walked across the narrow width of the corridor, rested her forehead on the opposite wall, and let out a sound somewhere between a snarl, a scream of frustration, and a whimper.

He scooped an arm around her waist just before she sagged to the floor. A frantic look around and he spotted a midshipman. "Do you know where our berths are?"

"Sorry, sirs." He looked at them uncertainly. "No one told us that you weren't both male. All I have allocated for your use is a two-berth bunk room."

That Carla didn't even reply told him how tired she was. "That'll be fine. Lead the way."

The room was classic Navy ship: two-tier bunk, hanging closet just four uniforms wide, and enough room to dump your gear and change your clothes, provided you did it one at a time. At least it wasn't open berthing space. Oddly, it had that rarest of luxuries: a private bathroom. A meter and a half square, it boasted a sink and toilet, and if you closed the door, the whole thing turned into a steel-lined shower.

He stripped Carla down, which wasn't as much fun as usual because of her near-somnambulant state, and shoved her in. When he didn't hear the water start, he stripped and followed her in.

She sat on the closed toilet and leaned against the wall, on the verge of sleep.

He turned on the overhead shower, which flashed cold, then hot as the pipes cleared.

She squawked and sputtered, sitting up but not rising. So, once they were wet, he slapped off the water and shampooed and soaped them both.

He dragged her to her feet and hit the water again.

She hung against him as he sluiced them off.

Rubbing Sergeant Carla Anderson down with a

towel, even an undersized, low-pile Navy one, was a worthwhile experience. Her skin glowed, her muscles shifted beneath the surface in enticing glides that he did his best to ignore. He was exhausted as well, but his body clearly had other ideas. The confined space was not conducive to keeping his distance.

He ached with need as he lay her down on the lower bunk, and not only his body. He was…happier for simply being near her. But it wouldn't be fair to go sharing his happiness, or his body's raging lust, not in her current state.

She stopped his escape to the upper bunk with a light hold on his hand. Carla shifted on the narrow mattress and tugged lightly until he lay down against her. There was no way in hell he was going to get any sleep with his body pressed up against hers.

She brushed her lips over his, a tickling sensation that ran right up his spine.

"Thanks." Barely a mumble.

"You're welcome."

"You smell good." Her voice was thick and sleepy as she nuzzled against his neck. "You feel good too." She snuggled up against him.

Okay. He might be a decent kind of guy, but there were goddamn limits to that code of gentlemanly conduct, weren't there?

He nuzzled her back.

And the damn woman purred. Carla was not the sort of woman who purred. She snarled and wrestled and laughed at the strangest moments, but she didn't go languid and feline and make low sounds in her throat that forced a man to try to cause more of them.

Kyle continued his efforts with surprising success. Rather than pushing him away or ramping it up, she brushed her hands lightly over his shoulders and slid them into his hair, guiding him to breast, belly, and beyond.

Sex with Carla was invariably an aerobic sport, but she didn't rise into one of her wild climbs.

Not this time.

Instead of sex, Kyle felt as if he was making love to her. Perhaps for the first time in the six months they'd been together. He evoked small murmurs and gentle pressures as she leaned in for more, rather than driving against him.

He took his time, investigating the terrain she offered for his study, a terrain he both did and didn't know. They had certainly used each other very thoroughly at every opportunity, but the heat always exploded forth, never allowing the time to appreciate more.

The skin at the side of her breast was as soft as her inner thigh. When she opened to him, she was warm, deep, and soft. When at long last he found protection and slid into her, she welcomed him with a kiss as gentle as a breeze and as deep as forever.

This time her peaks weren't shuddering mountains that slammed through her frame causing an avalanche in his, but ocean waves that rose, then rose again until they both finished on a sigh rather than a gasp. For all the skin contact she so readily offered, her hugs were typically hard and brief.

This time she held him to her and wouldn't let go. She kept her face buried in the crook of his neck, her arms and legs wrapped around him. It wasn't as if she was clinging to him, but rather as if she'd simply never let go because they fit so well together.

He'd had his fair share of sex, maybe more, starting with a blond and very flexible red belt on his father's dojo's padded floor on their shared sixteenth birthdays. Sally Ann McKay threw one hell of a fine party. And he'd made love to several of the fine women who had consented to share his bed.

Never before had he been *in* love when he did it. But there was no question, he was that far gone on Carla Anderson.

This wasn't some post-action fuck. That would have been wild and perhaps dangerous, considering how he was still feeling about the poor girl he'd had to kill. But Carla had let it not be about that. This had been only about them, as if they hadn't just had the busiest forty-eight hours of their military careers.

They shifted into a position so familiar now that it was hard to sleep any other way. He flat on his back, she curled against his shoulder with an arm and a leg flung across him. He brushed her hair back behind her ear, but knew it would shortly slide across her face as if she always slept safe behind its liquid brown shield.

He kissed her on the top of her head and lay back.

He'd never had to explain to his dad about Sally Ann; his father had simply known. He'd waited until the next weekend when they were standing thigh deep in a nut-freezing cold stream trying to tease breakfast onto their lures. Mom was sleeping in.

Then Dad had simply asked if the sex had been safe. It had.

"You'll know when it's the right one, Ky. Until then, you treat them as nice as you know how and you'll be well rewarded." Like most of his dad's lessons, it had been a good one.

That had ended "The Talk," though not the lessons that Sally Ann had offered in exchange for extra sparring practice. They'd lasted two years, until the night before she went to college and he went Green Beret, one heck of a fine send-off.

And now Dad was right again.

Kyle simply knew.

It was crazy, ridiculous, and stupid. Carla was a teammate. If they were anywhere other than Delta, they'd probably have had both their asses booted by now. They'd certainly have been assigned to different units. She was wild, chaotic, and shared almost nothing about herself or what was going on inside that beautiful head of hers.

Didn't matter.

Kyle knew.

Carla Anderson was the only one for him, which would only piss her off if he was dumb enough to tell her. So he'd keep his own counsel for now.

He kissed her once more atop her hair and let the stresses of the last couple days wash out of him.

—⁓—

Carla lay on Kyle's shoulder wishing she could cut out her brain and drop it into the closest garbage chute. It was so screwed up that she couldn't even imagine it would make worthwhile compost.

Her body was asleep, passed out, gone beyond the pale, and humming very contentedly to itself about what Kyle had just done to it. She couldn't move a muscle even if there was a hull breach and they were sinking. Between exhaustion and the positively magnetic attraction of her body to Kyle's, she might as well be riveted into place.

What he'd just done to her was impossible. She'd never let someone else take control before. She always had tabs on exactly what she was doing and what she wanted.

She wanted to blame what had just happened on the mission, on exhaustion, on finally being mission-qualified for the Combat Applications Group.

The raw heat that always drove them together was somehow still the Carla perched on the top of the cliff with her shirt open.

She might have been working it to distract the other soldiers, but she'd only been thinking of one man as she flaunted her distractions. She could still feel the spike of heat that had soared through her as Kyle grabbed her hard and rough with his worn-soft leather climbing gloves and slammed her back against that tree with such desperate need.

But that ravenous woman still lingered back in the Venezuelan jungle. On this bunk in the heart of this ship of war lay another woman.

There had been a release she'd never known. Kyle hadn't just satisfied them both; he'd worshipped her body. And he'd done it with a tenderness that she didn't know what to do with.

Tenderness was not in the experience of one Carla Anderson.

And she'd let him do it to her. Even worse, she'd encouraged him. She didn't want to lose control and let a man make her feel like…

No, that wasn't quite it.

Kyle Reeves didn't make her feel *like* anything.

He made her *feel*.

And that was the worst of all.

Chapter 11

KYLE WAS DEEP IN A SPLENDID DREAM OF BEING GENTLY teased awake. Of being so aroused that he could take a woman forever and ever, as long as that woman was Carla Anderson.

He could—

He opened one eye. Then the other. Or he could lie here, alone in a steel bunk bed on a ship of war and feel like a teenage idiot once again at summer camp and fantasizing about the head lifeguard—so awesome in her white one-piece and long blond hair, and at least half again his own daydreamy twelve. He scrabbled around in the darkness for his watch, but his stomach told him very clearly what time it was.

The CIA hadn't been big on food during debriefing, which had accounted for both breakfast and lunch chow times. Making love to Carla had been a wise choice over dinner, but now his body was insisting that man did not live by sex alone. Too bad. When it was the best sex of his life with the woman he loved—

That woke him up. He sat up and clipped his head sharply enough on the upper bunk that the dark room was now alight with bright stars.

He held on to the top of his head, cursing, but now glad that he'd woken alone so that Carla wouldn't know what a complete dolt her lover was. He switched on a light, which clashed brutally with the stars already swimming before him.

He shut his eyes and waited for everything to calm down. In love?

How the hell had that happened? He'd made it this long and never fallen in love before. This was nuts. Wasn't that something that women did? Half his lovers had said they were "in love" with him, not that he'd actually believed a one of them.

But about Carla Anderson he was definitely…an idiot.

She'd welcome a declaration of love about the same way she'd welcome incoming gunfire. As an excuse to shoot back. Hard.

Then what the hell was he supposed to do?

The darkness held no answers.

His stomach was so mundane that it began to growl in alarm at his continued inaction. He tested one eye against the light; it had calmed down to merely painful.

He found his watch. Oh-six-hundred. First time he'd slept twelve in a row in forever, probably since submitting his application for Delta. At least it felt that way. Best sleep he'd had in a long time.

A quick shower washed off the last of his haziness and made him think about sudsing up a woman who wasn't out cold on her feet. He spotted a small night-light and flicked it on to spare his head any other unexpected affronts when he came back to the room. He made the bunk then wandered out looking for the rest of his team.

They were grouped in a corner of the mess hall. There was a chow line and enough tables to seat half the hundred-person crew at a sitting; thirty were eating right now.

Carla, Richie, and Duane were there. Chad showed up in the chow line close behind him.

"How'd y'all sleep, buddy?" Chad slapped him on the shoulder in a friendly way that was almost hard enough to make Kyle eat his still-empty tray.

"Like we just kicked a piece of drug-lord ass."

"Damn straight. How long did they keep you?" No question who "they" were. The CIA had ganged up on them all last night.

"Don't even know." Kyle hadn't been thinking about his watch when he crawled out of the debrief, then into Carla's bunk. "Long damn time."

Chad nodded and started grabbing calories at random. Guy didn't have any taste buds, at least not ones that were connected to each other: deep-fried fish, a burger, hash browns, apple pie topped with a dog-poop-sized plop of soft-serve chocolate ice cream, and breakfast sausage. He put a puddle of ketchup on one side of his plate and of tartar sauce on the other.

Kyle went with breakfast: eggs, sausage, bacon, and trimmings. A cup of coffee and he headed to the table.

Chad then hit the soda machine and was making a graveyard: about an inch of soda from each tap. He also liked to chew his ice, loudly.

"If you break a tooth, dude, I'm not doing any god-damn oral surgery in the field. Just so you know."

Chad grinned at him.

They arrived at the table together. Carla sat in the corner with Richie beside her and Duane across, which left Kyle to grab the diagonal, forcing Chad to perch at the end.

"Hey, beautiful!" Chad called out.

"Go to hell, Chadwick," Carla said without much heat. Oddly, she looked as if she'd hardly slept a wink.

She sure didn't offer him a coy smile, not that she ever had when they were together as a team. Or alone for that matter. Avaricious? Yes. Insatiable? Oh yeah. Coy wasn't her style. So why was he being disappointed all of a sudden? Dumb as a thumb? Definitely.

"You're cute, sugar, but I was talking to Duane. He's so pretty."

Duane didn't even bother looking up from his mixed stack of pancakes with waffles. He never woke up fast unless there was a mission. He just flipped a finger at Chad and kept eating.

"Wait a minute." Richie looked up. "If she's cute and he's beautiful. What am—"

"Pathetic," Chad offered. "I heard you left a half mil in good American cash on the table."

"Two million-five if they used standard bundling. And it wasn't me, it was him." Richie pointed at Kyle with a french fry. "What we left is burned up now anyway."

Right. Once again, Kyle had forgotten about the money he'd pocketed. Maybe he could use part of it to bribe some-one else to turn it in to the CIA's grill squad. Actionable offense to have kept it. He didn't think he could sucker Chad into fronting with the CIA for him, but Richie was a distinct possibility. Actually, he had an uncomfortable itch that he wasn't done with the need for bribe money yet. He'd turn it in at end of mission; that worked.

"Hey, hotshot," Kyle called across the table.

Carla looked up at him. Definite dark smudges under those lovely eyes. She cradled a mug of coffee between both hands like it was gold, no sign of a tray anywhere. She didn't meet his eyes, which he didn't like one bit. Kyle dropped his plate and fork in front of her.

"I don't—"

"Eat." To cut off any argument, he rose and went back to load up a fresh plate.

By the time he returned, she'd started eating, which he took as a good sign. Her body knew what to do even if her brain didn't. The mess hall was holding steady at over half-full, but not packed. There was an odd perimeter of empty tables near theirs, as if all the slack in the room had been gathered to isolate them.

"What's with the empty tables? One of you idiots forget to shower?" He pretended to sniff around the table.

"You've crossed over, Kyle." Carla already looked better for the calories. "Delta eats alone. No one knows what to do with us, so they leave a wide space."

"How—"

By her look, he knew that the source of information was once again the deceased brother. What the hell had he been into? Whatever it was had screwed Carla up but good. Somehow her brother was at the core of it each time she went strange. Not something to drag out in front of the team.

"It's still weird." Maybe something about her experiences in last night's operation had brought the brother up, bugging her the same way shooting the girl had been bothering him. Still did, but he did his best to ignore that—the long-barrel S&W 686 she'd been digging for went a long way toward appeasing his angst. So, he'd give Carla a break and not push.

Richie looked around the room. "Yeah, it is kind of weird. Surprised I didn't notice before. It is far beyond random probabilities, isn't it?"

As if to prove them wrong, a long, leggy woman with

mahogany hair spilling down past her shoulders walked right across the invisible line. She grabbed a chair and pulled it up between Kyle and Chad. She had one of those fashion magazine smiles, which was appropriate because her face went right along with it.

He'd somehow crossed over into a world of hot military women. What the hell? If he'd known about them, he'd have signed up for Delta long before now.

"You shot jocks conscious yet?"

"I am now. Chad Hawkins." Chad held out his hand and offered that deceptively sweet smile that he pulled out for the ladies. Yet another reason the "Reaper" tag had stuck—if Chad was in the bar and on the prowl, no one stood a chance until he'd picked his choice from the crowd.

"Chief Warrant Lola Maloney, that's *Mrs*. by the way." She shook his hand, but he didn't let go.

"Damn. Too late, huh?"

"Unless y'all want him to shoot up your ass. He's a crew chief gunner on a DAP Hawk."

"Okay." Chad grinned his retreat but released her hand quickly enough at that.

"You the one who hauled us out last night?" Kyle figured two female crew chiefs, maybe female pilot.

"Got it in one."

"Nice flying."

"Thanks." That really lit up her smile. "You'll be glad to know we dropped your prisoners and the spook squad onto a handy neighborhood aircraft carrier about an hour ago, so they're out of your hair. At least for now."

A round of a prayer circled about the table, mostly in the form of "Thank you, Jesus!"

"Yeah, they get a little hairy. But you must have done good for them to keep you so long, so count that as a job well done."

Kyle nodded his thanks and ate his eggs. "You wouldn't by any chance know what we're supposed to be doing next. We were sent out without a whole lot of direction."

"A little. Mine says to be at your disposal until otherwise directed." She pulled out two sheets of paper, one folded up, the other tucked in an envelope. She waved the folded one. She handed him the envelope. "What does yours say?"

Kyle glanced around the table; no one was paying any attention to their food. Carla was watching the envelope with a hungry look, hungry even though her plate was clean.

He peeled it open. And glanced at the two lines.

"We're going back in is my guess. Mission briefing at sixteen hundred. That's all it says."

—◦◦◦—

Carla started to rise with the others to leave the mess hall, but Kyle sent her a field "Stay!" signal with a pointed finger, then a closed fist.

She fooled around with her empty coffee cup and tried not to be pissed. There was no way she was going to discuss their goddamn sex life in the USS *Freedom*'s mess hall, whether or not it was just the two of them inside the "table buffer."

The only thing that was going to clear her head was some action, action involving another on-the-edge mission. Otherwise, she'd start thinking and, as she'd proved through a long sleepless night, that was a dead-end road to fucking nowhere.

The other guys didn't even offer looks of sympathy. Well, screw them. She didn't need any sympathy.

"Carla. Hey. Talking to you." Kyle's voice was soft and kind. He had that nice smile that said he was amused by her not paying attention faster.

"So talk." She didn't want soft and kind.

Kyle scrubbed at his face for a moment, then looked at his watch.

She so wasn't gonna be helping him out here. It was only at that thought that she wondered why she was being such a consummate bitch. Kyle didn't deserve any of this. She was bringing her own shit to the table and that wasn't fair. Carla opened her mouth to apologize but Kyle cut her off.

"Look, Anderson." His voice had turned that strange harsh again.

Not as harsh as he'd used on Major Asshole Gonzalez last night, but it wasn't a voice she was used to hearing from Kyle, especially not aimed at her.

"I don't know what bug crawled up your ass, but if you don't sleep eight of the next ten hours, I'm leaving it and you right here on this ship tonight. We clear?"

He didn't wait for her answer. Instead, in one of those fluid Kyle moves that normally fired up her more carnal instincts, he was up from the table and gone across the mess hall before she had a chance to even think about a response.

"Oh yeah?" didn't really cut it.

She staggered to her feet but had to keep a hand on the table while the room did a quick tilt and whirl. Once that settled, she managed to drop her empty mug and plate at the scrub tubs.

It seemed like every single person on the ship was in motion. Last shift leaving their meals and heading for stations. Next shift headed in for their breakfast. The corridors were about a person and a half wide, and by the time she rediscovered her berth, she'd managed to ram her shoulder into the wall about a dozen times while trying to avoid being run down by every last one of them.

She wanted…what?

She wanted to take back last night. Erase it. She wanted Kyle to undo what he'd done to her.

Carla Lesson Sixteen: *Can't change the past*. She'd learned that one many times, especially as she held the folded flag and watched her brother being lowered into the ground.

Her last ever words to him had been a teasing promise to steal his brand-new motorcycle while he was overseas.

He'd smiled and called back over his shoulder as he walked away, "Over my dead body." She hadn't touched it while he was gone, but that hadn't kept him alive. Now she'd ride it as long as she survived.

That was the problem. There was no place in her world for what Kyle had made her feel.

Death awaited.

Simple as that.

It was easy to do the impossible when you knew death was coming. It didn't matter anyway. She was ready.

What's the worst that could happen?

You die.

Old joke. Old truth.

Since she already knew the future, it meant she could try harder than anyone and it didn't matter much. No stupid risks; that was a waste. But you could run at maximum effort all the time because there was no need to hold back for a future that didn't exist. End result was the same, but she got something good done in the meantime.

So how much of a joke was it that Kyle had made her feel…

She closed the berthing space door, and the dim room wavered along the edges of her vision.

…so alive.

She pitched facedown onto the bunk and was asleep before her face hit the pillow.

Kyle found his way to the *Freedom*'s missile deck. The big RAM surface-to-air missile launcher dominated the space. It was a massive piece of hardware swinging twenty-one missiles on a rolling armature. Fifty-caliber machine guns were perched at the corners, complete with curved shields to protect the gunner from return fire. But there was still some space for him to lean against the stern rail and stare out at the sea rolling lazily off the stern.

As his pulse slowed, as the haze of anger at Carla that he hadn't been able to control cooled, he became aware of the rising heat of the early morning air. Even on the sea off Venezuela, they were too close to the equator for the temperatures to be reasonable. They were far enough offshore that no birds swirled above hoping for scraps. The only sounds were the rumble and vibration of the big Rolls-Royce gas turbines as the ship idled slowly toward the rising sun across the endless liquid plane.

Looking down at the afterdeck, Kyle could see that the rear third of the ship was a big helicopter landing platform marked out in broad white lines that would show up even in a raging storm. Under the stern was a pickup ramp for cargo and small watercraft. And under his skin was Sergeant First Class Carla Anderson.

Damn her for making him lose his control. He should go find her and apologize. He'd never spoken that way to another soldier, not even the asshole ones. So why had he done it to her?

He knew why.

Which only made it worse.

"Going to be a warm one."

He hadn't heard or felt Chief Warrant Lola Maloney approaching as he leaned there.

She was dressed in standard desert-camouflage ACU pants and plain T-shirt. Woman's body went just fine with that smile and that face.

She stared out over the stern at the rolling wake of the *Freedom* as she worked through the seas, but not hurrying on her way. No other ships were around. A smudge to the north might have been an aircraft carrier or destroyer, somebody big, but he couldn't tell more from here.

"Aren't you supposed to be asleep?" The Night Stalkers, like Delta, did most of their work at night. He'd slept too long last night and now had to stay up for a few hours and then find somewhere other than with Carla to take a nap before mission briefing.

"Thought you might need a shoulder."

"Am I that obvious?"

"Not to most, no. Met my husband, Tim, on my first full mission with the Night Stalkers. I qualify that because I did a partial mission while still in training. I hauled back your girlfriend's brother."

"No shit? I met the Colonel."

"Gibson? Yeah, you know for sure that if he was in on it, it was way bad and seriously major on the priority scale."

Kyle nodded. He'd figured that one out himself.

"I made sure her brother had a flag over him after I brought him home. And no, I don't know what happened, and no, I can't talk about even the bit that I do know."

"Uh, thanks for doing that."

"We give them honor in death." Lola shrugged at how little that made up for, but it was something. "Anyway, Tim was a handful. Of course, so was I. Looks like you have a dose of that on your hands."

"Maybe." And maybe Carla wasn't just reacting to something that had happened on the mission. Maybe it was a reaction to him. But for the life of him, he couldn't think of what he'd done—other than falling in love with her.

Not that he'd said a word about it.

And her look this morning clearly said that, at least for now, the feeling was not at all mutual.

Kyle stared out at the stern waves, then up at the blue sky, then back down at the helideck.

"Wait a sec. Where's your helicopter?"

Chief Maloney stamped her heel against the deck. "You're standing on the roof of a two-bird hangar. You don't think we leave stealth gear out in the daylight if we don't have to? And you're avoiding the topic."

Stealth? What the... But then he remembered the

way that the helicopters had sort of showed up out of nowhere. Almost as if they arrived overhead in the jungle before their sound did. Well, that would certainly explain it. Even an idiot knew there were other stealth birds besides the one that went down in bin Laden's compound, but he'd never expected to meet one. *Welcome to Delta, boy.*

Now that he actually had, it had serious implications. It meant that last night's and tonight's missions were important enough to call for the release of those very special assets.

"Gather round, folks. He's starting to put the pieces together."

He eyed Chief Maloney, but she was just grinning at him.

She was lead pilot, flying the very best equipment of a high-powered outfit like the Night Stalkers. Which meant...what?

"Still not getting it, Chief."

She clapped him on the shoulder. "Then just do like Mama Rici always say: 'Fry up the next chucklehead, girl!'" She said it in a thick Creole roll.

"Chucklehead?"

"Where you from, boy?"

"Washington. The state, not the capital."

"What do you call a catfish up there?"

"Uh, we call them catfish."

"Heathens! It means stop worrying at what you can't fix." With that, the Chief offered him a smile and strolled off. "Got to go get me some shut-eye and dream o' my man." Then she laughed a crazy-woman laugh that sent chills up his spine and made him wonder if someone had just pricked a pin into a voodoo doll of him.

If that's what had happened, he hoped to hell Carla wasn't doing the pinning.

However, she might be.

For reasons he still wasn't sure of, Kyle guessed that his waking-up dreaming of Carla was what had caused the trouble in the first place.

Chapter 12

"AGENT SMITH. YES, THAT'S REALLY MY NAME. I'LL make it worse. My given first name is Fred. Honest to God. Fred Smith. And, please, I've heard every single joke there is about being a CIA agent named Fred Smith." He held up his hand. "Especially the ones from *The Matrix*, so please try to resist the temptation, and this will go a lot faster."

All Carla cared about was that he wasn't one of the three CIA sadists who had questioned her last night. The night before. Yesterday. Whatever.

They were back in the same briefing room she'd been stuck in for so long last night. Steel table, steel chairs, no windows, no air.

She hadn't been near a single piece of intel during the whole mission and hadn't interacted with the prisoners except to offer to shoot one in the butthole if he jumped off the waterfall. She didn't even know Richie and Kyle had extracted any documents until she saw the two of them sorting through paper after the hike out.

But she had been the one to cover the most ground, crisscrossing the compound several times. The CIA apparently wasn't going to be happy until she personally identified every stone and bush she'd met along the way.

Any other evidence extractable from the Venezuelan General's drug-fort hacienda had died along with the men in the explosions. The vehicles were, without exception, U.S. military purchased through a FMS—Foreign Military Sales—package to the Colombian antidrug effort and then moved to the Venezuelan military, which had really pissed off the debriefing team. This morning's satellite-pass photos had shown that the destruction Carla had wrought with her explosives and Kyle's "kill the copter" ploy had totally burned out any remaining evidence.

The guys resisted harassing Agent Smith, but it was a close thing. Duane and Chad were trading dangerous smiles... They'd get him later if he ticked them off the least bit.

"We're offshore Venezuela," the agent started.

"Been there. Did that." Chad started the riff that wasn't going to end well. They had to do something to suppress the "Agent Smith" jokes that must be rolling through their brains. If he hadn't made a point of it, she'd just have taken him at his word about his name and moved on.

Smith rolled right on. "The country with the largest oil reserves in the world."

"Which is why we're here." Duane wasn't about to be one-upped, not by Chad, at least.

"And"—Smith was tenacious—"one of the three worst drug-trafficking countries there is."

"Which is why *we* actually were there night before last," Kyle said softly and calmed the whole team down. He did that somehow and made it look easy and effortless.

Usually Carla appreciated it, just went along for the ride. Tonight was different. Tonight she didn't want to cooperate.

Introspection wasn't exactly her long suit. So, she kept her own fit of unvoiced rebellion against Kyle quiet, because she knew one thing for damn sure—it was personal. Aside from the fact that it wasn't the least little bit appropriate, it was totally ridiculous. The briefing continued while she did her best to beat her feelings back into the box where they belonged.

"Their networks are built in layers that we haven't been able to crack. We knew General Carlos Vasquez was a major player in the Cartel de los Soles. He—"

"Wait." Carla popped a hand. "What? Cartel of the Suns?" Focus on the briefing. Good idea. And it helped.

Agent Smith turned on a screen on the wall behind him and flashed up an image. It was a close-up of the man they'd dragged through the jungle last night, but in happier times wearing his full uniform.

Damn it! Carla hated being predictable almost as much as she hated whatever Kyle was doing to her.

"Note the epaulettes on his shoulder boards. Their military doesn't use stars like we do; they use suns. He wears the three suns of a major general. The Cartel de los Soles isn't a typical price-fixing single cartel like the Mexican and Colombian cartels, nor is it restricted to command tier. It's actually a series of competing drug cartels that exist in every division and rank of the Venezuelan military. There have been many migrations of Colombian drug cartels into the country, but this is Venezuela's homegrown version."

"How effective are they?"

"Twenty percent of U.S.-consumed cocaine and fifty percent for Western Europe transports through Venezuela."

That earned the room's attention.

"As I'm assuming that the five of us aren't expected to take on a hundred metric tons of cocaine traffic ourselves, what's our part in this?"

Carla kept meaning to ask Kyle how he did that. She'd been on the verge of whining, maybe even pinging Agent Smith about being a block of CIA code, and Kyle had jumped past that and put it in perspective.

Of course, talking hadn't ever been a big part of their relationship. Every time they were alone together, the heat exploded into sex. On the rare occasions that they remained conscious afterward, they ended up reviewing missions, assignments, training, and all that other noise. She'd have to put "talking to him" somewhere on her Kyle to-do list. Maybe. What if she didn't like the answers?

She looked over at him: calm, ready to proceed, and still too goddamn handsome. Even now, in the briefing room, she wanted to jump him. Or kill him for crimes unknown. Christ, she was a total basket case. If anyone ever managed a good look at what was inside her head, they'd lock her away in a padded cell for sure.

"Your part in this"—Agent Fred Smith went to the next slide—"are these."

The image he put up earned the room's silence.

It was a submarine, thirty meters long and three or four across, based on the man standing beside it in the photo. It was painted in a pattern of blues and grays that looked like water. Or a camouflage that would work well if it was just under sun-dappled ocean waves. It had a proper conning tower and looked very well done.

"It's made of wood framing with a fiberglass and

Kevlar shell, so it has almost no radar signature. It can carry up to ten metric tons of refined cocaine. Diesel, ten days en route to the southern U.S."

"That means it needs air and we can take it on the surface." Richie put the tech pieces together even faster than Kyle.

"Sounds like a Navy job if they're out on the ocean." Carla wasn't about to be outdone.

"The subs also have batteries for fourteen hours submerged operation, so they only have to surface at night for running the diesel and recharging. They can run at a depth of sixty meters."

Crap. How were they supposed to fight something like that?

"To make it worse, they're disposable."

"What?" Richie bolted upright in his chair. "That thing must cost north of a million dollars to make and they throw it away?"

"This one was closer to two million." Agent Fred smiled and waited for someone to take the next step.

None of the guys had a clue. Carla saw Kyle's lightbulb go on, damn him. He traded a smile with Agent Fred.

Wait a sec!

"What's the street price on ten metric tons in the U.S.?"

"A billion dollars U.S. per ton, more or less. Trafficker's take is usually thirteen percent, so call it a hundred and thirty million, times ten tons. Double that if they also hold the in-country U.S. or European upper-level distribution. Per trip."

That's why a two-million-dollar sub was disposable. Hell, you could run a fleet of them.

Carla started thinking about the kind of military force

that would be hanging around to protect an investment of that size. Suddenly it didn't look so amusing.

"That's why we're here." Her voice was a whisper, but the nods around the room confirmed her conclusion.

The DEA could find and take down a submarine, or at least a percentage of them.

But to take down the command structure behind them…

"Shit!" She put the pieces together and sat up to look at Kyle.

His nod of agreement was grim.

"You want"—she had to ask the question—"the five of us to take down the Cartel de los Soles?"

"That might be asking a bit much," Agent Fred acknowledged, "but we certainly want you to handicap them."

Three hours later Carla was little clearer about what was going on. Fred Smith was gone, and now it was just the team sitting around the steel table in a black hole inside the USS *Freedom*.

"How can they use so many words to say so little?" Carla wanted to know. Her head was torn between a desire to spin and an equal need to throb.

"Special training," Chad replied.

"Spook training," Duane followed on.

"Deep, dark secret-agent training."

Carla put her head down on the table. With Richie joining in, they were jumping from *Mutt and Jeff* to *The Three Stooges*. Wasn't that just too perfect.

"If we go into Venezuela directly, it will appear too obvious," Kyle said as if that clarified anything.

"So…" Carla didn't bother raising her head but

continued talking to the table. "We're going to swim to Aruba with fake passports, pretending that we're tourists who haven't just been dropped offshore out of a Special Operations helicopter."

"Then we rent a sailboat," Chad began the round-robin again.

"Sail it to Venezuela."

"Pretending that we're tourists, but only as a thin disguise for being drug lords looking to expand their business with local contacts in the drug-transport business."

"And then we leverage those contacts to start a war inside the cartel." What the hell, she might as well join in with the other lunatics. She raised her head to look at Kyle. "And this somehow makes sense to you?"

He nodded.

Carla put her head back down on the table. It would be really convenient at the moment if she didn't trust the man so implicitly.

But she did.

Kyle found Carla at the same back rail overlooking the stern of the ship where he'd spoken to the SOAR pilot this morning. It was as if he'd blinked and the scene had simply changed.

Chief Warrant Lola Maloney shifted to Sergeant Carla Anderson.

Day for night.

Night had fallen over the tropics while they were in the briefing. The ship used limited lights in these waters—running lights to warn other ships and soft lights by the doorways. The few ship's spaces with outside windows were darkened to allow the ship's officers a clear view out at the night, though there was not much to see at the moment.

It was dark enough on deck that only the silhouette of his teammate showed. That and the slash of the Milky Way like a white band across the heavens.

"Hey, girlie." He went for light.

"Hey, tough guy." Her voice was soft and amused. Or soft and relieved?

"We okay?"

He could see her nod as he joined at the rail. "Sure. Why wouldn't we be?"

"Want to talk about it?"

"Not so much. You?" She sounded as if she'd dealt with whatever had cost her a night's sleep.

Kyle considered.

Shooting a naked girl maybe not even into her teens. He didn't want to discuss that for a second.

Being in love with Carla? Yeah, that was going to get him absolutely no mileage. "I'm good."

"You're very good. Think we can do it quiet enough here for no one to notice?"

"Sure."

She sidled toward him until they were a breath apart.

Kyle nodded back over his shoulder at the ship's superstructure. "If you don't mind entertaining the deck watch officer up there wearing his night-vision gear."

"Spoilsport!" She leaned back against the rail. "Crap. I tell you, Kyle, the military does have drawbacks."

"Serving with you isn't one of them, Wild Woman."

"Aww. You really know how to sweet-talk a girl, Mister Kyle. Right back at ya, buddy."

Buddy? Yeah, guess he deserved that.

"Hey, Carla."

"What?"

Kyle opened his mouth, but that was far as he got. He never chickened on anything. So why was he chickening on this?

Because she's the best thing that ever happened to you and you're scared to death of screwing it up. So his body came up with a comment when his brain didn't supply one.

"Bet we're not headed into the land of personal privacy."

Lola Maloney was going to be dumping them back in-country at 0300. Six hours from now.

"Well, time's a-wasting, sailor." She turned and walked away from him.

Even the woman's silhouette slayed him. The heat pounded into his body as he imagined taking her that way, walking away from him. It didn't take much effort to let himself go with the flow.

Kyle caught up to her just as she entered their bunk room. She didn't want to think. And she sure as hell didn't want to explain.

She *did* want to feel. Not in her heart, but very much in her body.

His heat had followed her down the corridors of the USS *Freedom*. The passageways that had been so cluttered before were blessedly empty. Which was good because their mutual awareness would have scorched anyone who passed too close.

She peeled off her T-shirt and bra in a single motion as he closed the door to their quarters. She managed to loosen her slacks before his hands wrapped around her from behind.

He was so strong, so powerful. Kyle Reeves could keep the world at bay. One hand scooped up onto her breasts; the other plunged down the front of her pants. She braced her hands against either side of the closet door as he took her.

The soft wash of a night-light came out of the bath. It made her body look as if it were glowing softly in the mirror mounted on the closet door. His tanned arms, dark serpents against her reflected skin, snagging and ensnaring her.

But, oh God, what they could do to her. She thrust back harder and harder against him as he drove her upward with his hands. Then, with a vile oath quite unlike him, he dragged down both their pants, sheathed himself, and drove into her so hard that it took her breath away.

Just as her eyes slid shut, she caught a reflection of them. A man lost in the shadows behind her, consumed by the fire of his need for her. And a woman—held safe by his powerful hands—with a look of purest ecstasy shining across her features.

Normally she would think of her control over the animal side of man, or her power to humble even a warrior like Kyle.

But this woman in the mirror, the one who opened her eyes once more to watch herself climb toward a sky-high release, she was lost in the simple joy. Not the "Wild Woman" caught up like a hellfire that would never let her come back to earth, though her body vibrated and shook until it seemed the ship was under attack.

The ship wasn't.

Nor was it only her body that even now burned in waves so hot and powerful that an ocean's worth of cool water wouldn't be enough to douse the fires building within.

There was a woman inside her who she didn't know.

Hidden behind a layer of the carefully nursed char that Carla had stoked and banked around her inner self for a lifetime. It was being blown away like the finest dust, as if it had never been.

Carla exploded from within at Kyle's hammering release.

The aftershocks nearly sank her as the waves slammed through both of them again and again.

A warrior had shattered her shields as if they weren't even tissue paper.

And now a different woman lay back against a man whose arms enveloped her with an infinite tenderness after being so rough just moments before. Tender, but no less powerful. His strokes were now soothing and comforting, and sent a warmth into her as strong as any frantic release, but transformed into ocean-long waves.

He remained shadowed, his face buried in her hair.

All that showed was the new woman exposed in the mirror for everyone to see, everyone including Carla herself.

A woman Carla didn't recognize.

Chapter 13

"NO WAY IN HELL!"

The four guys stood around in the ship's ready room wearing little more than Speedos; they also wore wristwatches. Carla admitted that they looked damn good that way. Four men at the prime of their lives and their training, so impossibly fit and handsome, parading around the room most of the way to naked. Kyle stood out, of course, even discounting her personal bias.

But there were limits!

"I am not wearing a goddamn bikini in front of you jokers."

"Ba-kaw! Buck buck ba-kaw!" Chad started doing a chicken dance around in circles. Duane picked it up and Richie blushed—either on her behalf or because he too wanted to see her dressed...undressed that way.

Only Kyle was standing there with that goddamn, patient half smile of his.

"They're going to drop us a dozen kilometers off the beach in Aruba. We're going to arrive on the beach with the morning snorkelers and week-old entry stamps in our Spanish passports. Then we're going to peel off our wet suits. What are you going to be wearing?"

"When James Bond crawled out of scuba gear, he didn't have to wear a goddamn bikini!"

"No," Richie acknowledged.

"Thank God someone's on my side." Carla sat down

on a bench and crossed her arms solidly over her T-shirt and sports bra. *Which she'd be keeping firmly in place, thank you very much.*

"He did climb out of a semisubmersible alligator wearing a full suit, tie, and dress shoes. I guess it was a dry-suit alligator, though it certainly didn't look it in the film."

"Thanks, Richie." So much for having someone useful on her side.

"No one on the boat has a one-piece." Kyle kept his voice level. "We asked around."

"I'm not wearing one of those either. Wait! You've been discussing my body with everyone on the whole goddamn ship?"

"Nope, just the women." Chad offered a leer and then did another chicken-dance circle, actually making a tune out of his chicken noises.

When he passed too close to her bench, Carla kicked him hard in the shin. That sent him hopping off in a new direction making a different kind of noise. She still had her combat boots on.

"Okay, Anderson. So what are you going to wear instead?"

"A goddamn cast-iron suit!" She clambered to her feet and snatched the impossibly tiny bag that Kyle had tried to hand to her at the beginning of the conversation.

Then she struck him in the solar plexus. He'd been ready for her, so her fist merely bounced off his rock-hard gut.

"What was that for?"

"For thinking this is in any way funny."

"I find it"—he hesitated and bit his lower lip for a

moment—"intriguing. You'll be far more appropriately clothed than you were crossing the General's compound two nights ago with your shirt open to your navel."

"Two nights ago," Carla managed between gritted teeth, "I was a soldier. Now I'm just going to be a girl on show."

"You're going to be a woman who will look beautiful."

"Aw shucks, Mr. Soldier Man. I feel so much better now."

She stalked off to change.

Duane and Chad had finished prepping the drop bag and were double-checking it by the time Carla came back.

Kyle had seen her naked many times: indoors, outdoors, daylight, starlight, firelight, just hours ago reflected in a mirror. That he'd somehow had the power to cause Sergeant Carla Anderson to come apart like that still awed him. It was as if she'd transformed within the circle of his arms. He couldn't wait to try it again.

But the woman who walked back into the ready room was a revelation despite her grim expression.

"Aw, spoilsport!" Chad called out when he noticed that Carla had indeed changed, but then pulled on a white, large-sized, V-neck T-shirt over the swimsuit.

"Can it, Reaper." Kyle gave it just enough heat so that the guys would know that while they'd had their fun, they were done now. And using Chad's Unit nickname would remind them all that this was a mission, not a fashion show.

Though what Kyle noticed was how the T-shirt hem teased and enticed. Her legs looked longer, and it almost suggested the lack of bikini bottoms entirely, though he occasionally caught quick flashes of bright yellow to prove they were indeed there.

He did his honest best to keep his expression neutral.

Her arched eyebrow told him he'd done a lousy job of it.

"Thanks, Carla," he managed to choke out and turned to pull on the neoprene shorts and jacket of his wet suit because there were some things that a Speedo was never going to hide.

Two hours before dawn, there was negligible boat traffic off the west coast of Aruba, which Carla appreciated. Being run down by a coastal freighter while swimming to shore wasn't really her idea of a good time.

They had just jumped out of Chief Warrant Maloney's helicopter as it hovered a single meter above the waves; the swim should be a straightforward task. They covered the first ten kilometers rapidly using DPVs. The small diver propulsion vehicles had very quiet electric motors to drive the small propeller, a leash that hooked to the front of a simple waist harness to tow them along, and two handles for steering.

When they could see the coast as a shimmer of resort lights on the horizon, they disconnected the DPVs, opened the devices' small flotation bladders to the sea, and let them sink out of sight along with the harnesses.

The last five kilometers was a snorkel-and-fin job, made pesky by the big rollers of the open ocean, but not problematic.

Dawn found them a couple hundred meters offshore.

The soft morning light—simple pinks shifting gold, orange, then yellow—shone through the crystalline water down to the coral reefs. Carla wished she had time to stop and watch, or, better yet, was wearing tanks so that she could go down and enjoy the spectacle.

The only tank diving she'd ever done had been for Delta training. They'd started in a swimming pool and then rapidly moved into the most turgid, dark, and brutally rough water they could find. Puget Sound was deep, muddy, deathly cold, and rife with rip currents.

The Aruban sea life's changing of the guard on the coral reef a dozen meters below her was a dance visible through crystal-clear water. Nighttime fish were seeking their hideaways, and the daytime species began nosing their way out of theirs. Angel, sun, grouper, and a hundred others she didn't recognize, exotically attired in oranges, blues, and yellow stripes. A two-meter sand shark lazed along the bottom, moving in a languid fashion meant to fool other fish into thinking he was harmless. A great ray—as wide as Ms. Shark was long—flapped its wings as it rose out of the sand and sent her scooting off in a new direction.

When they hit the lifeless sandy bottom of the surf zone, it was a rude and abrupt shock.

A quick glance showed Carla that she was in among several early-morning snorkelers, none of them her team. A family of four paddled happily past her. A couple swam along holding hands. By the way they did it, you could just tell that they were newlyweds. *Better them than me.*

Carla kept paddling for shore. Marriage had worked out so well for Mom and Dad. He'd been a useless drunk long before Mom's National Guard unit went to war. Mom had been shocked by her abrupt deployment. It was supposed to be a weekend a month and some extra time if there was a sudden disaster. There had been one, and it was called Afghanistan. After her one-year deployment was over, she'd returned a better, happier person. She'd wanted to go back and the only way was to go full Army.

Carla could still remember the conversation.

Clay had been seventeen and already working two jobs to eke out a helicopter license at the local airfield. He was shooting for the 101st Airborne on his eighteenth birthday, Carla had just turned fourteen and was already spending as much of her time as she could hiking in the mountains.

There had been no need to comment about their home life. Dad wasn't a part of this family meeting.

"It's up to you, honey. Clay will be gone soon. You still have four years to go. If I sign up, you'll be mostly on your own for at least two years." *With Dad the sullen drunk* the unspoken part of the conversation.

"Mom…" Carla hadn't wanted her to go, but she knew what her mom needed to survive. "You *have* to go. I'll be fine."

A year later Clay was indeed flying with the 101st, Carla had managed to find a small place of her own, and Mom had come home in a wooden box. Dad had refused to go to the funeral in DC, even refused the delivery of the flag.

Carla had only been home by chance.

Shoving her father into bed to sleep off yet another night, then sitting on the couch to watch the dawn, she'd

fallen asleep. She'd woken to her father fighting with
the poor lieutenant who'd been trying to deliver the
folded flag. She'd taken it herself.

Now she had two flags, Mom's and Clay's. She wondered who they would go to when her own flag, folded
down to a triangle, joined the other two. Her father
wouldn't be sober enough to care.

"Cheerful thoughts for a beautiful morning," Carla
muttered to herself as her knees grounded on the soft
sand. She flipped over to sit on her butt as she slid up
her mask, spit out the snorkel, and removed her fins.
The sun was well up, and while the resort beach wasn't
crowded, it was active. Perfect.

Per plan, they'd come ashore in the land of the well-
tended. The resort itself was made of ornate towers
surrounded by lush plantings dotted with sharp-peaked
giant umbrella shapes made of darkest thatch. The resorts
weren't crowded together here like the photos of Waikiki,
but spread along the shining sand in stately array.

Richie and Kyle were already ashore. Chad and Duane
were just arriving a hundred meters down the beach.

Carla stood and, before even wading ashore, rapidly
shed her neoprene in the warm morning air that would
soon be trying to bake out their brains.

———∿∿∿———

"Oh. My. God!" Richie's voice had Kyle turning.

Kyle couldn't have said it better. His mouth, dry with
salt water, was suddenly parched past speech.

"Ursula Andress in *Dr. No*." Richie's deep immer-
sion in Bond films made the point perfectly.

Carla Anderson, rising from the surf, didn't brag

Ursula's impressive build or blond locks. But she most certainly boasted that same centerfold wet look, advertising exactly why you should come snorkeling in Aruba.

Her long hair, black from its soaking, glittered wetly in the morning sun. Her white T-shirt had become wholly transparent when wet, each place it clung merely emphasizing the incredible fitness of the woman within. The lemon-yellow bikini, merely a suggestion beneath the T-shirt when dry in the ready room, now shone through brightly. There was far too little of it for a woman of Carla's form, and Kyle blessed the lack of every single millimeter. Her dusky skin glowed with fitness and sunshine.

She strode up the beach until she was standing right in front of them. "What?"

Kyle could only shake his head.

Chad, never at a loss for words, joined them. "Damn, Anderson. I knew that Kyle was an asshole lucky far beyond what he deserves, but I had no idea how far beyond."

Duane had arrived beside Chad and merely nodded his agreement, silent for once.

Carla's brow knit for a moment, then she looked down at herself and cursed. She dumped her swim gear to the sand and tried pulling the T-shirt away from her body. She wrung out the bit in front of her belly. When she let it go, it wrapped back around her body with a nearly audible slap.

Another guy stopped to stare until his newlywed wife shoved him along on his way.

"Is this a *Sports Illustrated* photo shoot? Could you introduce us to the director or whoever?" A pair of shapely bleach blonds, severely straining the scant material of their swimsuit tops, stopped and asked. Then they looked at the steam pouring out of Carla's ears and scooted on their way. Normally Kyle would have at least watched how the two of them walked off. All four of the guys would. Not with Carla Anderson standing in front of them; they weren't even in the same league as the reality of the soldier woman standing before them.

"If…" Carla took a deep breath, which caused several truly amazing shifts in her anatomy.

"Lucky" didn't begin to cover how Kyle was feeling at the moment. "Awed" came much closer. How was it that a woman like her was with him? He just couldn't make the pieces connect.

"If," she started again, "you assholes keep looking at me that way, you're going to end up being the laughingstocks of this beach while I demonstrate just how much I really know about hand-to-hand combat. I will start handing out personal, customized lessons in five, four, three…"

She wasn't looking at the others, though of course she'd be tracking them in her peripheral vision. She was glaring directly at him.

He got the message, but he couldn't do anything about it. "You're gorgeous," he managed to breathe out.

She rolled her eyes. "You are all such guys." She bent to gather her swim gear, not kneeling, but thoughtlessly bending right over at the waist, and then began walking up the beach.

None of them could do more than stare, and Kyle couldn't begrudge them one bit of it.

"Oh my God." This time Richie managed no more than a whisper.

Carla walking away from him in her leathers had been a treat.

But this was…

They followed as soon as they were able to move.

Carla hit the first stall off the beach that sold women's clothes. Aruba was Dutch. The beach was lined with orderly resort hotels. Their lobbies in turn would be lined with frigidly air-conditioned shops that catered to the ridiculously wealthy. She'd be even more uncomfortable there than she was crossing the beach so close to naked that guys were having trouble walking past her.

She was surprised that the heat rising from her anger didn't simply bake the T-shirt dry. Of all the goddamn jerks. Okay, she could understand the others, kind of. In their world, women either belonged in khaki or were something found in stateside bars.

But, damn it! She'd thought Kyle was better than that.

Since when did stunned puppy-dog eyes have any part in her world?

He said she was gorgeous.

He was full of shit!

Though there was no denying the heat between them. She liked that he wanted her…when they weren't in the middle of a mission!

Man but he was making her nuts.

So, she avoided the resorts and worked her way back into the areas inland from the beach. They still catered to the tourists, but they did it without the ostentation and Gucci labels.

Despite Aruba having been a Dutch colony for centuries, a Latin feel pervaded the air. There was a mix of small shops, restaurants, and cheaper hotels without their own beach front. There were also dozens, maybe hundreds of stalls, carts, and even blankets rolled out on the sidewalks. It was too carefully quaint, testifying to just how much of their economy was based on tourism, but that didn't concern her at the moment. There was still a sleepy feel, as it was only shortly past sunrise, but most of the locals were already in place to garner every dollar they could.

She was hailed in Dutch, English (which she pretended not to know), German (which she really didn't), then Spanish. She hoped to God she could find something in the stall that wouldn't plaster the word "Aruba!" or worse, "I *heart* Aruba!" across her chest.

Carla bought a floppy straw sunhat, big sunglasses, sandals, and the most covering sundress that the woman had, which wasn't saying much. It was a wraparound in a bright floral pattern whose yellows were far too reminiscent of the despised bikini. It plunged down between her breasts and stopped short of mid-thigh, but it was better than the T-shirt and bikini that had earned her so much attention, including a small band of ardent followers, in just the two blocks she'd stalked from the beach.

She'd left it to the boys to clear out any of her sudden fans. If it was left up to her, she'd probably end up in jail on a murder-one charge. Actually, no *probably* about it.

At least her guys had gotten their shit back together

by the time she was done shopping. Two had hit a couple stalls and come back with shorts and touristy T-shirts—Duane had actually fallen for the "I *heart* Aruba!" trap, which did look pretty good stretched across his muscles—while two others stood guard on the stall she'd entered. The old Arawak proprietor with her wrinkle-buried eyes and matronly bosom had clucked her tongue knowingly when Carla had eyed the rear exit of the stall as a potential means of escape.

A grimace, a couple dozen euros from her waterproof money belt, and she rejoined the guys. They dumped their swim gear at the back of a still-closed rental stall. The guy would simply assume that someone had accidentally returned their gear to the wrong place, and he'd quietly add it to his inventory when none of the other vendors squawked.

Kyle had been first shift to guard the stall where Carla had shopped. Had tried not to imagine what was happening while the *matrona* was holding up a nearly sheer swatch of cloth as a temporary dressing room.

When the other guys came back, he'd gone and bought clothes for himself. Creating even that small amount of distance from Carla was a relief.

He couldn't afford to get stupid about her or it would damage the team. It would fall apart if he was worrying about her rather than his own role in this. Well, that certainly sounded like his problem, not hers. And Dad had taught him how to deal with such things. He would pound the problem aside, find his center, and stay focused on Carla's capabilities as a soldier, which were awesome. He'd still place her as number one on his list of who he'd want guarding his back.

But then he returned to the booth just as she wended her way out of the shadowy rear—past piles of T-shirts and racks of dresses and handbags—to once more stand in the sunlight.

Offset by the bright floral flirtiness of the dress, her darker skin simply glowed. Her hair had already dried in the arid heat into a thick tangle that he couldn't wait to run his hands through. The dress covered more than the bikini and wet T-shirt, but what it hid, it implied and the impact was equally powerful.

Lucky beyond what he deserved? No question!

Fear he was going to screw it up…

Well, there was a new thought. Until two nights ago, it had simply been the best relationship of his life. But everything had ramped up and now he couldn't imagine not being with Carla.

He offered her his arm. She glared at him, then on a huff of exasperation, slipped her hand around his elbow.

The five of them had entered one end of the market wearing swimsuits and not much more. They exited the other wearing tourist outfits and small backpacks. Carla also carried a colorful straw bag that he'd bought for her.

They each now held a variety of clothes, sunscreen, toiletries, a couple of guidebooks, and several ridiculous geegaws that clearly labeled them as tourists traveling light. Personally, he'd been unable to resist a small, fuzzy moose toy with "Aruba" stitched into one of his broad antlers. Would it be breaking security if he gave it to Mom for Christmas? Probably, but it was still too damn cute.

They'd laughed together over Indonesian curry chicken and fries from the curiously named Mrs. Kelly's food truck, but that didn't make it any less delicious. Indonesia and Aruba had both been Dutch colonies for well over three centuries.

At one moment, Kyle and Carla were wandering alone, the other three guys off this way or that.

"I'm sorry it upset you earlier. I want you to know that you look absolutely fabulous in that dress." She now owned slacks, shorts, and several tops, but she hadn't changed into them, for which he was eternally grateful.

Carla looked over at him, her eyes hidden by sunglasses and the wide straw brim of her hat.

"Um, thanks. I'm sorry if I overreacted, but I've never worn girl clothes before."

"Never?" He tried to imagine that. Women in bars, especially the ones who hung out in the Green Beret bars seeking the target-eager environment, always wore girl clothes—though often so scanty that the word "clothes" might be an exaggeration.

"Come on, Kyle. Do I look like a senior prom kind of girl?"

He inspected her as she stopped to look at a vendor of local jewelry. He could tell that she wasn't really browsing, that it's just what she thought a girl was supposed to do, to maintain her cover. A glance revealed that Carla had no piercings. Couldn't even buy his girl earrings. Then he spotted a fine chain of silver from which dangled a small sailboat of carved amber wrapped in silver filigree. It was actually quite pretty work.

He waited until Carla grew bored with the inspection

of earrings and necklaces, less than sixty seconds, and wandered off to see what Chad was up to. He was probably purchasing a pink Swiss Army knife labeled with the inevitable "Aruba!" because the man simply couldn't breath right without having some sort of weapon.

Kyle quickly purchased the tiny sailboat necklace. The vendor's smile said he'd just been ripped off, but Kyle didn't care to take the time for a bartering session.

He slipped up behind Carla. Lowering the sailboat down in front of her just long enough to hear her brief gasp before he secured it around her neck. The boat sailed just between the first rise of her breasts.

She turned to study him and he took both of her hands.

"No, you don't look like a prom girl. You look like someone who was the prom queen and has now grown into a stunning woman. And—" He cut her off on the verge of interrupting.

She scowled.

"—no, it does not make you one iota less the soldier I want fighting beside me." Then he did something he'd never done before. He kissed her in broad daylight in front of others.

With a soft "damn you" against his lips, she melted against him. The woman who flowed against him was as unexpected as the soldier in form-clinging leathers. This time she didn't grab and devour. She didn't take control and demand. Instead, she simply slid her hands around his neck and held on.

He felt a desire to protect rather than plunder. If he were rich, he would set her up in the penthouse of one of these towering resorts looming above the market. He would lavish her with—

Kyle was going mad.

He curled his arms around her. A sigh, he swallowed. He…

…opened an eye and spotted Duane, standing there with arms folded across his "I *heart* Aruba!" chest and a grin on his face. He opened the other and saw Chad and Richie in similar stances.

"There's a cliché here just waiting to happen," Duane observed.

"Something about getting rooms, or were you thinking of the girl cooties one?" Chad asked him.

"The name is Bond. James Bond," Richie offered up.

That broke them up and everyone laughed.

Everyone except Carla, who had pulled in her arms but remained nestled against Kyle's chest.

Nothing to lose?

He had the whole world to lose and it was curled up in his arms.

———— ∾ ————

Carla wished for heat to rise to her cheeks. She wanted to feel embarrassed, put upon, something that she could fight back against.

Instead, she stood in the circle of Kyle's arms among the bustle of the now lively market and felt desirable and beautiful. No one had ever bought her jewelry. A tiny sailboat of hope that someday she could sail free.

Jewelry and a dress. And a kiss that hadn't fired her up, but rather melted her down.

She was such a write-off. They should decommission her and sink her at sea like a wreck for people to dive down and wonder at.

For a moment longer she let herself remain curled against Kyle's chest and breathe in his smell of new shirt and salt air, let herself be…

She was not ready to finish that sentence. "Loved?" What had her brain been thinking? That was so not going to happen. Well, at least she knew which part of her had died first. The only ones she'd ever wanted love from were dead and buried in Arlington.

Pushing back from Kyle's chest, not so fast that he'd be offended or think her ungrateful, she moved from the circle of his arms.

He let her go, but kept hold of her hand to tuck back around his elbow.

She needed that at the moment. Needed to stay grounded. A quick glance at the guys showed that they weren't offended or jealous or even looking at her as if she'd somehow changed from the soldier who'd spent six months training close beside them. Rather, they smiled as if somehow it had been their doing that she and Kyle were together. It made the…a mushy word tried to sneak in but she suppressed it…bond she felt for them that much stronger.

She offered her first true smile since coming ashore and found it returned, and it was one of the best feelings she'd ever had. Right up there with the kiss she'd just received.

"So—" She hated that she had to clear her throat before she could continue. She stroked the bit of jewelry lying so consciously on her chest. "I heard there was a real sailboat around here somewhere."

Chapter 14

AGENT FRED SMITH HAD ARRANGED A SAILBOAT CHARTER for them at the Oranjestad waterfront, a short taxi ride from where they'd come ashore. The capital city of thirty thousand was a teeming metropolis compared to the resort communities along Palm and Eagle Beaches, but they passed through it too quickly for her to form much of an impression.

They picked up the fifty-six-foot sloop from a worried-looking rental agent.

Kyle and Richie both spoke sailboat to him until he relaxed.

Carla had never sailed. She'd been on transport ships and could pilot a small rubber Zodiac through a storm in the dark of night with a dozen of the world's deadliest warriors aboard just fine. Sailboats were a new experience.

So she did her best to stand there, be a pretty airhead, and not grind her teeth overmuch while the rental agent went through the boat with the guys.

Aruba claimed two other small islands well to the east as a part of its territory, and the guys spun a story about wanting to show their sister the other islands.

The agent wasn't buying it.

As soon as he was gone and they had started preparing to depart, she stepped lightly aboard and settled in the cockpit to watch them.

"You know..." She lounged back in her short

sundress, stretching out her legs to rest on the bench across the cockpit. She was starting to appreciate the advantages to girl clothes, like torturing guys. "You boys need a better cover story if you don't want everyone assuming we're going to sea to have an orgy."

Duane and Chad grinned at her wickedly. They'd caught on right away that their story wasn't working and had done what they could to really twist the agent's mind.

Kyle's head shot up from whatever line he was working on and then cursed when he finally connected the truth of that.

Richie blinked at her. "Why would they think that?"

"If we're all friendly and cozy as brothers and sister, Richie, Mama led a very wide-ranging sex life, a fact the agent clearly noted."

He looked around at their varied complexions—New York Jew, darkly tanned Georgia, and Scandinavian white. She and Kyle were the closest to possibly being related, but not really. She expressed a lot of her grandmother's Cherokee genes, and Kyle was just gorgeous Anglo-Saxon mutt.

The look on Kyle's face verged on horror at impugning her virtue, as if they weren't screwing each other at every opportunity. He mouthed a "sorry."

She wanted to make him suffer, but couldn't keep it in and laughed.

"Like I care what an Aruban rental agent thinks."

—⁂—

Kyle had settled in at the helm. He'd taken first shift. Carla leaned back against him so that he had one hand on the tiller and the other around her waist. He'd almost

broached the boat side to the waves, earning a surprised
scowl from Richie, who'd been cleaning up lines on the
forward deck.

"You sure you know how to sail?"

He knew how to sail, and he knew what to do with
their mission. They were on course and on schedule.

What he just didn't know how to deal with was this
particular woman in his arms. It wasn't that his blood
went to his crotch every time they drew close together...
Okay, it wasn't only that. It was that his world became
impossibly full, and other small concerns, like sailing,
became secondary at best.

He also had a very nice view from above as her sailboat necklace slipped side to side between her breasts
each time the sloop rode up over a wave and back down
the other side.

"How long do we have?" Her voice was little more
than a pleased murmur.

Kyle glanced up at the sails, which were now full
and drawing well. If the wind held from this quarter,
they could almost sail a single tack all the way to
Maracaibo, Venezuela.

"A hundred and fifty sea miles. Twenty, maybe
twenty-four hours. We'll show up looking just like tourists tomorrow morning, exactly as planned."

"I could get used to this." Her voice was warm and soft.

So could he. Drag her off to his cave and never let her
get away. Never in his life had he enjoyed a woman so
much. Not even close.

But there was still a shield, a layer, something there
that he didn't quite trust. And he'd learned to listen to
his instincts, a skill honed by his Delta instructors.

Time. For once they had time and perhaps this was the opportunity to figure out how to drive forward his questions of what drove Carla, without…appearing to be doing precisely that.

He almost cursed as Chad and Duane produced a lunch from down below using the foodstuffs they'd bought at the market. He sighed. Later, but soon.

Carla may have sat up, but she still wore that sundress, so it wasn't a total loss.

"You guys are really such dweebs," Carla informed them.

"The few. The proud," Duane mumbled around a mouthful of a *bitterbal*, hissing at the spicy-hot mustard he'd dipped the deep-fried meatball into.

Kyle had known what she was doing from the moment she purchased the slacks and blouse back at the market but hadn't changed into them. But he'd been more than happy to play along.

"For the last two hours"—she took a large bite of *arepa* roll stuffed with cheese, ham, and slivered papaya—"you've been treating me completely differently. I left the dress on to tease you. Instead—"

"Instead we're treating you like the total babe that you are." Chad's grin was almost a laugh.

"I wondered how long you'd put up with it before the true Carla surfaced," Duane added, then shifted to a thick Southern accent. "Would y'all like youse bottle of pineapple juice freshened up, missus?"

"Eat my shorts, Jenkins!"

"Gladly!"

Kyle found himself joining in the round of laughter. In this moment the years rolled back. No longer were they Delta commandos who had just pulled off one deadly raid and most likely were headed into another. They weren't ex-Army, ex-SEAL, ex-Special Forces. They were just a group of friends hanging out and enjoying each other's company on a beautiful sailing day in the southern Caribbean.

That he was about to lead his team into harm's way, that part he was used to.

Not so used to doing the same with the woman he loved. Hell, he'd have trouble holding her back if he were dumb enough to try. He'd only end up pissing her off and wasting one of his best assets.

Something drove Carla Anderson and drove her hard. And he was slowly beginning to get it through his thick skull that it wasn't all about her dead brother—her brother who had flown helicopters and died at Colonel Gibson's side, another topic they'd never discussed.

The rest of them were laughing over Richie's attempt to eat a stack of banana chips as if they were caviar-and-toasts at a British high tea. The loud crunching completely ruined the effect.

Kyle didn't know what the hell to do with it.

Mom and Dad were a happy couple in Redmond, Washington. He taught martial arts, she worked her corporate gig, and most weekends still found them fishing together.

Richie had grown up a couple hours north of New York. Well-to-do family, IBM engineer and housewife.

Duane was a lot like him, Dad was ex-Marine and an executive at Coca-Cola in Atlanta. Mom was a lawyer.

Chad might look Iowa, but he was Detroit, downtown, the bad side. He'd earned every inch of his way out of there.

Carla was…Army. Her brother was dead and her mom and dad… He didn't even know if they were dead, alive, or missing. They must have been one hell of a couple to produce a girl like the one sitting next to him.

Then he remembered, no girl clothes. Ever. No one had given her jewelry before. Ever.

He rubbed the back of his neck and shut his eyes for a moment on another bright laugh from the group, Carla's voice ringing like a clear bell above the others.

There was a purity to her joy that he couldn't doubt. It filled her from the inside. Overlay the veneer of a woman who attacked everything as if it was the ultimate and final challenge. Even making love.

He heard the sail slap—hard. He opened his eyes as the boat slowed and the heel leveled out. Only a quick slam of the tiller kept him from an unplanned tack.

"You awake, man?"

Kyle had slept after making love to Carla. But that was now a day and a half ago. He rubbed his face again, but it didn't help. Figuring all of the mission angles had sliced right through any attempt to catch even a few hours' shut-eye last night.

This time he wasn't fast enough and they tacked hard and without warning. The boom slammed across to the other side of the boat, nearly clipping Chad in the head. The jib was now backed against the mast. His attempt to recover was too little too late and only made matters worse.

"I got it." Richie moved in across from him and laid a hand on the tiller. "Go get some shut-eye."

Kyle nodded and headed below.

"Whoops! There goes any chance of that happening."

Chad's voice sounded behind him as he descended the short ladder into the main cabin.

"You wouldn't hear me complaining," Duane responded. "Go get him, girl."

Kyle glanced back up toward the cockpit. Carla was about to climb down the ladder. Her short dress looked even shorter from down here. It looked as if… "What the hell?"

She arrived on the plank flooring beside him. "The lady didn't sell underwear, only dresses and things. Why, are you complaining?"

Because she'd been sitting there with them and… He shook his head. He had no idea and he didn't know why he bothered. Not a chance of winning an argument with the woman. He aimed for the forward stateroom.

The boat was laid out with a generous galley to one side and a comfortable pilot's berth to the other.

Carla's fingers pressed lightly on his back, moving him along. The companionway continued forward between two wide settees to either side that could each seat four people on bench seats across a table. One of the bulkheads sported an impressive array of electronics, GPS, radio, wind and speed, radar, depth…all the cool toys.

A bunk bed nestled in a tiny room opposite a comfortable head and shower. The forward stateroom boasted sun-yellow walls, shining mahogany trim, and a double bed with generous pillows.

He crashed down into them.

Moments later he felt Carla's weight depress the mattress beside him, and strong hands began digging into his shoulder muscles.

"Carla, I don't know if I can—"

"Shut up, Reeves. Do I look that stupid?"

"No. Most beautiful woman on earth, maybe. Stupid, no."

"You're biased." She dug a knuckle hard into a locked-up trapezius muscle.

"Totally," he groaned as it let go. "Doesn't make it any less true." And it didn't. She was a knockout beauty, a knockout soldier, and a knockout lover. Three knockouts definitely counted for something. In boxing you only needed one to win. That meant Carla was...

He lost his ability to speak or even think coherently as she dug into successive shoulder muscles and forced them to let go. For a long time he let himself float and groan as she worked his neck, shoulder, and back until he was in a near-liquid puddle of happy soldier.

For everything he *didn't* know about Carla, there were many things he *did* know. First and foremost that there would never be another woman for him. She was it. He was lock, stock, and barrel in love.

"Love"—it was like a whisper through his soul as sleep took him under—"you."

———～～～———

Carla froze with her fingers on Kyle's latissimus dorsi near the base of his shoulder blades.

No fucking way!

"'Love you'! Are you full of shit, Reeves? You did not just say that to me!"

In answer, Kyle released a soft snore.

She raised a hand to pound it down on his back. To roust him but good and make him explain that.

Take it back!

Say you were dreaming of doing the two blonds on

the beach, both at once. He wasn't. He hadn't even had the decency to ogle them, just kept watching her in her damned wet T-shirt and fluorescent bikini.

Then she caught sight of her hand silhouetted against the midday light streaming through the skylight hatch above the bunk.

It wasn't flat to smack down. It was a fist and it was clenched bone-shatteringly hard as if she could trap his two words there until they were crushed to sand, and then bludgeon them back into the man.

"Breathe! Goddamn it! Just breathe!" Her orders to herself were barely managed gasps that cost her more air than they recovered.

She couldn't unclench her fist. Already it ached. It was going to sting like mad when she managed to open it. She did manage to bring it down into her open lap and clench it with her other hand.

Love you?

"That was nowhere in the bargain, Reeves."

He slept on.

Maybe she'd misunderstood him.

In her dreams. He'd spoken it and she'd heard it.

Maybe it was in his dreams. Yeah, and maybe he was…thinking of the great food here. Maybe he'd been poisoned by… They'd eaten the same food and drunk the same drinks for the last six months.

Six months? She'd only had a couple lovers who lasted that long. Okay. One. And he'd run off with a singer and it had been about time. She'd never wanted a lover for that long in the first place. Her heart had died long ago, just her body and her brain didn't know it yet so she was getting good use out of them.

How was she supposed to give something to a man like Kyle after her father had disowned his family and Mom's heart had long since stopped beating? Kyle deserved more than she'd ever—

"You okay, Carla?" Chad stood right in front of her.

Somehow she'd escaped Kyle and wandered halfway down the companionway. A cautious glance behind her showed that she'd closed the stateroom door on Kyle's sleeping form.

"Look like you've seen a ghost."

She nodded, though she wasn't sure which question she was answering. Shaking her head didn't make it any clearer for either of them.

Chad was starting to look worried. The roughest soldier on their team was being solicitous; she must really look a total mess.

"He's asleep," she kind of blurted out.

"You should get some shut-eye too, while he gives you a chance." He offered a wink.

At her blank nod, he looked even more concerned.

Without another word, he guided her into the bunk room, the other only space on the boat with a door, and nudged her onto the lower bunk before closing it behind his exit.

She lay down on her side, could feel her eyes stinging with the strain of staring at the blank wall. She forced herself to blink, which did nothing to ease the burning.

Rather than get eyestrain from staring, Carla finally forced her eyes closed. She curled up in a ball around the fist she still didn't dare unclench.

Chapter 15

"Here we go!" Kyle called out.

An hour after sunset, Lola Maloney had flown her Black Hawk by, a hundred meters ahead of the sailboat at less than five meters above the waves. They were getting close enough to the Venezuelan shore that they didn't want her flying overhead to lower their cargo because she'd show up on the Coast Guard's radar. Dead ahead, she tumbled out the two bundles of gear that they'd assembled while still on the *Freedom*.

Kyle kept his gaze on the packages' blinking lights. It was just like a drug delivery, which was an amusing parallel.

He eased the sailboat to a near standstill, bow to the wind, coming even with their supplies to the lee side. Duane and Richie manned boat hooks. When they drifted down on the bundles, they snagged them and heaved them over the lifelines and onto the deck.

He eased off the wind. The boat leaned back in and began making way once more. Lola flew by once more off their bow, far enough out to not rock the boat overly much. With a side-to-side wobble of her bird, the equivalent of a wave, she disappeared back into the darkness. She'd turn on her running lights when she reached the LCS ship steaming slowly a hundred miles offshore—out past where she'd draw any Venezuelan attention.

"What did we catch, boys?" Kyle called forward.

Boys? No Carla visible. Man, he'd slept like a baby after the massage she'd given him. Solid right up to the moment Chad had knocked on the forward hatch above the stateroom bed and told him the helo was inbound. He'd crawled out the hatch and taken over the helm. Carla must be down below; he'd have to remember to thank her. He rolled his shoulders again. They felt good and loose.

"Caught us a load of good shit." Duane peeled open the waterproof cover and flotation ring from the first big pack. He toted it to the companionway ladder and handed it down to Chad, who'd gone below. Man probably couldn't wait to get his hands back around a gun.

Richie hauled back the next one and handed it down as well. "What should we do with the covers?"

"Sink 'em. We don't want any signs that we were picking up cargo."

"Roger that, boss. We don't want a country rife with corrupt cocaine smugglers to think that someone else is doing smuggling on their turf, do we?"

Duane went forward to lose the delivery packaging. Kyle handed the tiller off to Richie; he wanted to see for himself that the gear had arrived intact and was stowed out of sight.

He swung down the ladder. Chad had a big pack set out on each table and already had one open.

"Where's Carla?"

Chad nodded toward the bunkroom. "Probably still sacked out."

Kyle had bolted from the bed so fast that he only now registered that he'd been sleeping alone. That was odd.

"I'll get her. We need to go over this gear carefully."

When he went to move past Chad, the man didn't give way.

Kyle went to push by, but the man didn't budge as if he was anchored in place despite the bob and sway of the sloop as she cut once more through the waves.

"What?"

Chad studied him for a long moment before speaking very softly. "Not sure. But you might want to think about walking softly there."

"We're Delta. We always walk softly." Kyle's attempt at making a joke of it fell flat. He took a breath, then nodded.

Chad studied him again before moving aside.

As Kyle squeezed past, he spoke softly. "Thanks, buddy." Whatever was awaiting him, he'd have to face it.

Chad nodded and turned to pull a stack of C4 blocks from the open bag.

<hr />

Carla had slept.

How in the world had she slept?

At least until the guys started running up and down the decks like a herd of elephants. The packs hit the deck with a wet splat right above her head, resounding through the thin fiberglass.

She heard the helicopter whisper by once more and knew it was gone.

Kyle was coming. She heard him clambering down the ladder like it was second nature to him. The sailboat had remained foreign to her though she'd picked up a lot watching Kyle and Richie. The boat was both too big and too small. It felt large and clunky compared to the high-speed rubber boats they often used. And it felt too small because there were only the five of them rather than a hundred on a ship of war. No guns, no torpedoes, no radar watch officer. Just them. And its normal state wasn't level, but rather heeled over. She was lying as much on the hull as the bunk.

Kyle was still coming, and she still didn't know what to do about it.

There was a discussion that she couldn't make out through the stateroom walls. A long silence followed by a soft knock on the door. And then it cracked open and Kyle peered in at her.

"You awake?"

"No. Duh!"

"The gear is here."

"I heard."

Kyle squinted at her carefully. The light was behind him, so he was in silhouette in the doorway. "You sleep okay?"

"Sure." Much to her surprise. *No thanks to you!* But she kept that thought to herself. "You?"

"After what you did for me?" He rolled his shoulders to make his point. "You're fantastic."

Carla closed her eyes for a moment. So, he didn't remember speaking the words as he fell asleep. Could she pretend everything was unchanged and somehow make it be?

She was Delta. She could do anything.

Sitting up, she nodded to Kyle that she was ready. The space was small enough that she couldn't really rise as long as he was standing in the doorway. He backed off and held the door wide for her.

She looked down at her right hand, still clenched closed even while she slept.

Sure, pretending was something Delta trained for. It was a key part of infiltration and recon—the fine art of blending in. But no matter how much she wanted to pretend, those two words had been spoken.

She unclenched her fist and set the words free, could almost see the whisper of "Love you" slide out into the light.

The one thing she couldn't pretend away was that the words weren't out in the world.

Now if only they didn't make a circular run, like a bad WWII torpedo, and destroy her.

Chapter 16

KYLE AND CARLA WERE FIXING BREAKFAST IN THE galley down in the main cabin. They were about four hours out of Maracaibo, and everyone had gotten at least six hours of sack time. The other guys were on deck and all the gear from the packs was stowed where a casual inspection wouldn't find it.

If a customs agent tried a more thorough inspection, well, Kyle had a plan for that as well.

They worked together in easy familiarity even if the ingredients were strange. Breakfast was going to be strong coffee and a bowl of yogurt filled with some of the strangest fruits he'd ever seen. Pineapple and papaya were normal enough, but the others…

It was fun, tasting two similar round, red fruits, one like a plum and the other a sour cherry.

"Wow." Kyle saved his comment until after Carla had tasted the unholy combination that made her eyes cross as well. "There are two fruits that should never be eaten together."

"You got that right." She rinsed her mouth out with a glass of pineapple juice. "Ick. That's even worse."

"Try this one. Vendor said it's called a *mispel*."

"You try it." So he did. It was egg-shaped, but the size of his fist. The flesh was dark brown. He bit the edge carefully and was almost overwhelmed with flavor. He swiped at the juice dribbling down his chin and licked his fingers.

"That good, huh?"

He held it out to her and she took a bite right over where his had been, causing more juice to dribble down his hands. He licked them clean again and still the flavor washed across his senses: powerful, sweet, almost a woody taste, but more like liquid sunshine.

"Wow! That's almost as good as sex."

"Nothing's as good as sex with you." That earned him a smile, but nothing stronger. Normally he'd get a saucy smile, a deep kiss, a quick grab. Something.

Instead she turned to the counter and began cutting more of the vari-shaped fruit. The next one was conical and peach yellow inside. She tasted a small piece and nodded her approval before she started cleaning out the center seeds.

"Is this what normal couples do, normal families?" she asked without looking up.

"What do you mean, cook together, treat each other decently?"

She nodded once, tightly, without looking up from her knife work.

"What the hell kind of a past..." He clamped down on his tongue. He could feel the impossible tension in the air. Could see it in her white knuckles. In fact, if she kept cutting that way, she was going to end up with several fewer fingers.

Chad had been right about walking softly.

Kyle rested his hand over both of hers to stop her before she hurt herself. With a brushstroke along her cheek, he turned her gaze toward him.

Carla was putting up a good front about something. She looked straight into his eyes, brave as ever, but he could see the caution there. No cringing as if she expected a blow, so her past hadn't included that kind of abuse. It was something else. Well, he would hope that offering her the truth somehow helped, even if he wasn't ready to risk the truth that he loved her.

"Yes. This is what a normal couple does together. Cook. Take time. Talk."

She bit down on her lower lip before speaking. "I—I don't know how to do that."

"It's like girl clothes. Wear it for a while. See how it fits."

She nodded once, then again. And then she returned to cutting up the fruit for breakfast as if everything was exactly as it had been moments before.

He might have even bought into the show, if he hadn't seen the salt stains where she'd wept against the dark pillow. He hadn't known Carla to ever be even sentimental. To have wept…

Well, whatever it was, knowing Carla, she'd find a way to swallow it down and be back to normal soon. Or it would explode full force when she finally decided to let it out.

Two things were for certain: no matter what it was, it wouldn't affect her performance as a soldier one iota, and no matter how rough the ride, he'd be there for her. One of the best lessons he'd ever learned from his dad.

⁓⁓⁓

"We've got incoming."

Carla heard Duane's call from up on deck and stopped slicing the *mispel* to peer out the small galley window. It was still a smudge, but it was a fast-moving smudge.

"We're still too far offshore for a customs inspection. It's not moving like Coast Guard."

Carla would take Kyle's word for it. "Who else is in these waters? Agent Smith said there were no other U.S. operations in the area."

Chad squatted at the head of the companionway ladder. "They're pleasure-craft size: ten meters long and throwing a big bow wave. No way to outrun them. I'll give you one guess."

"Or two guesses, but the second one doesn't count." Duane was standing behind Richie at the helm so that he'd be mostly hidden, looking through binoculars. "Yup, bad news. At least three aboard. All *hombres*, at the rail, one with binocs."

"What would pirates want with us?" Richie called from the tiller.

"Not pirates, Richie," Carla called out to him, "smugglers. Okay, sure, pirates. Attacking on the high seas and all that. They see our hot sailboat and think it's perfect for the first leg of the Maracaibo-Aruba-Europe cocaine run. So smugglers and pirates."

"Problem is" — Kyle peeked out the windows at the rapidly approaching craft — "that means that they want our boat for their own uses. Best scenario?"

"They take the boat and then they shoot us," Chad answered.

"Worst case?" Duane continued to study them through the field glasses. "They shoot us first."

Carla had studied piracy as part of OTC training. How to counter it and how to retake a ship. They'd practiced on oil tankers, cruise ships, and pleasure yachts. But now they were on the receiving end.

"Well, they've certainly seen the three of us," Chad reported. "If we go below, they'll just shoot up the hull. What's the next bright idea?"

"Get them talking," Kyle called out.

"Great advice, dude." Duane turned away.

Kyle pointed to the row of windows behind them on the opposite side of the cabin.

Carla nodded and pulled the curtains across them. Now she and Kyle wouldn't be silhouetted from behind. It would be very hard to see into the shadowed cabin through the other windows. Kyle was already pulling up the bunk that they'd stowed the rifles under.

She went for handguns first, then she pulled out a Milkor MGL. The U.S. Marines had been the first to get the Multiple Grenade Launcher…after The Unit. Like a revolver on steroids, it shot six 40 mm grenades as fast as she could pull the trigger. It had been one of her favorite toys in training. She pulled out a box of six more loads and set it on the cutting board, close at hand though she couldn't imagine using it.

Kyle handed her an HK416 rifle that she set across the galley counter in front of her. He slipped a trio of Glocks onto the top step of the companionway ladder, but there was no way to distribute them topside under the watchful eye of the approaching pirates.

Carla hoped they were wrong but could feel in her bones that they weren't. A vessel in distress would radio or signal, and they wouldn't be approaching just astern so that their last turn would place them close alongside.

The cruiser pulled up on the port side and almost ate a sail boom as Richie performed an "accidental" jib and it slammed across. The pirates' boat had a main cabin and a small flying bridge up high. There would be helm and engine controls in both places, but they couldn't see which the boat's driver was using. Three men were lined up along the lower rail.

"Douse your sails!" someone shouted over a loud-hailer in Spanish. "This is an official Venezuelan inspection."

"Nice of them to talk first," Kyle commented.

"It is. Doesn't strike me as very official. It's not your average Coast Guard who runs around in a Carver 38 sport boat," Carla offered drily. They had no official logo on the boat. Instead, it looked very civilian, as if it too had been recently captured.

"They might at least have thought to say 'please.'"

"It was rather rude of them, don't you think?" Carla was searching through the scope. With only the small kitchen window to aim through, she didn't have a lot of options. "The sail boom is really in the way."

Kyle pitched his voice low to Chad, who still stood at the head of the ladder. "Into the wind. Get the boom amidships."

Chad passed the instruction to Richie. They looked like tourists, each of them still in their "I *heart* Aruba!" T-shirts and baggy shorts. They made a show of wrestling the boom into place as if they didn't know what they were doing. Chad managed to slip one of the pistols into his waistband in the confusion.

"I still count three unsavories along the rail. They're keeping their right arms out of sight, but I spotted the butt of a rifle stock on the leftmost guy," Carla reported.

"Roger, three." Kyle was sighting through the next window down, which wasn't open.

Her window was open, but it had a bug screen across

it that she'd have to punch out before firing if she didn't want the grenade going off right in her face.

"Go for the wheelhouse," Kyle told her.

"Now, or when they're in motion?" Carla loved Kyle's perfect calm and perfect patience. It steadied her and made her a better soldier every single time. He was screwing up Carla the woman, but that didn't get in her way right now.

"I'm seeing rifle stock on middle unsavory."

No longer any question what to do. "In one," Carla said and felt that connection between them as they fired in unison.

Middle bad guy was just lifting his rifle as Kyle fired. The first shot shattered the window; the second passed through the man's forehead.

Carla punched her weapon a half step forward, knocking out the screen. She fired the first High Explosive round at the side of the cruiser's cabin. The HE punched a hole in the fiberglass. Half a second later, she sent the second one through the new hole in the side of the cabin where it would shred whoever was inside. For good measure, she shot one onto the flying bridge.

She dropped the MGL and swept up her rifle, but it was over. No one remained at the rail. Well, one did, flopped over it with a gaping hole in his back directly behind where his heart had been.

Winding back in her memory, she counted five shots from Kyle and two from Chad with the pistol he'd managed to grab.

Coming from the galley, she was closer to the ladder than Kyle and sprinted up the steps. She tossed the remaining handguns to Duane and Richie, and then she and Kyle covered their teammates as they jumped across the gap and swarmed the boat.

There were the sharp single spits of "security" shots and then a call of "Clear." They tossed over a couple of lines so that the boats didn't drift too far apart.

"Just need a couple of strip breaching charges and a timer to clean this up," Duane called back. "Shit! Bloodstains still on the interior carpet. Whoever they grabbed the boat from didn't do so well." He leaned out to glance over the stern. "Panama is now shy a couple of tourists."

Carla ducked back down, dug out the charge, and tossed it up to Kyle.

They weren't in position to report the location of the boat without having to explain themselves. And after their treatment of it, they didn't want anyone else seeing it either. The bad guys were dead, but...

"Hey, Richie," she called out the window she'd fired the MGL through. He was still on the Carver 38 and she'd been reloading the MGL six-shooter. "See if you can find some info on the real owners. Name of someone we can notify."

He disappeared into the cabin.

"Hope y'all signed the damage insurance before we hired our boat," Chad called out. "Mr. Rental is gonna be ticked about having his window shot out."

Carla had also dropped the Milkor grenade launcher right in the middle of their breakfast, scattering the yogurt and most of their fruit to the floor. That was probably the least of their worries, but it meant day-old sandwiches for breakfast.

They cast the derelict boat adrift, Carla's grenades

had destroyed both control stations as well as two more bad guys. Richie handed her a small packet of papers for a Panamanian couple. She'd have to find something to do with them. If they went to the CIA, no one would ever hear a thing.

Once they were clear of the boat and about a hundred meters out, there was a loud *krump!* and a splash of water around the sides of the boat.

"She no longer has a bottom and is going down," Duane announced with obvious satisfaction.

"Bye-bye." Chad waved at the boat as the Carver slipped rapidly out of sight with its load of dead bodies, tied to the craft to make sure they stayed down. "Assholes."

She and Kyle returned below, reloaded and re-stowed the weapons.

"Nice job, Wild Woman."

"Good shooting, Mister Kyle." The smile was easy between them.

She *loved* working with Kyle.

It was safe to think that, wasn't it?

Chapter 17

COMING INTO MARACAIBO HARBOR WAS QUITE THE spectacle. Around the breakwater and past the Faro de San Bernardo. The red lighthouse towered above the sandy lump of San Bernardo Island and the narrow channel leading into the ten-kilometer reach of a lagoon. The water was a crystalline blue, and the air was thick with the scents of palm and arid soil. The wind that had carried them so smoothly continued to favor them and promised hints of high jungles and a friendly city.

Kyle was once again at the helm and guided them up to the customs dock. The city towered ahead of them. Being on the far side of Lake Maracaibo from the rest of Venezuela, it had evolved in its own way. Other cities were a mayhem of conflicts, violence, and corruption. Maracaibo boasted a mostly peaceful culture and one of the finest universities in South America.

One of the world's longest stressed-concrete suspension bridges now connected it to the rest of the country, built to avoid the thousand-kilometer detour around the lake. That historical separation from the rest of the country and the harbor's position at the sea access to the largest lake on the continent also made it one of the most popular drug-smuggling ports in the world. Right up there with Buenaventura and Cartagena before Colombia finally started its crackdowns.

This time the team had a different story to tell the customs

man. Richie, Duane, and Chad were each in a black T-shirt,
dark sunglasses, and khakis. They'd been told to not say
a word. Kyle wore a dress shirt and Carla was back in
the killer sundress. A man and his woman moving carefully, a man who needed three bodyguards to go sailing.

They didn't try to disguise the bullet holes of the shattered window he'd shot through. Instead, they'd simply
cleaned up any evidence that the bullets had come from
inside rather than outside and run an obvious strip of
duct tape over the window.

You didn't arrive at a customs dock bearing guns, at
least not visible ones. But Chad, Duane, and Richie did
each have a large military knife strapped to their thighs.

The customs official started out, well, officious.
Then he found the thousand in worn U.S. bills, from
Major Gonzalez's stash, folded into Kyle's passport.
He pocketed the money but didn't become much more
cooperative. Five hundred each in Kyle's "bodyguards'"
passports helped somewhat. Kyle wondered how much
of the couple thousand he'd pocketed would be left to
turn in at the end of this mission.

They'd debated how much money to put in Carla's
passport—none or the most. He'd thought she should
have no money, just be the clueless lady along for the
ride. That would be safest for her. That way the customs
agents would assume she knew nothing.

Carla had been strangely quiet and offered him only
a pleasant smile at the suggestion.

Now she moved forward and Kyle's eyes nearly
bugged out. Where the wraparound ties of her sundress
met over the small of her back, she'd stuffed a Glock.
She was going to shoot the damned agent.

The woman had lost it.

She sidled up to the man until his eyes were bugging out trying to look down her cleavage. She tapped her passport on her lower lip, drawing his attention back up to her mouth, then fumbled and dropped it.

She didn't squat down to pick it up, she bent from the hip with the flexibility of a ballet dancer revealing the scant covering of the yellow bikini bottoms beneath the sundress, which would disorient any man.

She stood back up with her back to the agent. She winked at Kyle and cocked a hip—which Kyle could see had a hundred percent of the agent's attention, though oddly every bit of the color had just drained out of his face. Then she slowly turned back to face the agent and handed over her passport.

That's when Kyle finally focused on the handgun tucked in the back of her dress, the weapon she had just flaunted at the customs agent.

She'd painted it hot pink back on the ship though he hadn't understood why, and he'd been sidetracked by something before he'd thought to ask. Her weapon was the same color as the notorious AK-47 that belonged to the Empress of the Antrax kill squad.

With her coloring—it was a sure bet that the customs agent had never met a Cherokee woman before—her long, dark hair, and the surprising things that the sundress did to her cleavage, she was more than a passable imitation of a Mexican drug cartel leader, especially to someone who didn't follow such news too closely. He probably didn't see anything past the cleavage and the hot-pink weapon.

"My man and I," she purred in English with a thick

Mexican accent to the agent still white with shock, "are so looking forward to doing business in your country. And we are always so glad to show our appreciation to anyone who helps us." Then she reached into the cleavage of her sundress and extracted a thick wad of hundred-dollar bills. Negligently she split it in half, tucking one portion back in her dress. Folding the rest—at least five grand, maybe ten—which she then took her time stuffing well down into the man's pants.

It was so perfect. Word of the takedown of the General's hacienda would have rippled through the military very quickly. It had been three days, almost four since it happened, plenty of time for rumors that it was a Sinaloa drug hit to percolate down to even a mere customs agent.

The man positively stumbled over himself to cooperate and stamp their passports.

If Kyle had to judge, the man's attitude was equal portions of avarice for more bribes, terror at thinking he faced the actual Empress of Antrax, and the desperate lust that Carla was somehow able to evoke at will. No question who the agent would be dreaming about next time he bedded a woman. Kyle liked that his own fantasy woman was the one he got to *have* in his arms.

Could make a life's plan out of that. Their schedule really needed to slow down for a minute so that he and Carla could talk about where they were going, but he didn't see it happening anytime soon. Their arrival in Venezuela was the end of their idyll, such as it had been.

The agent sent them to the small, exclusive Club Náutico marina for one of the slips held for the most-special guests of the towering Hotel Ventura. The agent had supplied his cell phone number should they ever be pulling in again and "require" an inspection. He never did look below. Their stowed weapons and other supplies remained unobserved.

Once the man and the port of entry were out of sight behind them, Richie let out a whoop.

"You go, girl!" Chad slapped her a hard high five.

"Remind me never to mess with you." Duane repeated the high five.

Kyle did the only thing that came to mind. He dragged her into his arms and kissed her for all he was worth. Her body hummed against his.

The kiss built until it burned, searing away the niggling concern that had rippled through him on finding that Carla had wept into her pillow. This woman was so powerful and the way she felt was so right, no questions could remain about her—not as soldier, woman, or lover.

She unwrapped herself from around his body with a high laugh that sparkled out across the shining water. She did a cha-cha-cha dance around the deck.

"Guys and girl clothes. Who knew the power?" Again the laugh.

Watching her hips sway and her hair swing as she danced, Kyle could feel the power firsthand.

"And how much you want to bet"—she did a hip bump with Chad, who was snapping his fingers in applause, and continued speaking a bit breathlessly—"that rumors of our arrival are even now spreading out through the underworld. I expect we'll have drug traffickers begging for our services within the day."

"Or a hit squad." Kyle considered. "I can imagine

that the General's friends would welcome the opportunity for a serving of revenge."

"You're forgetting Major Gonzales."

He was. That sobered the group even though it meant that the Major didn't have a lot of folks willing to avenge his death.

Mr. CIA Fred Smith had found many things in the Major's electronic files on the two USBs that Kyle had grabbed. One of them was a list of where the hostages he'd taken were being held. On the General's behalf, the Major had kidnapped daughters, cousins, even wives, and stashed them away under guard to ensure their relatives' cooperation. That had won the cartel a great deal of power, but very few friends.

And most of the women were under guard at a single location in Maracaibo.

"Freeing them is our next task," Kyle decided.

"How does freeing the Major's hostages help us? Not saying we shouldn't, just asking."

"It's either because I'm a soft mush who takes pity on them." That got him the laugh he was after. Soft mush wasn't really in his personal profile except around Carla. "Or it's because of the mass of confusion it will cause among the cartels as they try to figure out who is doing what and why." That got the confirming nods from the others.

Besides, Kyle had an idea to up the ante even more.

When they pulled up to the hotel's dock, two dock boys in pressed white shorts and shirts were awaiting their arrival, apparently warned by their tame customs agent.

Yes, word of their arrival was going out far and wide very soon.

———

The Hotel Ventura was luxurious, discreet, and had them installed in a suite overlooking Lake Maracaibo in a matter of minutes. Another wad of the Major's money cleared away any questions.

Kyle had grown up comfortably but had to work a couple of jobs for his first beater car. This "lifestyle of the rich and famous" was so not him, but the view was damned nice. Their hotel room commanded a corner of the eighth floor with a view that included both old town and the northern entrance to the lake.

Eight kilometers of water spread to the east. If they leaned out of the balcony, they could see the great bridge spanning from downtown Maracaibo to the rest of Venezuela. To the north, beyond old town, lay the outer lagoon busy with commercial and pleasure boat traffic and, as a dark blue line, the Atlantic.

When Carla joined him on the balcony and leaned against the rail with her thoughtless grace, it was even better. He snugged a hand around her waist and pulled her in hip to hip. They watched the world in silence for a time.

"Where I grew up"—Carla's voice was soft enough that he wouldn't have heard her if they were even a step apart—"you could see the backs of a couple of bars to one side, and then dry sage and creosote covering Colorado hills to the other. This view is both breathtaking and claustrophobic. There are a million and half people in this city, and we can probably see a third of them out our hotel window. Where I grew up, there weren't twenty thousand people within a hundred miles."

Colorado. It was his first window into her past other than "Cherokee on Mom's side." Those two tidbits and a dead brother. At least having a place in the country to picture Carla Anderson settled something inside him. Colorado.

"No wonder you can hike the way you do."

She leaned her head on his shoulder. "I spent a lot of time walking those hills and mountains, just me, my rifle, and a pack. We should do that sometime, Kyle. Just you and me. It's beautiful out there."

"I'd love to, sweetheart." He kissed her on the temple.

—◊◊◊—

Carla wondered why she'd said all that. She was from the Army. Now she was from Delta. And suddenly she was spilling her guts to Kyle.

But she *would* like to take him out into the Colorado wilderness. Not the known places like Maroon Bells Lake or the Mesa Verde cliff dwellings, but into the true wilderness.

"There's a swimming hole a two-day hike up Crazy Woman Gulch where you can sit for a week and hear nothing but the animals who have always lived there. Or up on the thirteen-thousand-foot peak of Hesperus Mountain in La Plata with nothing but desert and mesa country to the west. You can sit up there until the sunrise itself has a sound as it cracks the tops of the San Juan Mountains far to the east."

Kyle nodded. "I'd like to see that."

They had crossed over somewhere, somehow. She wanted to share that wilderness with him. He'd understand. He'd appreciate it.

Carla had always trusted the men and women of her teams. You had to, or it came apart on you and often in the worst way.

Then there was The Unit. She understood now why they referred to it that way on their side of the wire. Delta was literally "The Unit." It was no longer a matter of trusting those with you because you had to. On the inside, you trusted because you knew you could. If it went down bad, there was no question that every last man, and now woman, would give their all.

Yet with Kyle it was more.

In The Unit she was as safe in life and limb as someone in their profession could be.

With Kyle, she herself was safe. She knew she could tell him anything about her past and it wouldn't change a thing. She wouldn't be doing that, but she knew he'd treat her exactly the same if she did.

There was a heat inside her, not the searing fire of lust, but a warmth that started somewhere deep and expanded through her. She had no experience with such a feeling, no word to pin it down with.

She wanted to grab on to the balcony rail and rant against it. She didn't want these changes.

But she hadn't taken the two words and rammed them back down Kyle's throat. Instead she had let them free, and that one act was changing her more than any other since joining the Army.

She felt things. Felt them for the man beside her. Beyond loyalty, beyond trust.

And it was real, not illusion.

It was also good. Really good.

It was just scaring the hell out of her.

She forced herself to turn to the man standing beside her and holding her as if she was important. His dark gaze was studying the city far below them, his sharp mind already deep at work on the next stage of what they'd come here to do.

But his arm around her waist spoke of far more inside him than being a Delta Force soldier on a mission. It spoke of more than lust or even companionship. It spoke of a deep caring that Carla hadn't experienced in years, perhaps never as deeply as now. This moment in this place.

She kissed him on the cheek.

He turned those dark eyes on her, and they warmed as they did every time he looked at her.

"What was that for?"

She didn't have the words, so she shook her head. "Just because."

Rather than hitting her with one of his soul-scorching kisses, he rested his lips on her forehead for a moment that stretched into forever before he mumbled against her skin, "'Just because' certainly works for me."

Oddly, it worked for her too.

Chapter 18

RATHER THAN EATING AT THE HOTEL VENTURA or one of the convenient nearby restaurants, Kyle led them farther into the city of Maracaibo.

The tall Hotel Castillo on the Avenida Cecilio Acosta was far enough from the lakeshore to be affordable for someone on a budget and close enough to Maracaibo's central core to be attractive to tourists. So, many of the folks brushed back by the waves of high prices along the shoreline washed up here.

Kyle led his team into the restaurant. They'd have dinner here as a preparatory casing of the place. The top two floors, nine and ten, belonged exclusively to General Vasquez's portion of the Cartel de los Soles, specifically Major Gonzalez's part of it. According to the Major's files, twenty-five hostages were tucked away there under guard.

It had been four days since their attack on the hacienda. It would help if they could get information on whether or not there had been any changes in status on those two floors. If they couldn't find out, they'd have to go in blind.

To keep up appearances, Kyle had bought Carla another dress. At the store she'd gone for the conservative rack and he'd cut her off at the pass.

This one was the epitome of a "little black dress" cranked up to kill. A short, flirty skirt over bare legs and strap-on sandals, thin straps over bare shoulders that met behind her neck, leaving her back uncovered, and the clean lines of a plunging cleavage that he could dive into and never be seen again. The tiny amber-and-silver sailboat dangled at sea there.

She was a delight from every angle. There were always dresses that only slender women could wear. With her soldier fitness on top of that, Carla made him wish that she'd never wear anything else.

As they entered the lobby—an airy mix of potted palms, marble floors, and decent woodwork—cool air washed over them. The fact that it was mid-January meant that the daily high was ninety instead of summer's ninety-five degrees. The air-conditioning plunged the room to seventy.

At Carla's shiver, Kyle could see that they both had a few things yet to learn about girl clothes, like when to also purchase a wrap. He shrugged out of his white Armani jacket and draped it over her shoulders, though he hated to cover up the fine view.

They proceeded toward the back of the lobby to the restaurant, marked by a wide but shadowy entrance. Duane and Chad split off to check the exits and security, which was wholly in keeping with their bodyguard roles. Richie maintained a watchful eye from three paces ahead.

Kyle selected a table set in the corner of the half-full room. It had fewer escape routes—though the kitchen was close at hand. But it had excellent sight lines from each place around the circular bench of the booth. Both the lighting and the conversation were subdued.

Once they slid in and had double-checked the room, they picked up menus. Carla had lightly clasped his jacket by the lapels to keep it mostly closed around her, though she hadn't slid her arms into the sleeves.

Yes, it might cover up much of what there'd been to see, but it showed a different woman. More than just the soldier embarrassed by scanty clothing.

Her face was quiet as she bent over to study the menu lying flat on the table before her. The dress's amazing cleavage glowed beneath the tasteful downlighting above the table. But wrapped in his jacket, she was somehow more his. Without him noticing quite when, they had made the transition from lovers to a couple.

He wished he had better words for it, ones she might be willing to hear, but he didn't. She just was as naturally in place with his jacket about her shoulders as she would be with her own. No longer lovers, now they simply belonged together.

Duane slid into one end of the circular bench and offered a short nod. Nothing unexpected, good.

"I don't see any guards on this floor," Chad informed them as he slid in the other side beside Richie. "I swung by the front desk; they still use keys tucked into cubbyholes. There are no keys and no messages for any room on the ninth or tenth floors."

"That's good."

If there were no unexpected changes in the hostages' situation, that meant that Delta Force would be the surprise.

—⁓—

Carla tried to study the menu, but her brain was doing nothing about distinguishing burger (*americano*) from beef tenderloin (*solomillo de vacuno*).

All she could do was hold on to Kyle's jacket and do

her best not to melt. She'd certainly been more uncomfortable than a brief shiver any number of times before. That wasn't what got to her.

Nor was it the delicious warmth of Kyle's body heat that enveloped her. And the smell of him. He'd been wearing the jacket for under half an hour, but it was filled with his heady scent of iron will and gorgeous man.

No, what absolutely melted her was the thoughtless consideration.

No one had ever taken care of her.

Her mother had been overwhelmed by just trying to survive her husband and keep food on the table. Clay had been protective of Carla, but at four years older, he'd always been in a different school with a different circle of friends—he'd been the sort of guy who actually had friends—and then he'd gone into the service.

Yet Kyle hadn't hesitated or even considered. She was cold and his jacket should naturally be draped over her bare shoulders. That hadn't been the soldier's doing; it had been the man's.

Carla kept her face aimed down at the menu but studied him in her peripheral vision.

He held the menu easily, looked as if he belonged. The smuggler king with his bodyguards and his moll. He also belonged here as the soldier and his team, for no matter his protestations to the contrary, he was this team's unquestioned leader. Richie always wanted someone to follow, and Duane was glad to go along for the ride. Chad was a hard case beneath that mellow exterior—yet he too looked to Kyle for guidance.

She and Kyle also belonged here as man and woman in a nice restaurant. When had she fractured into so many versions of herself? And how would they come back together? She didn't know the answer to either question.

He should look different as he pointed at something on the menu and asked Richie for a translation. He should look like her leader, not her lover. He should look like the experienced soldier, not the man who had somehow infiltrated past her guards until she was sitting here mooning over him like a teen dreaming of the lead singer of Maroon 5. Back in junior high, she'd scrounged up several Adam Levine posters, though she'd never been able to afford a concert.

Now she wanted a poster of Kyle Reeves to keep her company.

She laughed aloud and everyone turned to look at her.

Carla shook her head to fend them off. Why would she want a poster when she already had the real thing?

Had it and wanted to keep it.

Oh crap!

She'd never wanted to keep a man before.

Then why did it sound so good?

"What looks good to you, honey?"

"You," she answered before she could stop herself.

Kyle grinned and leaned in to kiss her. "I meant on the menu, sweetheart."

Carla hadn't noticed the arrival of the waitress, now displaying an amused smile. So, Kyle was playing a role and she'd better get with it.

"Oh." She looked at the menu and still couldn't bring it into focus. The last man to call her "sweetheart" she'd almost put in the hospital. She'd definitely left him lying in the dirt on the first day of Delta Selection.

Yet, from Kyle, the endearment was…endearing.

She finally just stabbed down a finger and landed on *pabellón criollo*, broadly noted as the national dish of Venezuela. Now there was a tourist move if ever there was one.

A tourist in Venezuela and a tourist into being a couple. She already had a map for the first one.

Kyle's knee was warm against hers beneath the table, as was his hand relaxed casually on her thigh.

She really needed a guide map for the "couple" part of this adventure.

"Incoming!" Duane announced as they finished the main course.

A lone person was moving toward their table with no weapon in evidence.

Carla's shredded-beef stew with rice, beans, and fried plantain slices had turned out to be a good choice after all. She wiped rather than dabbed her mouth, leaving a partial smear of lipstick on the napkin. What was left would be lopsided, so she did her best to wipe off the rest of it quickly. All this girl crap—she was so done with it. How had Kyle talked her into lipstick anyway? She hadn't even noticed that one going by.

"And how!" Chad offered in a breathy tone unusual for him.

Carla focused on the approaching woman. A tall and slender blond with serious curves of the sort that would have intimidated Carla in high school, if she'd cared about something as trite as who had screwed the quarterback. After Carla had—he'd been great—she'd had to stuff Barbara Jean Geller, the head cheerleader, into a school locker before the girl would stop threatening her. Maybe she should have let the girl keep her clothes. It had been a little harsh, because Carla had chosen to use the boy's locker room for B. G.'s sequestration shortly before the end of football practice. She'd carefully avoided Carla for the last two years of high school.

The woman walking up to their table was what the cheerleader should have been: walking like she didn't care and wasn't here to sell it. She was dressed immaculately and looked very feminine in tailored slacks, a shining blue blouse, and a simple silver chain. She exuded an elegant perfection that Carla would never achieve.

"*Buenas tardes!*" She looked right at Carla.

Carla responded in kind and the woman nodded to herself as if she'd just confirmed something, though Carla couldn't imagine what. With a quick scan she assessed the table, a brief hesitation at Chad's obvious interest—he looked like a hunting spaniel about to spring into retrieval mode—and then her eyes reached Kyle's and stopped.

Perceptive woman.

"You just arrived on the *Viento Salvaje*, the *Savage Wind*." She didn't make it a question. Her voice was German-accented English—clear but overarticulated in a way no lazy American would ever consider. Except Carla suspected the German wasn't authentic. The woman was pretending to be a German tourist; they were everywhere. But her clothing was a little too high-end for a German on holiday—they loved to dress down—and her act a little too polished.

Carla hadn't paid any attention to the sailboat's name.

The woman reached into her pocket, pulled out a

card, and slid it across the table to Kyle. "Tanya Zimmer, Société de Reportage International. May I perhaps join with you?"

Chad didn't wait for Kyle's answer and instantly made room, offering Richie a sharp elbow when he didn't move fast enough.

She waited until Kyle nodded his permission before sliding in beside Chad.

"What can we do for you, Ms. Zimmer?"

"I find you to pose an intriguing puzzle. Rumors of your recent arrival"—she nodded to Carla—"they have already swept the waterfront. As a reporter, I do try to keep a close ear upon such things."

"However…?" Carla asked. Clearly the woman knew something.

"Your Spanish is a little too Spanish. I have no knowledge of the Empress of Antrax ever traveling to Spain." Her ear was exceptionally well trained, which spoke volumes about just who had joined their table.

"*Mierda!*" Carla thought she had it down well enough.

Tanya laughed. "However, that most certainly was the right accent. And your figure is also not"—she waved a casual curve in the air—"Latinate. While the latter is far from ubiquitous across the culture, it is one of the Empress of Antrax's trademarks."

"You also are no Latinate, despite your exceptional figure." Chad offered a friendly leer, which evoked a smile in return. The air was practically shimmering between them.

Did she and Kyle look like that to others? Did she and Kyle look like that at all? She didn't want to shimmer at a man, but she knew she did more than that inside each time Kyle was in the same room as her. A feature that had been pretty much constant for the last seven months of their lives, OTC *and* living together hadn't offered them much time apart. Maybe she needed to find herself a little space from him. A thought she didn't like the sound of.

"No, she's Israeli." Richie looked at their guest closely. "Well masked, but that isn't a true German accent no matter how good she is at pretending. It has Hebrew behind it. Exceptionally well masked."

"You have a pet linguist." Tanya nodded the round to Richie and addressed Kyle. "Your group continues to become ever more interesting."

"And you are Mossad." Carla took a stab in the dark.

The Israeli woman shook her head. "No, I work for SRI."

Carla simply waited, could read the half lie.

Tanya Zimmer grew a bit uncomfortable and shifted in her seat.

Kyle waited with her.

Tanya sighed. "This would perhaps be easier if our cards were upon the table."

Kyle spoke softly. "We are on vacation from Aruba, seeking business opportunities. We're Kyle and Carla Javits." Keeping their first names made life easier.

"And you are registered at the exclusive Hotel Ventura, yet you are eating here. This food is good, but definitely second-rate in comparison. 'Business opportunities' are far more likely along the lakeshore. Should I mention that a window on your 'vacation yacht' has been shot out?"

"May I mention that pirates are a royal pain in the ass?" Kyle reposted smoothly.

"You may," she countered, "but you are here, they are not, and there is only the single sign of damage to your boat. The pirates in these waters are typically more successful."

"They were successful on the craft prior to ours," Carla said grimly.

That shifted something at the table.

Tanya opened her mouth, then closed it again when the waitress came to clear the plates and take coffee and dessert orders.

After their corner was quiet again, Tanya spoke once more over her *café americano*. "I'm assuming the pirates won't be troubling anyone else?"

"Maybe in another life."

Her nod of "good" won her more credit in Carla's eyes than any previous words.

Carla reached into the purse that Chad had insisted was a necessary accessory item and pulled out the documents they had taken from the powerboat. After a moment's hesitation, she slid them across the table.

The woman looked down at them, but did not move to take them.

"Can you, as a reporter, make sure that their family is notified?"

Tanya studied her closely for a long moment. "The Empress of Antrax is not noted for her compassion. I will see that it is taken care of." She slipped the documents into her own purse.

Carla could almost trust this woman.

"Okay, Mr. 'Javits' from Aruba, what sort of business are you interested in? I have been here a year making contacts and do, now, know many folk."

"We're exploring avenues into the export business."

Tanya scanned the table. Then she quirked a quick smile to herself.

Carla knew that smile.

"Your next question is a trap."

At that, Tanya beamed.

"Shit! As was your smile. I get that now." Carla was ticked that she'd fallen for it. "You are way too smart and far too well trained, Ms. Zimmer."

"As are you." Tanya's smile continued. "As you guessed, I was about to offer to put you in touch with a Major Gonzalez to see your reaction, but you clearly know he is no longer in operation. And the only way you might know that, unless it truly was a Sinaloa hit—which you aren't, so it wasn't—would be if you were either a part of it or your people were connected to it." She paused, looked at the group around the table, and finally shrugged when she couldn't get a read on anyone's reactions. "It was very nicely done, by the way."

Carla didn't know whether to thank the woman or very quietly escort her to the ladies' room and cut her tongue out. Chad's was hanging out so far, all she'd need would be a pair of pruning shears.

"That's why the rumors of your arrival moved so fast." Tanya Zimmer selected a *besito de coco* cookie from the generously mounded plate in the middle of the table. "Very few here would notice your two points of failure. They have had very little contact with Mexican 'businesspeople' to date. You may have more difficulties as you shift into the, ah, export trade itself, but, *ja*, it was still expertly done."

In other words, drug traffickers in Venezuela would

know Sinaloa and might have seen online photos from one of the Empress of Antrax's frequent social media blitzes.

Carla glanced at Kyle and received a double tap of his knee to confirm what she was about to do. So, Carla leaned back, let Kyle's jacket slip off her shoulders, which would truly expose her warrior physique to their guest's trained eye, and then stared up at the restaurant's ceiling for a long moment as if looking far beyond it before looking back down.

She could feel the ripple around the table. Richie, Duane, and even the starstruck Chad shifted forward pending Tanya's reaction. They understood the question Carla had just asked silently and were tensed to see which way it went.

Twenty-five prisoners—hostages of the missing, presumed-dead Major Gonzalez—were languishing on the ninth and tenth floor. Would Tanya Zimmer know of them and understand that the "businessmen" around the table were in a position to do something about it? More importantly, would Tanya prove herself to be of any use?

Tanya watched Carla a long time before she too inspected the ceiling of the restaurant prior to speaking once more.

"Regrettably, I can be of not much help in that question, except to say there have been no observable changes to the hotel room assignments on the top floors. Yet."

Now that *was* valuable intel. It also purchased Tanya Zimmer a level of trust around the table. Major Gonzalez's unwilling guests were most likely still in residence. Though Tanya's warning of "yet" meant that the situation was dynamic and could change at any moment.

Chapter 19

KYLE WOULD ADMIT THAT THE HOTEL CASTILLO HAD been well chosen by Major Gonzalez.

It was in the middle of the city, so a violent assault such as the one they'd perpetrated on General Vasquez's hacienda wasn't practical. The ten-story structure was isolated; most of the tall buildings of Maracaibo were along the shoreline or in a small business district. That meant that the top floors had wide views but were difficult to see into for recon.

The building was older, which meant only three elevators and one stairwell, all leading to a common central lobby.

Kyle considered food service, but the cartel's men would be watching for that. During their dinner, each of the team had made a point of going to the restrooms in order to pass close beside the swinging kitchen doors. Room service trolleys had been lined up for a massive order. When it moved out, Chad had taken Tanya on a casual promenade around the hotel.

"Freight elevator just past the corner from the other three," Chad reported once they returned to the table. "The trolleys went up in one load without a single escort. Stopped on nine and came back down fast." So much for sending up the team with the trolleys. They would become targets the instant the ninth-floor door opened. No hotel personnel went to that floor. Experimental taps on the buttons in the lobby's passenger elevator during a brief ride to the third floor and back had proven that the ninth and tenth floors were locked out, unless a special key card was used.

After their walkabout, Chad and Tanya had been pure business, but the Israeli's carefully presented crisp sophistication appeared a bit tattered about the edges. They hadn't been gone long enough to do much, but Chad had certainly taken advantage of the situation and Tanya didn't appear to be complaining as she surreptitiously straightened her blouse once they'd returned to the table.

With nothing more to be learned at the hotel, Kyle headed the team back to the boat. They left Tanya at the hotel, much to Chad's disappointment, but she was still an unknown and bringing her aboard the *Savage Wind* would be far riskier than leaving her out in the world.

In the boat, they reviewed the observations made by each team member in their various reconnoiters, spun out and killed off a wide number of ideas, and spent some time attempting to puzzle out quite why a Mossad agent was in Venezuela at that particular moment.

Finally Kyle had an idea. The memory of a woman leaping upward came to mind.

"I see one good option. What do you think, Carla?" Kyle cupped his hands as if ready to boost her foot up and into the training-room ventilation system.

Carla was the only one who entered the Hotel Castillo lobby later that night. As a contingency, Kyle had paid cash for a second-floor room and acquired the key as they left the restaurant earlier in the evening.

Now she floated through the lobby in a midnight-blue blouse and chic linen slacks like the ones that had looked so good on Tanya Zimmer, especially after Chad had rumpled her elegant perfection a bit. It was a new and different version of girl clothes. The night clerk was very appreciative of the result, never once looking at her face. Guys really were predictable.

She took the elevator up to her new room and opened the window. Seconds later a rope snaked up for her to grab. She secured it to the bed, and the rest of the team swarmed up to her room from a dark corner of the hotel gardens.

She changed to match the rest of the team, purposely not retiring to the bathroom to do so; she simply turned her back instead. Most were too busy checking their gear, but she caught sight of Richie twitching. When she finished changing and turned back, he was studiously inspecting his rifle and his ears were bright pink. Sometimes girl underclothes could be fun too, though he really needed to toughen up. She'd still worn a bra after all.

She offered him a slap on the shoulder to let him know it was in good fun, then they headed for the elevators of the Hotel Castillo second-floor lobby in ones and twos. She punched for the eighth floor. By the time the elevator reached eight, it was empty.

On the way up, Carla swung lightly out through the safety access in the ceiling of the elevator car. She tossed a line over a convenient structural support on the ninth floor and was tied off nine stories up in an empty shaft when the elevator returned to the lobby. In minutes, the five of them were dangling together high in the elevator shaft.

She unfolded a fiber-optic spy cam and poked it into the crack between the door and the frame of the elevator. The ninth floor appeared to be clear, which wasn't expected.

Richie who had climbed a dozen feet above her, was doing the same on the tenth floor. He held up two fingers, then made his hand like a pretend gun, two armed guards. Then he drew a square in the air and swung his hand as if to enter it. They'd just gone into a room.

But the food delivery had stopped on nine. The doors to the freight elevator fit too tightly to allow a fiber-optic view around them.

Not wanting to risk a radio transmission, she waved Kyle over and he swung across the shaft on his line.

"You think the ninth floor is empty except during meal delivery and everything is happening on ten? I really don't see them carrying that much food up the stairwells themselves. Are the guards here but outside our sight lines?"

"Perhaps they empty the freight elevator and then reload it on one of the other elevators called from the ground-floor lobby. We didn't check for that. Our problem is that we can't see around the corners past this floor's lobby."

Carla could feel the answer somewhere. The building didn't have central air; each room had its own air conditioner and heater unit.

"Let's go look at the eighth floor."

Kyle nodded, then signaled to the others to stay, and the two of them lowered themselves down a story.

At eight, they popped the release on the elevator door and stepped onto the silent floor. It was straight up midnight, so the halls were empty. Early risers had already gone to bed, and those out partying on the town wouldn't be back for hours.

They quickly trotted down the halls. The building was a simple rectangle with the elevators and stairwell in a hall that sliced across the middle of the floor and the rooms around the perimeter. She went left and Kyle went right.

In thirty seconds they met at the other end of the elevator lobby none the wiser.

"Dry hole," Kyle commented and was heading back to the elevator. "Dry hole" was the standard phrase for when bad intel said there was something there and there wasn't.

Then she spotted what had caused the itch and called him back with a low whistle. When he turned to face her, she led him back into the hall.

The bigger freight elevator had been turned so that its door opened out into the side corridor rather than into the same area as the passenger elevators. That meant there was an empty space in the walls beside the two passenger elevators on the other side of the lobby. Sure enough, there it was. On the other side of the back corridor were two chutes clearly marked *Colada* and *Basura*—laundry and garbage.

"Ladies first," she said and headed for the laundry chute.

"Thank God they open side by side to the same back hallway view." Kyle grinned at her. Which meant he didn't have to climb the garbage chute.

"Wimp!" she whispered and entered the chute. Inside, the chute's walls were rough enough that her rubber-soled boots gripped as she jammed her way upward, just like climbing a Colorado rock chimney.

She bypassed the ninth floor and went to ten as Kyle moved up below her.

This time the spy cam sent out the laundry chute revealed the tenth-floor hallway perpendicular to this end of the lobby. Two rooms with doors stood open, revealing the soft mutter and laughter of men playing cards. Drunk men if she was any judge, by the sound in the earpiece.

There was a chair at the head of the stairwell door, but no one sat guard in it. The guards had been here a long time and grown complacent.

She shifted back down the chute and Kyle met her halfway. There wasn't room to get side by side, so Kyle ended up with his head between her wide-braced feet, her back against the far side of the chute above his feet.

"Don't get any ideas, tough guy." His head was between her ankles and facing her crotch. Thankfully she wore slacks.

"Only if you promise to wear that black dress for me again sometime, girlie."

If she was going to have to wear the dress, what would she make Kyle wear in exchange? A tux? No. She wouldn't know what to do with a man in a tux. But he'd looked damned fine as the wealthy and casual sailor, confident at the helm. Yes, that was an image she could definitely work with.

Then with a flash of hand signs, sometimes faster than words, they laid out a plan.

They both shifted up to the tenth floor before Kyle softly radioed the rest of the team.

"Enter and sweep nine. Expect a dry hole, but make sure. Then hit the stairs to ten. We'll be waiting for you."

Carla moved quietly out through the chute door until she stood in the center of the hallway and could easily hear the guards' card game. There was definitely alcohol involved.

Kyle set off in a circular recon of the floor away from the card game.

She considered sitting in the chair at the head of the stairs and waiting for the others to finish checking the floor below her.

Then her brain did one of its sideways things and she saw it from a new perspective. The simple thing to do would be wait until all of their firepower was gathered and simply clear the room. But there was another possibility.

She moved close beside the door to the card game. The next room down the hall was also open, something on the television playing loudly enough to make conversation difficult in the room. Kyle came around the far side of the rectangular hallways, all clear.

He couldn't cross in front of the open door of the other hotel room without the possibility of revealing himself.

Carla shot a grin at him across the gap mandated by the two doorways that separated them.

He mouthed, "What?"

She tipped her head toward the open rooms.

Then she walked into the first room, the one with the card game.

Kyle just about swallowed his tongue.

He knew to trust Carla's instincts, but it wasn't like he had a whole lot of choice.

Taking a breath, he stepped into the open room in

front of him. Two men were slouched low on a couch
with their backs to the door. In front of them a television
was playing a Spanish soap opera. The rifles leaning
against either end of the couch told him these were not
people he wanted to get real friendly with.

He pulled out his silenced Glock and double-tapped
both of them in the back of their heads. A quick check
revealed no one else there. He gave them each a "security" shot through the heart, changed for a fresh magazine, and hustled to join Carla.

As he entered the hall, Chad peeked in from the stairwell. Kyle silently signaled him that the room with the
loud television was secure and to come forward.

Chad moved in to back him up. Duane arrived and
shifted down the hall so that he had a clear view along
the corridor. Richie remained in the stairwell doorway,
facing downward with his rifle at the ready.

Kyle stepped into the room Carla had entered.

She was leaning back against the hotel room's darkened window on the far side of the room, her arms
crossed comfortably, the lights of Maracaibo sparkling
behind her.

Six card players were facing her.

They had the look of troops who had been left in one
place too long and had begun to fester and rot. Their hair
was unwashed and long. Most of them just wore pants
and grimy, sleeveless undershirts. Cards, money, and
bottles of rum the color of maple syrup were scattered
about the table.

He tuned into what Carla was saying in a liquid
Spanish he could barely follow. "I *do* know why you
haven't heard from the Major. I've been to the hacienda

and can confirm the rumors. He is never going to be joining your card game again."

The sounds of dismay were universal.

Actually, after tangling with the CIA, it would be a miracle if he ever saw the light of day again.

"I only regret that though you've done your job well, this is a hostile takeover. I will give you two choices. One, you can get up and quietly walk away. If I ever see any of you again, you will be dead."

They laughed at her standing there in front of them with her hands empty. Kyle and Chad had their rifles unslung and ready. Standing in the darkened entryway with Richie and Duane guarding their backs, they weren't visible even as reflections in the broad windows behind Carla.

She smiled at the guards appeasingly. "Or choice two, you can end up like your…"

She glanced up at Kyle and he flashed two fingers at her.

"…two dead companions next door."

Their laughter ended. Kyle flicked his safety on and then back off. The tiny sound might as well have been a rifle shot in the otherwise silent room.

All six jerked around like puppets to face him. Two reached for weapons, whether out of instinct or intent didn't matter. He dropped one and Chad dropped the other. They both flopped facedown onto the table before sliding out of their chairs to land at the other players' feet.

Carla continued to lean back against the window with her arms folded casually over her chest. "Make that four dead companions. Your choice. Walk away alive and get out of Maracaibo permanently, or…" She tipped her head toward the two dead men on the floor.

The men looked at each other.

They started to reach toward the money spread across the table.

"Leave it!" Carla snapped out. "The deal is your lives and nothing more. Empty your pockets on the table, wallets, watches, room keys, everything. Take no weapons. Not even shirts or shoes if you aren't already wearing them. You simply walk away, alive. Now!"

They didn't walk away after they emptied their pockets. They ran.

As soon as they were aboard the elevator and gone, Kyle turned to her.

"I followed your play. Now do you care to explain it?"

She brushed her hand over the golden sun emblem pinned to the lapels of her Venezuelan military uniform.

It was the same uniform their whole team wore.

"Your plan was for the hostages to identify us as members of another faction of the Cartel de los Soles and for word to leak out that they had just had their first intramural war."

Kyle nodded.

"We had hoped that someone might ask if one faction was bringing in Sinaloa on their side. Someone big enough to wipe out the General and release the Major's prisoners. Rather than just rumors, there will now be solid reports from trained observers whose panicked messages will be trusted. Any pal they tell is going to head for the hills. And the stories they spread will only add to the confusion. Now no one will trust anyone else in the military drug trade."

"Woman is hot," Chad remarked quietly from close beside him.

"You'd best be referring to her brains." Kyle felt the bite of jealousy but kept it down.

"She is hot in many ways, bro, but her brain is on fire. That was a seriously slick play."

Okay, Kyle could acknowledge that.

"It was nice, Carla. Wish I'd thought it up." But that was her strength.

He didn't need to say anything about being glad he had followed her lead. That would have been something to say back in the Green Berets. In Delta it had been trained out of them. Inside The Unit it was a given that you trusted your teammate, even if you didn't know why they were doing something—especially then. They'd learned to completely trust each other's judgment. It was surprising how much that elimination of second-guessing accelerated the speed of an operation.

"Damn nice," he finally conceded. Chad was right. She was "hot" in many, many ways.

There were only two room keys on the table. Master keys hopefully. He tossed them to Chad. "Open the rooms, let's see if we can't get everyone out of here without bringing in doctors and police. Not a word, just herd them into the lobby. Then double-check the rooms on nine to make sure they're empty."

Chad came forward and picked up the handcuff keys as well. Of course, that's how they'd be kept in their rooms, which wouldn't lock from the outside.

"Let's clear the weapons." Kyle nodded at the vast array left behind by the departing guards. They'd definitely been into their toys. There were HKs, Makarovs, and Chinese knockoffs.

Carla grabbed a pillowcase and began ejecting magazines, clearing chambers, and dumping emptied weapons into the case. He started with the rifles, tossing them on the bedspread and the rounds into Carla's bag. A low babble of voices rose out in the halls.

By the time he'd stripped the weapons off the two dead guards in the adjacent room and collected all of their own shooting brass from where it had scattered, twenty-five people were standing in the hall. Everyone accounted for.

Kyle stepped to the fore and spoke.

"On behalf of General Vasquez and Major Gonzalez, I would like to apologize for your detention."

Several were sick, hanging on to others. A number of the prettier women looked as if they'd been roughed up many times, probably in the worst ways. They all faced Kyle grimly with hatred burning in their eyes. One person in a despised military uniform looked much like another.

"Neither one is able to be here to beg your forgiveness…nor will they ever be again. We have removed them from the equation."

Surprise rippled through the crowd. Tentative smiles flickered across the faces of one or two of them, but died quickly. They'd long since learned not to trust in hope.

"There is a line of taxis"—he didn't bother checking his watch, their timing had been good—"even now pulling up in front of the hotel. They are prepaid and will take you where you direct them—a relation's, a police station, a hospital. We suggest you call the elevators and go now. *Adiós*."

No one moved.

Richie came up the stairwell from the ninth floor and shook his head. It had just been a buffer zone, no prisoners on that floor.

The hostages still stood mute and waited, unprepared for the sudden change in their fortunes.

Duane moved far enough among them to hit the call button. He, Chad, and finally Richie held doors until all three of the elevators stood open and empty. At first sidling sideways and finally in a mad, jumbled rush, the freed hostages bolted into the elevators—the last few scuttling from one elevator to the next looking for any slack space they could squeeze into. In moments the tenth-floor lobby was empty.

Kyle hefted the bedspread filled with empty rifles and headed for the stairwell. Carla was struggling to shoulder the now three pillowcases of ammo and handguns. Six guards with more weapons than an entire company of Green Berets. He took one of the bags from her and added it to his own load.

"What about their money?" Chad cocked a thumb back toward the high-stakes poker game. Tens of thousands of Venezuelan bolivars were scattered across the table, along with a surprising amount of American money. Major Gonzalez had clearly known that he didn't own their loyalty, but that he could buy their allegiance.

Kyle traded smiles with Carla.

"Tip for the maids," she said for him. "These guys were just pigs." She gathered up the bulging pillowcase.

They trotted down the stairs to Carla's original room

on the second floor and exited out the window to the shrubbery below.

Kyle was last down and pulled the doubled-over line back down after him. No sign that anyone had been in the room, except for the window being left open.

—⁓—

Carla spun and drew her Glock as soft applause sounded from the shadows of the hotel's garden close beside her.

Tanya Zimmer stood just beneath a young coconut palm slowly clapping her hands together.

"You have caused much of a stir in the lobby this day. I perhaps happened to be enjoying a late-night drink in the bar."

Carla slowly holstered her weapon as the others gathered round.

"First, four men in T-shirts spattered with blood, rushed through as if chased by Cerberus, the three-headed hound of hell. After that a large group poured out of the three elevators at once looking elated, terrified, and sadly the worse for much wear. The night clerk is perhaps even now still on the phone trying to find an explanation from any persons. The line of taxis was a very polite thought, I might so speak."

Chad moved up close beside her. "We have no idea what you're on about, beautiful, but thanks for the applause anyway. Want to go somewhere private and discuss it in detail?"

She patted his cheek. "You are very cute, Romeo, but not cute enough to sidetrack me so lightly."

"Damn! And I try so hard."

"Yes, you do, and we do see that. And by what chance

would I be interested in a mere *teniente coronel*"—she fingered the shoulder pad of Chad's uniform—"when there is a gorgeous *general de brigada* standing right here before me."

"Because he's taken." Chad smiled. "I'm not."

"Perhaps that is so." Tanya was clearing enjoying the fun of teasing Chad. "Or perhaps it is her I was talking about." She nodded to Carla, who wore the same single *sol* of a one-star general that Kyle did.

Carla returned the smile as Chad groaned.

Tanya totally had his number. Then with an easy shift, she was suddenly pure business. "You must need to get out of here, now. Meet me tomorrow at noon at the Basílica de Nuestra Señora de Chiquinquirá. Perhaps we can talk business. Only you two"—she indicated Kyle and Carla herself—"should, I think, be visible."

"Hey!" Chad protested.

"You, my Teniente Coronel"—she slipped a hand through his arm—"I think that you will be with me."

Chad did a double check with Kyle, and he nodded.

It would be good. He'd be able to monitor the woman and keep an eye on her. If trouble arose, there were few men on the planet more qualified to deal with it than Chad Hawkins.

They had also back-checked Tanya Zimmer of Société de Reportage International through Agent Fred Smith during the pre-operation satellite radio check-in.

She'd been telling the truth. She had been a registered reporter with SRI in good standing for over five years, as well as a registered and active member of Reporters Without Borders. She filed stories sporadically, but sufficiently to support her claim.

And she wasn't Mossad, or rather not a part of Mossad that many, even on the inside of Israel's intelligence agency, knew existed. Richie had managed to grab a photo of her at their meeting over dinner and sent it to Smith. The CIA had matched her to a very grainy photo taken in the center of a Syrian riot against the government that indicated she might be Kidon—Mossad's elite counterterrorism unit and kill squad. The same ones actively murdering Iran's top nuclear scientists.

They shed their uniform tops into the same pillowcase as the guards' handguns and pulled on light jackets; the evening temperatures had dropped into the high sixties. The jackets also covered their holstered weapons.

"How does he get the babe?" Richie watched Chad and Tanya head off into the dimly lit parking lot.

"Lucky pissant," Duane grumbled.

"Then what about him?" Richie aimed a thumb at Kyle.

"Lucky pissant," Duane grumbled again.

Which pretty much described how Carla was feeling—damned lucky to be with Kyle. And this team.

"So, Duane," she drawled as they headed toward the Toyota Fortuner SUV rental they'd dropped in a dark corner of the parking lot, "how do you feel about being on this team?"

His smile shone brightly in the darkness. "Lucky pissant."

They all laughed and drove back to their own hotel with an SUV full of Venezuelan weapons.

Chapter 20

THEIR ROOM OFF THE TEAM'S SUITE IN THE HOTEL Ventura had a small private balcony that faced east over the silence of Club Náutico marina, their sailboat, and the lake. The darkness hid any sign of the far bank. There should have been lights from the docks and towns on the far side of this narrowest part of the lake, but they must have been hit by yet another of the rolling blackouts that plagued the country.

Kyle knew the infrastructure was collapsing on every side of the "elected" dictatorship, but he didn't want to think about that.

Instead, he sat quietly beside Carla and stared out at the stars that filled the sky. They were just six hundred miles north of the equator; he'd never been so far south.

"It's really lovely here, isn't it?" His whisper sounded loud in the still darkness. Not a single ship was moving in the wide channel.

"You mean other than the drugs and the hostages and the killing and that stuff."

They lay curled together on a double-wide lounge chair that strangely reminded him of the grassy bank at the end of the Forty-Miler. The angle was the same though the sky was different. Rather than the thick forest canopy of the Uwharrie, they lay facing the limitless sky over the largest lake in South America. He wore underwear and she an oversized T-shirt, and they'd dragged the light comforter off the bed and tossed it over themselves.

Each bedroom in the suite had a private balcony.

He'd thought to make love to her out here, some wild post-op sex. And it hadn't been picturing Chad and Tanya doing precisely that act somewhere else in Maracaibo city that had stopped him. He'd simply been too warm and comfortable with Carla curled against him to do more.

"Lovely?" she echoed his comment.

"Yes."

"Like love?"

"Sure."

"Like you love me?"

"Uh-huh."

"*Shit!*"

"What?" He tried to look down at her, but his only view was the top of her head, a soft cloud of shadowed hair leaning against his shoulder in the darkness. Why was she—

He figured it out.

"*Oh shit!*"

"You're a quick one, tough guy."

"I just said I loved you." Strategically bad move. Really bad.

"You did."

He tried to gauge the tone of her voice, but it was so neutral that he couldn't read much from it. Delta had trained him that sometimes it was wisest not to speak.

"You mean it, don't you?" She hadn't moved from her position curled against him, head on his shoulder.

Good sign, right? He waited a moment longer just in

case it was the silence before the storm. When the storm held off, he decided that his best course of action was confirming it.

"Yeah. Have for a while. Didn't seem like the brightest maneuver, but I'm past charting a way out of it. I'm noticing you haven't tried to kill me yet."

"I'm kind of noticing that too." She shifted back. Not far enough to be trying to get away from him though, still within the curve of his arm. She looked up at him with the starlight catching tiny reflections off her dark eyes.

"What do you think it means?" A part of him was screaming for her to say it back and fall into his arms — just like a goddamn movie cliché, which Carla had never been.

"I don't know." Her voice remained soft as she studied him. "I like being with you more than any other man ever. But there are a few things that you don't know about me, Kyle."

"Such as?" She liked him? Shit! He'd been crazy gone on this woman since the day she'd rolled into The Unit and fed a chunk of concrete wall to old Ralph Whoever. He'd been in love with her since…

"Such as, my heart died four years ago."

Had it been since the day he'd first seen her? Or when she'd caught his ass on the Forty-Miler? Or leaning back against a pane of darkened glass dressed like a Venezuelan general and chatting with a group of men walking along the verge of death or… A thousand moments filled his mind. He felt his brain fill simply thinking about her.

Carla was waiting for something. For what… For his brain to shut up long enough to hear what she'd just said.

"Wait? Your heart what?"

"I lost Mom eight years ago. I went Army the day I buried my big brother next to her in Arlington. I went Delta on the fourth anniversary of his death."

"Doesn't mean your heart died. I've heard it beating plenty." Doofus statement. Best he had at the moment. Mom and brother both military casualties, both while she was still a teen. And Delta required a minimum four years of service before applying. She'd done that to the day. And he'd thought before that she was a driven woman; he'd had no idea. It explained a lot of her reactions.

"I'm sorry, Kyle. You don't know how sorry I am. I wish I had more to give you. I really wish I did. But this is all there is. Good operations. Good sex. No love. No marriage. No happy ever after, and you deserve so much more. You're such an amazing man. I'm so sorry, but that's all I have to give you."

She climbed out of his arms and he did nothing to stop her. He couldn't. He'd never considered that she didn't love him back. He'd simply figured she wasn't ready yet or...

Good operations and good sex? That's what she thought they had together?

He heard her slip through the balcony door like a whisper in the darkness but couldn't speak to call her back.

He'd never been in love before, not once in his life.

And now she...wasn't in love with him.

His brain kept chasing around the impossibility of what she'd said until the sky lightened.

The sun was well above the horizon before he finally managed to move. He was stiff, cold, and the sun didn't reach anywhere near where the chill was radiating out from deep inside his body.

Inside the bedroom, he found Carla in the bed. Their bed. The side nearest him had the covers folded down in clear invitation.

She was offering him her body, just not her heart.

Well, that wasn't enough for him. Not with her. Not with Carla Anderson. She was the one for him…except he wasn't the one for her. How in this fucked-up world had that happened? How had he not seen this coming?

She lay curled up under the covers, every shape clear and so familiar beneath the draped landscape.

His body ached to go to her. To prove her wrong. To prove that he was even more of an idiot than he really was. He wanted to make gentle love that he now knew would never happen. He wanted to slam her down hard and shake some goddamn sense into her.

Of course she loved him.

She had to.

But she didn't.

His fists throbbed with how hard they were clenched.

He studied her face in the sunlight streaming in from the balcony, amazed that she slept so deeply that it didn't wake her.

Why should it? There were no tears on her pillow. No pain creased her brow. Gorgeous as a fairy sleeping in the sunlight.

The Wild Woman was proving that she was just fine without him. He needed to go pound something to make it better—like his head against a brick wall. Yep, he and old Ralph Whoever, both fucked by the same woman.

He dressed quietly and headed out into the living room before he did something he might regret.

—⁓—

Carla lay there and listened to the soft snick of the door closing behind Kyle as he left the bedroom. She had watched him standing there, unmoving in the sun at the balcony's threshold. His outline a shadow on her closed eyelids, framed by brilliant sunlight.

He stood still for the longest time, long enough for the sun to shift behind him as if he was moving away from her.

Then, between one heartbeat and the next, he'd been gone and she was alone in the room.

She pulled the covers over her head to block the sunlight.

Carla had never promised him her heart. She'd never lied to him or even told him it was a possibility.

There had been a night, one night, when she'd been exhausted past reason, that he had made gentle, perfect love to her. She should have known, should have stopped it then and saved them both the pain. But she couldn't. No one had ever made her feel like that.

Knowing that she had paid back such joy with pure pain, pain past imagining, shamed her.

Because the pain wasn't past imagining. She knew the awful silence of a heart being ripped out of your chest.

She had stood alone at the graveside in Arlington, Virginia, on the same day she was supposed to be graduating from high school in Durango, Colorado. Her father hadn't wanted to come witness Clay's internment any more than his wife's.

Carla had looked down at her mother's grave, the grass and headstone so perfect that they looked artificial.

And she'd watched Clay being lowered into the gaping wound of dark soil beside their mother.

Carla and the chaplain were the only ones to stand witness to the honor guard and the grave diggers. In the end, it had been her alone, the grave long since filled and the sod spread.

The folded flag had still been in her hands when, less than a mile from his grave, she'd walked into the Arlington Army Recruiting Station and signed and sworn.

Didn't Kyle understand that she'd long since given everything she had to give? Would give him more if she could?

No tears came.

She muffled her dry-heave sobs with the pillow that, because he hadn't come to her bed, didn't smell even the slightest of Kyle Reeves.

Chapter 21

KYLE LOOKED LIKE HELL AND CARLA FELT LIKE HELL, which, she admitted, made it a perfect day to go to church.

The Basílica de Nuestra Señora de Chiquinquirá stood in the heart of the city. This area was wholly different from the wearier northern section of the city that included the Hotel Castillo.

To reach the Basílica they walked through the Paseo de la Chinita, a four-block city park filled with trees and long, cool fountains that battled against the midday heat already shimmering off the city. The walkways were a dramatic mosaic of black-and-gray stone. The park was dominated by a shining white colonnade forming a half arc around a towering white marble statue.

The Madonna, the golden-haloed Lady of Chiquinquirá, stood and cradled the Babe Jesus in her arms, and around her feet were gathered the winged hosts of angels.

Carla had never been a religious person, but at moments like this, she almost wished she was. So much of the world's great art had been created with religious spirit that she wished she could feel it herself. But even before the loss of Mom and Clay there had been no place inside that was stirred beyond an appreciation for the beauty of what she beheld. And frankly, given her choice, she'd rather be looking out at the view of the central Rockies.

Madonna help me. The words were empty. It was just a statue, but she needed help.

Kyle had stopped beside her when she paused to study the sculpture, almost blinding in the sun. He fell back into motion beside her when she moved once more through the fountains on the way to the Basílica.

They had spoken no words this morning that weren't a part of the ongoing operation. They had watched the official state news in silence and had seen not a single word about their actions. The "free" stations had long since had their transmitter licenses pulled by the "elected" dictatorship. The newspapers hadn't proved any better when Richie had gone down and purchased copies of today's editions. Newsprint was only one of the many shortages afflicting the population, though the state papers still managed to receive at least a portion of their allotment. Even Twitter was silent.

Duane and Richie kept eyeing both of them but were far too wise to actually say anything. They cut back on even doing that after Kyle hit them with a fulminating scowl. It had been a relief when they headed off early to get in place at the church.

"Kyle." She spoke softly as they stood at the curb waiting for a gap to cross Avenida 12. It hurt to speak, and her voice came out harsh and harder than she intended.

"Yes?" He sounded little better.

"We need to get past this." Neither of them were functioning at even fifty percent, and who knew what they were walking into.

"Get past this." A flat, emotionless statement. "Get past this," he repeated.

Then he whirled to face her. She'd have stepped back

if his hand hadn't clamped around her arm so hard that she could feel her muscles grinding against the bone.

"*Get past this?*" he roared in her face. "Goddamn it, Carla. Maybe you don't have a heart after all. You've just ripped out my guts, and you want me to behave naturally as if everything in my world hasn't just turned to total shit?"

Carla had only seen Kyle angry once or twice before, or thought she had. Those had been nothing compared to the man now crushing her arm in his grip. She could break loose, but she'd have to really hurt him to do it.

"I thought we had something. Stupid, naive ass that I am. How was I so screwed up that I trusted the simple fact that a woman who filled me with such goddamn joy was giving me no more than just her goddamn body? Shit, Carla. I've never had any trouble finding someone to fuck."

The words battered at her as he spit them into her face like a weapon on full auto. She could feel each syllable slicing past her skin to shred her inside.

"If I'd wanted a casual fuck"—he lashed her with it again—"I'd have gone out barhopping with Chad and Duane. Plenty of women have been glad to spread their legs for me. But no, asshole that I am, I had to choose you. Then, even worse, I'm such a shithead that I fall in love with you. I've never done that before, ever. And now you want to behave as if—"

He cast her arm aside, causing a final shock of pain as blood rushed back into where he had squeezed it out. She'd have a line of bruises up her bicep in the shape of his fingerprints. She shouldn't have worn a sleeveless blouse.

Kyle strode out into the traffic along the Avenida. He stalked across four lanes of mayhem as if it wasn't there.

Carla refused to rub her arm though it was still zinging. *Ooo, you're so strong that you're hurting me*, a line she'd never use. She was a dangerous woman—one of the most dangerous anywhere, courtesy of Delta—and could defend herself just fine. But she'd never backed down in the face of pain or hardship. Had a thousand training and action bruises that were ten times worse. So why had none of them ever hurt so much?

She'd never felt like this. Had never before been so connected to someone that she cared how *they* felt.

Well, girlfriend, you just found out how important you were to him. What are you going to do about it?

Kyle stopped on the far curb of Avenida 12 and couldn't make himself turn back to look at Carla. Christ preserve him, he'd just made everything worse.

He'd used his superior body strength to hurt her. He'd known he was doing it but had been unable to stop himself. He'd never hit anyone in anger, not since that asshole Mitch Holmes who'd thought he was a hotshot for beating up on the tae kwon do instructor's kid.

Mitch and a couple buddies had been waiting for Kyle in the alley outside the dojo one night. Kyle had come out of their ambush battered; they'd come out of it with broken noses, shattered toes, and a dislocated shoulder. When he'd staggered into the house with cracked ribs, his dad had bound his chest without a word. Kyle had still done the classes, though he'd been excused from sparring until he healed. Mitch and his buddies had never shown their faces again.

Kyle had just handed out a load of pain to the one person he cared most about in the world. He could feel the pain beneath his hard grasp and been unable to do anything about it. He'd used his superior body strength as a weapon against—

He hung his head and closed his eyes as his world spun. He was so lost because of a quiet woman with dark eyes and a world of hurt locked away deep inside her.

Deep breaths. That's what you did when you were pushing limits, deep, slow breaths. Get the damn pulse rate down.

He'd never cursed out a woman either.

What the hell was going on?

When he opened his eyes, Carla was standing barely a foot in front of him. A glance at her upper arm already showed his fingerprints purpling against her dusky skin.

If she punched his lights out, he'd deserve it.

Instead, she stood there, looking at him, without judgment or fear. It would be easy to think that she was standing there calmly, but he knew better. You didn't spend six months so close to someone and not be able to read them.

She was just as lost as he was.

Cursing himself for being eight times an idiot, he reached out and slid his arms around her.

She let him. Not like a lover, but like a friend. She rested her head on his shoulder and held on. He rested his cheek on her hair, breathed her in, and tried to ignore the pain washing through him.

"I'm so sorry, Carla." His voice was barely a whisper. "I have no excuse."

"Shh. I'm not made of glass."

No, she was made of goddamn steel.

Yet around her, he felt so fragile that he wondered if his heart was going to break.

———

Chad Hawkins had been trained to see patterns, the gaps in them, and how to break them. He leaned back against the leftmost of the four big columns that guarded the entry to the Basílica de Whatever and watched the shifting crowd of tourists.

Tanya of the amazing body had booted his butt a couple of hours earlier. Rather than circling back to the hotel, he'd scouted the area. As the morning heat rose toward noon, he'd parked himself here to wait and watch.

Throughout his childhood, Chad had watched the constant power shift between gangs in school and on the streets. He'd learned to gauge that tipping point where the smallest action could swing the power in the direction he desired, with no one the wiser.

He'd never been the leader, never been interested in it. He could get what he wanted by using his skills in analysis from behind the scenes. Had never followed a particular leader, except in self-interest, until Kyle Reeves had impressed the shit out of him so many times.

The dude's reputation had carried from his 1st Special Forces Group over to Chad's own 3rd SFG—even though they'd been posted a country apart and fighting in wholly different theaters of operation. Reeves's

teams didn't just come out victorious every goddamn
time, which is what Green Berets were supposed to do;
they all came out in one piece.

Chad had been thinking that if he failed Delta, he'd
apply for a transfer to Reeves's Green Beret team. Then
Reeves had been in the same Delta class.

About the only way Chad made it through Delta
Selection was knowing he wanted to serve with the man
so obviously at the head of the pack. Chad had driven
himself past anything he'd ever done before to do it, and
it had paid off—even if he hadn't been able to talk to the
guy for his first weeks on base. "Mister Kyle" showed
his patterns loud and clear: *I'm going that way. I dare
you to keep up.* Chad was still pretty damned pleased
that he had.

Tanya was another one with consistent patterns, not
as the reporter who she purported to be, but rather as a
world-class shadow warrior for the Israeli government.
While they hadn't wasted a single moment together in
sleep, he'd learned impressively little about her—other
than her exceptional skills between the sheets, in the
shower, on the… His body hardened all over again at
the memory.

He'd spotted Richie, just because his pattern was a
touch too perfect—that, and his skin shone seriously
white-guy white. The dude had wandered into the
Basílica in shorts and a T-shirt, then gawked his way
through the entire church as he scoped it out before
taking a spot in the second pew from the back. There
he'd pulled out a Spanish-language guidebook. That
his pack lay conveniently open near his shooting hand
looked purely accidental.

Chad hadn't spotted Duane, which only meant he was here but specifically hiding from Chad to mess with him.

After checking the church once more, Chad had moved to lean casually against one of the four tall, yellow columns that supported the grand portico or whatever they called the big-ass front of this church. From here he could see the three arched doorways, as well as having a clear view across the vast, baking brick-yard in front of the old church.

He'd been idly eyeing the crowd and some of the fine Latin ladies done up ever so nice—there was a thing about showing cleavage that he could truly appreciate. He'd always been something of a T-and-A man, especially the T, and this culture just fed into that.

Then the pattern broke.

Kyle and Carla should be strolling casually forward, arm in arm and gawking at the architecture. Instead they were walking a foot apart, moving purposefully through the crowd, and the circles under their eyes were so dark that they looked like they'd both been slugged.

They were dragging.

Those two never dragged.

They made it so much fun to serve on this team that he wondered how he'd been wasting his whole life before Delta. Just being around them made a man feel good.

Carla offered a discreet nod as she passed him by.

She should have bought shorts and a flirty blouse, or worn that sundress and the goofy straw hat she'd looked so damn cute in on the boat. Instead, she wore the same slacks and blue blouse from last night, which were out of place and looked much the worse for wear.

Then he glanced down and saw the line of finger-sized bruises on her arm.

He flicked a glance to Kyle's hands and saw him clenching and unclenching the fingers of one hand.

Carla continued on into the shadowed interior of the church.

———

Kyle didn't even see Chad until the man appeared from nowhere, grabbed him by the throat, and spun to slam his back into a pillar.

"You the one who marked her, Reeves?" Chad's face was inches from his own.

The snarl of fury told Kyle he was moments from having his neck broken.

"Well?" Chad shook him as if he didn't weigh anything. The man was far and away the strongest man on the team; he could fight an ox and win.

Kyle tried to speak, but he wasn't even getting air, never mind able to make words.

Chad eased off and Kyle's heels landed back on the ground. No wonder he couldn't breathe. Chad had actually pinned him up in the air.

Kyle dragged in a breath, then another. Didn't think Chad would give him time for a third, so he held up his hand palm outward.

"If I could cut it off"—his throat hurt like fire and sounded worse—"I would. If I could take it back, I'd do that too."

"Did you hit her?" Chad's hold might be looser, but he'd shifted his grip on Kyle's throat. A quick squeeze and Kyle wouldn't have a windpipe.

He was about to scoff—he'd never hit a woman except in sparring or a battle—but he saw something in Chad's eyes. Kyle had come from a world where such things just weren't done. Chad clearly came from a different world.

Not trusting his voice, Kyle just shook his head in a sharp negative.

Chad understood and eased his grip about a millimeter, but not two.

He leaned in until his face filled Kyle's field of view.

"You fix this, Reeves."

"I don't know how."

"I don't give a shit. You're Delta; it's what we do. You fix this." Then Chad spotted something over Kyle's shoulder, and his expression altered from Death's personal assistant to lit-up all-smiles farm boy.

Kyle started to turn, but Chad shifted his hand to rest casually on Kyle's shoulder…and dug his thumb into the brachial plexus nerve junction on the front of Kyle's shoulder. Pain sliced into his arm.

"You go inside and fix this." Chad sounded positively cheerful, easing off his pinch just a moment before Kyle was going to knife-hand him in the solar plexus. "I have to go meet someone."

Kyle risked a glance around the column as Chad moved off.

"And try to look like the boss for the meeting." Chad spoke just loudly enough for Kyle to hear. Then he was striding over to wrap Tanya Zimmer in a warm hug and kiss. "Babycakes!"

Kyle turned for the shadows of the church and rubbed at his shoulder.

Go fix this?

Like he had a frickin' clue where to begin.

And then right on the threshold of the arched entrance, he had a horrible thought.

What if Carla wouldn't let him fix it?

<hr />

Carla had always hated churches, on top of the fact that her father loved them, the hypocrite. She especially despised the ornate ones. She saw them as symbols of a clergy who specialized in picking the pockets of the masses.

The only god she'd ever found had lurked somewhere high in the Colorado Rockies—the only place where beauty and peace had ever abided. Hoping for some feeling of connection, she'd once tried a vision quest in the Sawatch Mountains. All she'd ended up with was serious hunger from a five-day fast and a bout of near-hypothermia. That would teach her to watch stupid Hollywood movies or trust in dreams.

But this church was incredible, a work of art without crossing over into totally ridiculous ostentation. The high, fluted columns of dark brown were painted as if they were trees with vines climbing up their towering trunks, holding up the blue and white barrel-vaulted heavens. Blue-ceilinged, half-dome alcoves off to either side lightened the space, almost making it feel like outdoors. The back of each pew was a whitewashed, elegantly carved tracery of vines that again suggested the outdoors. Not small, discreet ornamentation, but large, cheerful vines with leaves as long as her forearm.

People flowed around her, often with quiet gasps of

relief as they entered the church's cool interior. Some sat to simply admire the church, others to kneel and pray.

She didn't need to turn to know when Kyle came up close behind her. That hadn't changed. Carla could feel his presence in the crowd of a thousand, as if their bodies did not belong to two separate individuals.

"This," she whispered to him without turning. "If I ever had a church, this is what it would look like."

"Too bad you're never going to marry."

She appreciated his attempt at being wry, even if she could hear what it cost him by the roughness of his voice.

"Come on, you." She reached back and took his hand. "Time to go play tourist."

His hand hesitated, then squeezed ever so gently.

She pulled him forward until they were strolling side by side up the dark marble of the center aisle beneath the blue-vaulted heaven. "I'm really not fragile, you know."

"But I—" he croaked out.

"No. Don't you dare apologize." She didn't know if she could handle it if he did. "I know you. That you're so upset that you'd..." She raised her arm and then shrugged. "There are things we need to talk about, but now sure isn't the time."

Kyle stopped walking, and by the connection of their hands, her momentum turned her to face him.

His face was concentrating, like when he'd just received new data he hadn't figured out how to process yet, and he kept swallowing hard.

"You want to say it, don't you?"

Kyle nodded.

"If you don't mind that I can never say it back, I don't seem to mind hearing it."

"How am I supposed to come to the bed of a woman who will never say she loves me? At some point you've got to—"

"No," she warned him, keeping her tone as mild as she could. "No, I don't."

He studied her through narrowed eyes for a long moment and then surprised the shit out of her when he burst out laughing. It rang off the ceiling and seemed to fill the church with light.

He pulled her into his arms and kissed her on the forehead. "Aren't we the two most ridiculous people ever born." It wasn't a question.

She nodded her agreement. He held her close and she buried her face in his collar. They'd been apart for hours, not days, and she'd missed him so much.

"God help us both, but I do love you, Carla Anderson."

Weird.

She didn't mind hearing it one little bit.

Chapter 22

"EXCÚSEME. I HATE TO INTERRUPT."

Kyle turned at Tanya's gentle voice, her English now liberally Spanish-influenced. They had decided that with Kyle's less-than-fluent Spanish and Carla's detectably non-Mexican accent, it was better to play an American card and pretend scant knowledge of the local tongue.

It was only their first-level intelligence-gathering meeting. If this went well, they'd have more information on how to continue their strikes against the Cartel de los Soles.

Chad chose that moment to rub his hand across his throat and smile at Kyle ever so blandly.

Kyle resisted the urge to gut punch the man.

Carla was still tucked close against him. They had a lot to figure out yet, if they could. But that wasn't going to be happening right now. They had a role to play.

Tanya Zimmer had her own arm around Chad's waist, so she had to be well aware of Chad's hidden Glock against her forearm.

Kyle appreciated having one of his own men "hidden" as Tanya's lover and bodyguard.

He spotted Richie studiously reading his guidebook about four pews back.

Duane, dressed as a caretaker, actually nudged Carla out of his way as he worked along the rows of the pews, laboriously dusting their ornate woodwork like a recovering alkie doing his community service, right down to the shaking hands. Kyle could tell that Carla also recognized Duane under his ragpicker guise of grimy billed hat and tattered clothes that appeared to be months from their last laundering. The only thing missing from his disguise was that he didn't reek, which Kyle appreciated.

It looked as if Chad had missed him, which Duane was going to love.

Beside Tanya stood a nondescript man in his middle fifties. Dressed in a good quality but slightly heat-rumpled white suit, he might have been a college professor—right down to the round spectacles that seemed to make him blink more often than normal. His hair and mustache had silvered, and his skin was on the lighter side of most of the city's natives.

"Ms. Zimmer." Kyle inclined his head. "A pleasure to see you again so soon."

"Mr. Javits." It was the only name she had for Kyle and was probably as genuine as her own. "Ms. Zimmer's" tone was polite and formal. "Allow me please to introduce Señor Bolívar Estevan. I have explained your interest in the local market opportunities. He is much of an expert in that area."

"Oh, not an expert, my dear Tanya. I simply have a personal curiosity about such matters. A curiosity that I indulge shamelessly with gossip and rumor." His English was meticulous and only lightly accented. It had a merry tone, like someone's favorite uncle. He sounded like the classic absentminded professor—too much so. Combined with the fact that Tanya, who might actually be a Mossad Kidon operative, had set up the meeting, that probably meant he was actually well up the local cartel's hierarchy.

"We would appreciate any insights you might offer us, sir." Kyle waved them to an area of open pews well clear of where any worshippers or tourists were sitting — except Richie, now napping in the corner of his pew.

He and Tanya sat to either side of Estevan. Carla sat to Kyle's other side. Chad came to stand in the pew behind them, directly behind Tanya. He was the only one besides Kyle who had an excuse to openly scan the room and remain on alert.

In the shuffle of taking seats and getting settled, Kyle checked the entrance. He spotted two guards by the main doors. Chad was facing toward the church's nave and flashed him a subtle "three."

Five visible guards. Bolívar Estevan was higher level than Kyle had first supposed. Unless it was a setup, a possibility that couldn't be ignored.

Carla started chatting about family and teased how she was mad at Kyle for not yet getting her with child.

There was an image designed to slam right past his libido and straight into his core. A child by Carla? Holy shit, Batman! He'd imagined love, proposal, even marriage. Child? Children? That would be so… He wished he had a better word than "awesome" but he didn't.

Idiota! A woman who insisted she couldn't love you, and you're jumping straight to children minutes after nearly snapping her arm.

Focus, damn it! But the image of a pregnant Carla lingered. It was too easy to imagine. She'd be pissed as hell throughout every minute of the pregnancy and absolutely glorious.

Thankfully the conversation was still ongoing while his imagination was being completely cross-wired.

Estevan's guards weren't in motion but were very watchful. Situation still stable at the moment.

The man himself, apparently charmed by Carla, admitted to three children of his own, who were probably fictitious. He even mentioned that his two girls were at the Universidad Rafael Urdaneta, right here in Maracaibo.

"I think it is so important that women are properly educated," Carla agreed fervently.

"As do I." He offered pictures from his wallet of two girls who had unfortunately taken more after their father than their mother, a very handsome woman whose picture Kyle saw for only an instant.

Even if the guy was being genuine, Kyle was wondering how to get this conversation back on track.

"My husband and I"—Carla clasped Kyle's hand in her feigned excitement—"already have a very lucrative distribution company based in Colorado. We truck into a dozen south-central states. We've expanded into the ports this year because we just hated paying ship-to-shore expeditors for work we could do better ourselves. This trip is our research for the vertical integration of our business model. And why not make an extended vacation of it! Kyle is always so much about business; I want to have some fun too. We would so appreciate any insights or suggestions you might be able to offer us."

Then she turned and practically batted her eyes at Kyle.

"Can't you see it, honey? A condo here in town near the nightlife and a quieter place along the lake, out of

the fray when we want to work. Ooo! I just love the way
that sounds."

Bolívar Estevan blanched before her onslaught. But
the shift in expression was gone too fast to interpret.

Before Kyle could catch a breath to respond to Carla's
painted "dream," she continued on in a rush to Tanya.

"And you." Carla leaned toward Tanya until she was
practically in Kyle's lap. He noticed that her sleek, dark
blue blouse had somehow become unbuttoned a notch
further than it had been when they entered the church.
The tiny sailboat swung forward on its chain, catching
light and drawing attention downward. A frilly red lace
bra he'd never seen before peeked out between the falls
of darker fabric.

"I simply can't thank you enough, Tanya, for showing me this church. Is it true that it's three hundred years
old?" The last question she placed firmly to Bolívar
Estevan without leaning back.

The poor old guy's libido didn't stand a chance when
Carla was in this mode. Christ—whose mother's image
was sitting up by the altar watching him—neither did
his. Carla was magnificent.

There had to be a way to convince this woman that
she loved him as much as he loved her.

He was Delta. He could do anything, maybe even
change Carla Anderson's mind.

—◆◆◆—

Carla tried to keep her balance within this fluttery, over-
excited character she'd created. Oh God, she was chan-
neling B. G., the airhead cheerleader she'd confined in a
high school gym locker. Someone shoot her now. Please.

Had she gone too far? Or did guys actually buy into this kind of shtick?

Estevan took off his glasses and wiped them delicately before putting them back on and blinking a few times as if seeing the group of them clearly for the first time.

Then he turned to Kyle.

"Your wife is a very passionate woman, *señor*. I congratulate you on that."

"She is, *señor*. In many ways."

They traded guy smiles. That Kyle would pay for later—dearly.

Estevan inspected her for a moment and then turned to Tanya. "My dear Ms. Zimmer, perhaps this would be a fine opportunity for you to show Señora Carla Javits more of this beautiful church."

Ding! Carla wanted to do a victory dance. Too bad she hadn't worn the sundress with the swirly skirt.

She didn't like being dismissed for "the men to talk business," but the boy looked old school despite educating his daughters. The old phony, he'd probably bought the picture at a flea market.

Still in "excited cheerleader" mode, she kissed Kyle on the cheek and gushed at Tanya. "Oh, you must tell me about these lovely carved vines."

They moved off arm in arm leaving Kyle alone with Señor Estevan.

Don't screw it up, sweetheart.

Chapter 23

"YOU LOVE YOUR KYLE VERY MUCH, DON'T YOU?"

Carla made sure that their backs were to the men before she glared at Tanya. They stood arm in arm inspecting the fourth alcove along the Basílica's south wall. It held yet another gilded icon shining in the sun that streamed in through the stained glass.

Chad had moved along well behind them, clearly torn between his role as Tanya's bodyguard and his responsibility as a team member who should be supporting Kyle. He compromised by drifting along well behind them but scanning the entire church constantly. Richie had "woken back up" and returned to his guidebook and Chad had finally spotted Duane, so he didn't appear too worried.

It afforded a degree of privacy that Carla deeply appreciated at the moment.

"I wish people would stop saying that."

"It is only what I am seeing." Tanya moved onward, ignoring the icy tone that should have warned her off the subject. Carla could really get to like this woman who didn't scare easily.

They passed one of Estevan's guards, who eyed them carefully as they went by. High-end guard, Carla decided. He wasn't leering at their bodies; he was actually inspecting them to see if he could spot any weapons and making sure he memorized their faces.

Maybe Estevan was higher up the food chain than they'd even hoped for. It would certainly simplify the mission, though somehow things never became simpler when they were going well. Just like her and Kyle.

"What you see is a man who claims to love me."

"Whereas you care about him *gornisht*." Tanya signaled toward a side door and Carla gladly moved out into the sunshine with her. "Not at all."

Close beside the beautiful Basílica was a very cubic, modern glass building.

"The hospital associated with this church," Tanya told her. "I also note that you are not agreeing with my statement of how unmoved you are by such a man."

Carla hesitated just outside the door to let her eyes adjust to the daylight and scan to see how many other guards Estevan had scattered about the compound. She spotted two: one close, and one at the front corner where he could keep an eye on the front door as well as his companion near their side door.

Chad stepped into the sunshine and pulled down a pair of shades before confirming Carla's assessment of two additional guards.

"I like Kyle, more than I've ever liked any man." Which she had to admit to herself was true.

"But…"

"There is no but." Carla headed toward the rear of the building. Three tall, white domes, painfully bright in the sunshine, towered above the apse of the church. She'd forgotten her sunglasses in the miseries of this morning, though she noted that few locals wore them. Beyond the domes a two-story residence had been added on, painted church yellow but with a low, red roof of curved Spanish tile. The neighborhood past the residence did not look particularly interesting or savory.

"There must—"

"No." Carla turned to face Tanya.

Chad was well back and watching her curiously. She tried to keep her voice down but wasn't having much luck.

"No, there mustn't. He's wonderful. I wish I could love him, but it's not in me." She could feel the heat building that she hadn't been able to unleash on Kyle. She could feel the anger locked up inside her threatening to break loose like a tidal wave.

Tanya watched her with a calm sympathy that was making her beyond furious.

"I. Can't. Love. Okay? Are you happy? I'm a broken bitch and—"

Something was wrong. Beyond Tanya's shoulder there was...

No guard at the side door.

"—and?" Tanya hadn't picked up on anything yet.

The guard at the corner was missing as well.

"Carla. You can tell me to—"

"Turn around." Carla circled around Tanya so that it would look as if they were still talking, but now Tanya faced back along the broad paving between the church and the hospital, back toward the doors.

Tanya squinted her eyes at Carla's strange instruction and behavior.

Carla could feel an itch behind her. An itch between her shoulder blades that was growing by the second. And if Tanya didn't catch on to it in the next few seconds, Carla was going to take her down and take her down hard. Because either Tanya would see the shift in what was going on by the church, or she had set it up herself.

Three. Carla braced herself for a hell of a fight.

Two. Because if Tanya really was Mossad Kidon, she was as well trained as Delta.

On—

"*Bt-zwyn!*" the words hissed out between Tanya's full lips as her eyes suddenly shot wide.

"I assume that was pretty foul."

"Yes! I would say there is a hit about to go down."

Carla shifted quickly sideways to separate them as targets before moving back toward the church's side entrance, and to also shift out of Tanya's immediate reach in case she was playing two sides.

Chad noticed Carla's odd pattern of motion and spun to face the building. It took him less than a second to catch on to what was wrong.

By the time she and Tanya came up alongside Chad, they were moving at a full sprint.

"Chad, Alpha."

He ran past the side entrance and headed for the front of the church. In Delta training, the front of a building was the A side, B was to the left, and so on.

She hesitated long enough to pull her ankle piece.

Tanya was wearing shorts and a tight top that accentuated her generous cleavage, but she produced a Beretta .22 from somewhere.

They ducked in the side door, Carla peeling right and staying low. She hoped Tanya had gone left and was watching her back, rather than about to shoot her in it.

No guards.

No Bolívar Estevan.

No Kyle.

Shuffling along gently as if there was nothing out of place, tourists were watching her sudden arrival with alarm. Whatever had happened had been fast and quiet.

Richie once again appeared to be asleep in his pew. Slack-jawed—out cold—not asleep.

In the third alcove, close by Richie, she spotted the heaped bundle of a ragpicker.

Duane was down as well.

A glance back revealed that Tanya had indeed circled wide. Her searching pattern told Carla that she hadn't spotted any hostiles either. And apparently didn't have any guards of her own. It had been worrying Carla that she hadn't spotted any. Maybe Tanya really was working alone here in Venezuela. Major *cojones*. She liked that in a woman.

Chad rolled in from the front entrance as Tanya reached the D side of the building and looked out the side door there.

The roar of a large car's powerful engine rocketing down the *avenida*, running close along the north side of the church, told Carla more than she wanted to know.

Chad doubled back outside, stood in the entrance as a silhouette for a long moment, and then came back into the church more slowly with a shake of his head. The car was too far gone to chase. No need to identify it; neither Bolívar Estevan nor any of his guards were still in evidence.

Carla moved up to Richie, terrified of what she would find.

He had a pulse, thank God, but didn't react when she shook him. A sharp pinch of his earlobe brought a

mumbled protest—drugged. He'd be out of it for at least
a few more minutes, hopefully not for hours.

Chad had followed her flashed signal. She heard him
curse loudly and foully, despite being in a church, when
he found Duane.

"He's breathing but out," Chad called over. "Tranq
dart." He held up the offending object.

Tanya came up close beside her, shaking her head.

Carla awaited her moment. With a growl, she slapped
one hand over Tanya's pistol, trapping the woman's
hand against it and directing it toward a side wall. She
had her own weapon up against the underside of Tanya's
jaw. The woman's blue eyes widened, but she was smart
enough to freeze and then slowly release her Beretta.

Carla held it out behind her, and Chad was there to
take it.

It was the first time any tourists had seen their guns,
which had been purposely kept low and to the side.
All attention had followed their sprinting movements.
Now, at the evidence of a weapon, cries of fear echoed
throughout the church. It emptied in a small stampede.
In moments there were only the three of them standing
in the aisle beside the pews, Duane still out at their feet
and Richie groaning his way back to consciousness.

"Were you in on this?" Carla kept enough pressure of
her Glock's barrel against the soft underside of Tanya's
chin that the woman was making an effort to swallow
without jarring to Carla's trigger finger.

The tiniest shake of her head side to side.

"Then how?" Carla eased off enough to allow Tanya
to speak…if she whispered.

Again the tiny head shake.

"Uh," Richie mumbled as he came to.

Neither of them so much as glanced over. Tanya's bright blue eyes were mere inches from Carla's own. Her gaze didn't skitter about looking for an answer or an escape. She returned Carla's gaze directly.

"It should clean have been," Tanya finally whispered, her syntax decaying briefly when confronted with Carla's fury. "Your arrival. It was perfectly orchestrated: attacks on General Vasquez, release of Major Gonzalez's prisoners. One was favorite daughter of Estevan. That is why he agree to the meeting, I thought. I say without saying that I was offering him a meeting with the team who had done both these things. Even your arrival by sailboat was perfectly done. Customs agent has spent much time bragging about meeting La Emperatriz."

"Uh," Richie said again from behind her. "Shit!" His voice was still slurred. Then a brief silence before he continued more clearly, "You're going to want to see this."

"What?" Carla didn't turn or ease off. She figured that the local *policía* had been notified by now, and she only had seconds to make a decision about whether or not to drop "Tanya Zimmer" where she stood.

"It's a note that some bastard stuffed in my mouth after drugging me. Sorry about that, Carla. It's addressed to the 'Empress of Antrax.'"

Chapter 24

WITH DUANE STUMBLING BETWEEN CHAD AND A hardly better-off Richie, they managed to clear the area past the residence building behind the back of the church. Even as more sirens sounded, Carla was leading them between dusty sheet-metal shanties propped up by barely more solid houses. Definitely the less attractive side of Maracaibo.

If they had created any alarm among the local residents, the Marabinos were remaining thankfully quiet about it. The locals watched them pass, two very white women and two equally white men pretty much dragging a man tanned dark enough to be a local between them.

Then the residents melted back into the shadows with a skill born of long practice at self-preservation, which was apparently just as effective as Delta training. Their passage through the neighborhood left almost no ripple, and after a few blocks, Carla started them on a long circle back toward the Toyota at the far side of the Paseo de la Chinita park.

Duane shook off the worst of the drug and was able to move on his own by the time they reached the vehicle.

She didn't dare lead them back to their comfortable suite at the Hotel Ventura. For the moment the boat must be assumed to be under observation as well. The car was a risk, but they had parked it several blocks away before starting their approach to the Basílica.

It was also her best choice, as the back was still laden with the weapons they'd taken from the guards in the Hotel Castillo. For now, they were cut off from their other weapons. She just hoped no one tripped the booby traps, or there was going to be a large hole in the middle of Club Náutico's marina.

Duane had driven them here, but she plucked the keys from his fumbling hands.

They put Tanya in the middle of the backseat. Chad went to move in beside her, but Carla shook him off, ignoring his look of hurt.

"Richie, Duane, give your weapons to Chad and get in on either side of Tanya."

They didn't ask; they handed them over and climbed in.

"Chad"—Carla waited until the back doors were closed, but she and Chad hadn't opened their doors yet— "you're riding shotgun, literally. I don't want her grabbing someone else's weapon, especially until the guys finish shaking off the drugs. She so much as squirms in a way you don't like, you waste her. We clear?"

Chad blinked. "I thought… Shit, Carla. I'm sorry. I thought you didn't trust me because I'd slept with her."

"No, I trust you to be the best judge *because* you slept with her. You know her best so you'll be able to read her better than any of us. What does your gut say?"

He watched her closely over the hood of the car for a long moment, then grunted and muttered, "Old habits."

Somewhere along the way, Chad had learned to trust no one. She'd seen his trust of Kyle, his devotion to him, but even Delta training didn't erase the deepest of the old tapes.

There was a lesson there for her somewhere. Later.

Now he stared down at the roof of the car as if he could see the woman sitting in the backseat. Then he looked back up at Carla. Perhaps it was the first time that he'd truly looked her right in the eyes in the six months they'd been on the same team.

"Gut says trust her, but I'll keep my eyes open."

She nodded. That matched her own first-level assessment.

"And, Carla..." His gaze didn't waver.

She looked over at him. His fair features were twisting strangely as if he'd bitten down on something surprising and didn't know what to make of it yet.

"Uh, thanks." Then Chad mumbled something that she was only able to interpret in afterthought as they each opened their doors and climbed into the car.

"Goddamn son of a bitch has no fucking idea how lucky he is."

Carla could only hope that the "goddamn son of a bitch" was still alive. It was a fear that had twisted deep in her gut at that first instant when she'd spotted the missing guards, like the final, fatal slice of an enemy's blade.

She started the car and drove away, amazed that she remembered how. Because she'd sure as hell forgotten how to breathe the moment Richie read the note aloud.

To Empress of Antrax,

I now have something of value that is yours. We will proceed most carefully if you ever wish to have it back in one piece. Tanya will know how to reach me in five hours. If all does not go

*well, that which you value will return to you in
many pieces.*

Estevan

—◦◦◦◦—

Unsure where to go, Carla let her instincts take her to
the Hotel Castillo. She stared up at the sign and tried to
figure out why they'd come back to where the hostages
had been confined.

"Are you nuts, Carla?" Richie asked from the backseat.

Her throat was too tight and dry to form an answer, if
she even had one. Kyle would know what she was thinking.

It hurt to even think his name.

Kyle understood her decisions, even when she didn't.
Why didn't he understand that there was no love left
inside her, not even for him?

"No," Tanya answered for her. "It does make actual
sense. The group of hostages in this hotel was the power
base of Major Gonzalez. The other cartels would not
have assets here. The risk of discovery too great, too
dangerous. This hotel, it is a nearly guaranteed blind
spot. And Estevan, knowing you are the ones who
pulled off the raid, would think it too obvious that you
return here."

The explanation worked as well as any other Carla had.

She left them in the car as she went in to reserve
rooms. They didn't have any suites except up on the
tenth floor, and there was no way she was going up
there. She opted for three rooms on the sixth floor,
though they'd only be using one—the one she'd asked
for by number hoping each floor was numbered in the

same way. The sixth floor was also too far for Tanya to escape out the window.

During the crossing from car to lobby elevator, Carla took Duane's hand and Chad took Tanya's. Richie appeared clearheaded and had taken back his weapon before shifting into a rear-guard position.

Duane felt steady enough through their linked grasp, though he still blinked too much. Clearly he'd had a much bigger dose of the drug than Richie. Carla finally assessed his condition as sufficient for a crisis event. An adrenal rush would clear off the last of his fog. She returned his weapon as they rode up in the elevator.

The room numbering was the same. Their unremarkable room was directly across the hall from the laundry and garbage chutes if they needed a quick escape. The stairwell also was close at hand.

The room itself was pure hotel blah. Two queen-sized beds, three chairs, TV, and desk.

Chad sat Tanya in the middle of one of the queen-sized beds. It was much harder to get leverage for action off a soft mattress than an armchair or other solid object. Especially these mattresses, which were not in the best condition.

Chad pushed a chair into a corner of the room offering him the best range of fire. Duane sat on the edge of the second bed, and Richie straddled a desk chair backwards that he'd placed right in front of the only door.

Carla turned on the television and flicked it to a talk show to mask their conversation, then pulled up a chair to the foot of the bed.

"Okay, Tanya Zimmer, we know who you work for. So, start explaining."

"I am a reporter for—"

"—Mossad's Kidon counterterrorism kill squad carrying a Beretta .22LR Bobcat." She held out a hand and Chad dropped Tanya's gun into her palm—still fully loaded by the weight of it. Carla inspected the small weapon, which was absolutely lethal in the right hands. Without its seven-round magazine, it weighed about twice as much as a smartphone and wasn't much larger. "You think that like doesn't recognize like? What are you doing here in Venezuela? How did you end up so conveniently in our path?"

Carla didn't scream. She didn't rant. She didn't beg to know where they'd taken Kyle. She was serving the team, wasn't she? The fact that she was dying inside with each second, emphasized by the loud ticking of the analog bedside clock, didn't matter. Did it?

Tanya glanced once around the room and nodded. She wasn't exactly in a position to be making choices.

Carla liked the woman, which made her twice as suspicious. She wasn't above leaving a pretty corpse spread out on the bright blue bedspread of room 603 and walking away.

"Cocaine usage is climbing rapidly in Israel's population. Soon our young people will be so bad off as you Americans. Most of Colombia's and Bolivia's exports are run up the Pacific coast to Mexico and the western United States. Most of the exports to Europe are first sent into Venezuela. They then travel by boat to various points inclusive of Aruba to the Florida coast and New Orleans. Or by planes to Africa."

Carla nodded sharply. They knew this; that's why they were here.

"Once the drugs are in Aruba, that's a Dutch country and passage into the Netherlands is very straightforward. I was sent in to investigate the back trail of what is entering our country. I have spent most of the last two months living in Cubiro near General Vasquez's hacienda, befriending the workers there. I was within days of getting inside with hopes of gathering good intel for a strike there. Then two nights ago the people I knew up at the hacienda came streaming into the village in fear for their lives."

Carla nodded for her to continue.

"They came to the village with tales of the fanged skull of Sinaloa and a beautiful woman who walked without fear and killed without hesitation. Confirmed kills of everyone in the main house except the cook and her children. When I reported it, I was informed that Claudia Ochoa Felix had been in a Guadalajara nightclub at the time, and the two equally lethal Torres sisters were also accounted for within the last twenty-four hours. I had learned the location of Major Gonzalez's hostages. I decided to come here and see who showed up."

"That's why you greeted me in Spanish in the restaurant." Carla listened to the TV rattling away behind her with some chagrin. That was more the sound in her head than what Kyle used when cursing. She'd forgotten to also think in Mexican Spanish while speaking it.

Tanya nodded. "I suspected by then that you were not Sinaloa. When your Mexican was so shaded with true Spanish, I knew you had to be SAS or Delta. Your distinct lack of an accent when you speak English was indicative of the U.S., western region. I have walked through the hacienda's compound after your visit. It was a most effective and total destruction of the place. The fire of course destroyed any bodies and…" Then she laughed. Four people seated around ready to waste her ass at a moment's notice, and the woman leaned back against the pillows and laughed.

And Carla had thought she herself was tough.

"What?"

"You did get the General out first?"

Carla merely raised an eyebrow.

"And the Major. Oh my, you people are so good. I don't know if we could have done that. Even walking through the rubble, I never guessed. I entered the remains of the compound along with the locals doing scavenging. There were many of very upset police on the grounds, but no military."

"Those police were on the take, upset at the loss of income. The military were afraid to be associated with the, ahem, deceased and departed." Carla offered her blandest smile.

Tanya nodded that she'd made the same assessment.

"So, you just happen to team up with us," Carla observed. "And by purest coincidence, you just happen to have contacts throughout the Venezuelan drug industry."

It was perhaps the first time Carla saw heat rise in Tanya's eyes.

"Two years. I have been in this country for *two years*. Embedded…" She caught herself and took a deep breath. She looked little calmer but regained partial control of her English. "That meeting for you today… I risked every contact I had to make it happen."

She waited while Tanya regained her poise of careful

control, but there'd been no mistaking the anger and frustration at what had happened. Tanya had been the one to set up a meeting that had put them in harm's way, and it made Carla furious that it had turned out so badly.

She didn't need to glance at Chad for confirmation; she could feel him relax. There had been an absolute honesty to Tanya's fury.

Carla tossed Tanya's handgun back to her. With a sleight-of-hand that was hard to follow, it disappeared back behind the woman's waistband.

The guys relaxed.

"What's next, Carla?"

She turned to look at Chad. Why was he asking her? They should be asking Kyl—

Shit! No Kyle.

She closed her eyes against the fresh stab of panic that tried to slide up her throat and choke her to death.

She'd only once before lost someone in the field that she'd been sleeping with, the only other time in her life she'd slept with a soldier. A bullet did a bad ricochet along the concrete wall of a godforsaken hideout along the Congo River. Courtesy of Delta she now knew that hugging a wall might feel safe but was a deadly choice—bullets had a habit of skimming along walls. Now she'd even practiced the art of making it happen on purpose, ground skip too. He'd bled out in her lap and she'd been helpless to stop it.

It hadn't felt like this.

Waves of panic kept washing through her. Thinking clearly…thinking at all was impossible. Every time she closed her eyes, she pictured Kyle coming back to her, one piece at a time.

But Delta was about flexibility, not dependent on any one individual.

The team waited for her. Even Tanya.

For some idiot reason, they thought she was the one most likely to figure out what to do next. They were fucking nuts.

Carla glanced at her watch.

"Four hours and six minutes left. You have no way to contact or find Bolívar Estevan prior to the five hours he mentioned?"

"No." Tanya shook her head. "He must still think I am but a reporter turned go-between. He has granted me three phone interviews before, with no direct quotes, but I had never met him before today. I call a specific number at a certain time of day. I leave my number and hang up. And it has to be a landline so that he knows exactly where I am. So, we can't be on the move until after he returns the call."

"So much for Plan C," Chad muttered.

"Yeah, especially since we don't have a Plan A yet," Duane followed up. He must have finished shaking off the drug because the two of them were back to their Mutt and Jeff routine.

"I get a call back from a blocked number. Last year I managed to have it one time traced back. It led to a burner cell phone purchased in Italy. He's very careful. He must have had every step planned at the church right down to the prewritten note. The outside guards weren't there to protect Estevan. They were there to track your team."

"That fits." Duane spoke up. "They hadn't spotted me any more than you did." He cuffed the back of Chad's head and received a grin in return. "I saw one take out Richie and tried to move in. That's when another of them darted me." He nodded over to Richie. "If it makes you any happier, bro, the guy who dosed you, I broke his ribs bad before I went down. He was definitely spitting blood. Expect a corpse to show up somewhere soon."

"No pity from me, man. Thanks." A thumbs-up confirmed it.

Four hours. It was one in the afternoon by the bedside clock that continued to count each relentless second aloud.

"We can't just sit here while Kyle's—"

Carla held up a hand to silence Chad's protest. She had to think.

Bolívar Estevan. Everyone's favorite uncle. A meticulous planner, which meant at some level he would be predictable, a fact she filed away for later. Two daughters at university, but he'd mentioned three children. The third would have been the one they'd freed from this very hotel.

Where would he take her? Back to his family home, wherever that was. Certainly not close to the city; that would be too exposed, too indefensible.

Damn! She'd seen his flinch but not understood it.

"Can't you see it, honey? A condo here in town near the nightlife and a quieter place along the lake, out of the fray when we want to work. Ooo! I just love the way that sounds."

Her idiotic gushing had struck too close to home; that was exactly Estevan's setup.

Stupid! Stupid! Stupid! But how could she have known?

Yet he'd been here in town for the meeting.

There was something there, but she couldn't come at it head-on the way Kyle did. She'd have to circle around it for a bit and then jump the idea when it wasn't looking.

She thought back to her first day at Delta. The "inde-fence-ible" fence that was in reality so well protected. How did you find protection here? Not protection, safety.

Why did Estevan need safety?

He didn't just have a place out on the lake. He didn't just have a drug business. He had a drug *trans-port* business.

And that had been the exact niche she'd talked about moving into. Estevan would have millions or billions of dollars tied up in something that…the Empress of Antrax had just threatened. That's why he hadn't simply taken her out. He thought he was neutralizing her by taking Kyle.

"He didn't neutralize me. He's pissed me off!"

"What was that?"

She ignored Chad. Bolívar Estevan needed safety for his drug transport business. Why? A place along Lake Maracaibo. A place where you could…build submarines?

"Estevan builds the submarines himself," she guessed aloud. "Our move masquerading as Sinaloa to horn in to the drug export business was a mistake, because it's a direct threat to his own operation. His own operation out on the lake."

Carla glanced at Tanya, who nodded her agreement. "It would make sense. I should have been surprised that he accepted the meeting. He is very powerful and very well-known. It was a dangerous move for him to come out in public. I should have seen he had special reason to come—to defend his territory. Against you."

"He knew that nothing less would draw out the Empress of Antrax." Then a chill ran up her spine.

"What?"

Carla sprang to her feet, unable to sit still. She paced from Richie's chair by the door over to the window beside Chad. Seven very unsatisfying steps but even that was better than sitting still.

"My disguise was not designed to hold up to the level of scrutiny he will bring. I intended to fool a customs agent, not a drug lord. Clearly they haven't met, or he would know I'm a phony. But he'll know it soon. Then he won't be giving Kyle back." *Not even in little pieces*, a truly sick part of her brain pointed out. "Kyle is bait to draw me out of the city where Estevan fears I have other forces. He plans to capture me and eliminate the Empress of Antrax. Or, as soon as he finds out we're phonies, kill us both anyway." She didn't know where the chess pieces were now—but maybe she could control where the crucial ones were going to be.

"Who has a map of the lake?"

Richie pulled out his guidebook and turned to a fold-out map.

She studied the terrain. Maracaibo fronted the narrow mouth of the roughly circular 150-kilometer lake. Before the bridge was built, there had only been a ferry to cross the gap or a thousand kilometers of road. Now that the bridge was in place, most of that thousand-kilometer perimeter road would be abandoned or little used. There were dozens of streams and rivers draining into the lake, but only a few were big and deep enough for a submarine.

Where in a hundred miles of lake was Estevan hiding?

His camp only had to be big enough to build a craft a hundred feet long. His material supply chain would be even more easily hidden: fiberglass, Kevlar, an engine; nothing to stand out.

She needed detailed bathymetry, not a tourist map. Where was deep enough? Where too shallow?

She needed Kyle.

The blow of that thought was unexpected and knocked the wind out of her.

She started pacing again, past the blabbering TV, into the bathroom, back out until she reached the windows, and turned once more. She hated that the others were waiting for her, watching her, could probably see the panic on her face.

She needed Kyle. The feeling had nothing to do with her inability to plan her way out of this.

The impossible ache was wholly personal.

The Carla Anderson she knew never needed anybody. Waves of fear and need crashed together in her gut. If she'd eaten in the last twenty-four hours, she'd be barfing it up right about now. The room spun worse than during her single drinking expedition. After burying her brother, after carrying his flag into the Army recruiting office and signing up, she'd gone on a bender before reporting in the next morning.

She'd drunk and eaten and been sick and drunk more. She'd woken up on somebody's sagging couch in a run-down apartment with peeling paint and no idea of how she gotten there or who her benefactor was. Her clothes had been cleaned and were laid out neatly beside the couch, with her brother's folded flag on top that she'd somehow managed not to lose. By

its careful placement, she guessed that a retired soldier had kept her safe from herself that night. There'd
been no sign of the small backpack she'd shoved a
change of clothes into before flying to her brother's
funeral. Didn't matter, the Army would be clothing
her in the future.

She'd left before the snorer in the one-bedroom woke
up. Left a thank-you note and slipped out. And, my
God, her father did that to himself every night? Even
now, standing in a Venezuelan hotel room, she couldn't
fathom his state of mind.

Whatever disease he had, she didn't. She was strong
and—

She stopped her pacing. Closed her eyes until she
forced the whirling madness in her head to a stop
through sheer will power.

When she opened her eyes, she was facing the television. For a disorienting moment, her inside turmoil
appeared to have transferred to outside turmoil.

The talk show had shifted over to news, which was
showing weather footage. A storm was coming. A big
one. Not a hurricane, but nasty.

A glance out the hotel room window confirmed that
the sunny day was already darkening to the north and
winds were starting to shake the fronds of the palm trees
in the small garden beside the hotel. The sun still shone
brightly, but it wouldn't for long.

Tonight. Under cover of darkness and storm.

She always worked better with a deadline.

Carla turned back to the rest of the room.

"A storm is coming. I think"—she pointed at the
three guys—"you three should go for a sail."

—∿∿—

Kyle woke slowly and then wished he hadn't. His head hurt like hell. He'd sensed the coming blow at the church, but too late.

It had come from his most protected quarter, which he should have been ready for. Just as the lights went out for him, he'd twisted enough to see Richie unmoving on the bench. Totally unmoving.

God, he hoped Richie wasn't dead.

Kyle fought against nausea, did his best to suppress any noise. He was…alone?

He went to open his eyes, only to realize that he already had, but to no effect. He tried blinking but could sense no change. In a blackout cell or gone blind? He'd assume the former for his own peace of mind.

He wasn't tied. He'd been dumped here. Wherever "here" was.

His head pounded out a rhythm like a bad Venezuelan cover band trying to do Swedish pop music. If only Carla was here to soothe it with the cool touch of her strong hands.

Carla!

Kyle jerked upright, only remembering to duck his head at the last moment, but he didn't hit anything. No warship. No Navy bunk bed where they'd…

A gentle testing found a thin mattress, steel floor, and corrugated steel walls. He didn't try to stand but instead crawled about his cell. If he was under observation, he wanted to appear weaker than he was…which was pretty pitiful, considering how every movement still sent sparklers into his vision from where he'd been clipped at the base of the skull.

His cell was three meters long, piss pot in the corner, and twin steel doors at one end. He made a show of using the door for support to struggle upright. Reaching upward, the ceiling was right at the limit of his reach.

He was in a cargo container. He hoped he wasn't being shipped somewhere, though he could sense no motion through the whirling nausea that had resulted from the head blow. His ear against the steel revealed no noise except his own pulse and breathing.

The air inside the container was hot and thick, but breathable. At least he wasn't out in the baking sun. If he were, he'd have been cooked alive by now.

He slumped down against the right-hand door as if too weary to return to the mattress, which wasn't far from the truth. His head hurt like hell. Not knowing what was happening to the rest of the team made the panic rise. It took all he could muster to keep it down.

He'd failed them, hadn't been smart enough. Were they drugged? Injured? Tortured?

If he simply knew they were dead, it almost might be easier.

Except Carla. He couldn't imagine the world without her in it, even if he wasn't. He pulled up his knees and rested his head on them. He didn't dare be caught lying down or asleep when the container door opened.

If it opened.

He didn't have long to wait.

Chapter 25

IT WAS A RISK TO THE TEAM, AND CARLA HATED IT. BUT it was the best she could do without Mr. Master Planner Kyle around.

Richie would take the sailboat out onto the lake. He'd use the comm gear to squirt a message back to Agent Fred Smith.

Duane and Chad had taken most of the remaining cash from Major Gonzalez's safe and were going to buy, rent, or steal the fastest small powerboat they could find. They would meet Richie somewhere out on the lake, away from prying eyes, and transfer the weapons and other gear into the high-speed boat. It would take a minimum of sixteen hours to sail the length of the lake, and they were going to have far less than that…once they knew where they were going.

Carla had finally snuck around and tackled the idea in a way it hadn't expected. Now if they could just pin it to the map…

She and Tanya got on the phones to the cab companies that the team had hired the night before to carry away the hostages from the raid on the tenth floor.

Thirty cabs from six companies.

Twenty-two used by the hostages, eight went home paid for but empty.

Cabs with single women in them, nineteen. No question where the Major's taste in tactics lay—focus on the women.

Nine had left Maracaibo city. Six cabs had returned within the hour. Two had only returned a few hours ago from a long drive far around the lake.

Carla marked the drop-off points of the hostages on the map.

One cab was overdue and not answering his radio or his cell phone. It could be a coverage problem. Or a breakdown.

Or it could be that Bolívar Estevan had his favorite daughter back and wanted nothing leading back to them.

Her instincts said that was the case.

She managed to charm the cab's radio frequency and the driver's cell number out of the dispatcher. It had taken a trip to the office, a deeply unbuttoned shirt, and a surprisingly small wad of bills to get the information, which was good because that was all she'd kept from the Major Gonzalez stash. She'd of course been issued walking-around money, but with the reports that she'd have to file about every damn *céntimo* she didn't turn back in, she'd rather not touch it.

Once Carla was back in the hotel room, she crossed out the other two cabs that had gone partway around the lake.

Sorry, Mister Cabbie, we may have just sent you on your last ride. Now, where did you go?

Tanya did what any smart operator did while stuck in a hotel before a mission. She ordered room service. Carla marked it down on her mental list of advanced techniques they didn't teach you in Delta.

The maid who delivered their food was cheerfully talkative, and Carla wanted to gag her and shove her out the door. Tanya was clearly on another tack.

"My sister and I have been in Venezuela a week," she told the maid.

And if the maid bought that, she was both blind and stupid. Carla's lean-and-dark build had not a single thing in common with Tanya's built-and-blond look except that they were about the same height.

The maid was neither blind nor stupid and instantly assumed they were lovers. She relaxed even further, as if they were suddenly just gals together. Actually, by the woman's manner, maybe she swung both ways despite the ring on her right hand. She was young, pretty, and there was no fucking way.

Carla was about to shoo her from the room before she got any bright ideas.

"We were wondering," Tanya cut her off smoothly, "does anything interesting happen in this town? We only just arrived in Maracaibo, and it seems so quiet and safe…and dull."

Carla took a bite of a *tequeños* to stopper her mouth before she said something stupid. Tanya was asking for news on the aftermath of their raid last night. Just last night? Back when she'd still thought everything would be okay between her and Kyle. He could say he loved her as long as he kept coming to her bed.

But no, that wasn't good enough for him. Well, she wasn't going to lie to him simply to sleep with him.

Kyle was such a pain in the ass!

She dipped the deep-fried soft cheese into the green sauce and bit down.

Damn him anyway!

She gasped.

Her mouth was on fire!

Tanya rose, fetched a bottle of water, and opened it for her.

"My dear sister doesn't recognize *guasacaca* from guacamole."

Despite the water, the sauce's fiery heat—on top of the still molten cheese—had tears streaming out her eyes.

Tanya dabbed Carla's eyes with a Kleenex, gave her shoulders a hug, and kissed her on top of the head, just the way a lover would, continuing the myth for the maid.

Just the way Kyle would. Which brought back the seasick feeling in Carla's gut that—in a way she'd never understand—she had betrayed him.

"Oh, things happen in Maracaibo," the maid offered in a suggestive tone.

Tanya returned to the bed and stretched out on the top of the covers like she was posing for a men's magazine ad. Or in this case a lesbian one.

Carla had been using "womanly wiles" a lot in the last forty-eight hours herself. Which were also the first times she'd ever used them. She was disgusted that they worked, disgusted at herself for using them, and wished that the whole world could go back to the way it was when they were merely jumping out of a speeding jetliner in the middle of the night. Back before she strode across the hacienda compound with her blouse open down to her belly button and way before the goddamn yellow bikini.

The maid breathlessly recounted an outsider's view of what had happened the night before. A few new details, but nothing substantial, other than the first hostages arriving over a year ago.

"Really?" Tanya had gasped breathlessly with wide eyes and bosom heaving in all of the appropriate places.

Carla did her best to look surprised. "In this very hotel?"

"Right here, on the tenth floor." The maid sounded oh so pleased at being able to shock.

Carla expected Tanya to offer a shiver of delight, and then the maid would probably try a tumble onto the bed.

Carla wished the guys were here; a little testosterone to clear the air. She was going to leave if the maid and Tanya started anything. This also reminded her of just how little she knew of this woman she had chosen to trust. How far would she go? Was Tanya actually interested, despite having slept with Chad? Wouldn't he be bummed. The thought almost made her smile. Almost.

Instead of simpering, Tanya glanced over at her. "I don't know, sister. Perhaps we should look for a different hotel. It sounds quite horrid."

The maid finally realized her gross indiscretion. The mood in the room shifted abruptly as she politely backpedaled, reassured, and escaped as fast as she could.

Tanya simply smiled at Carla once they were the only ones left in the room.

"You're a manipulative bitch." Carla could never… but she had. Perhaps not at another woman, but she had nonetheless.

"Guilty, sister. Whatever works on an assignment." Tanya remained stretched out on the bed and pretended to send her a kiss.

Okay, so being "girlie" had its uses, which she was going to do her damnedest to keep to a minimum. And she'd never use them on Kyle. Not ever. Though an image of wearing that black dress for him and having him take it off…

Shit! If the jerk was still alive. If he'd gone and died

on her, she'd resurrect his ass just so that she could kill him herself.

"Hardly worth the effort on that one. Too easy." Tanya flicked her fingers toward the door.

"She knew." Carla was disgusted. "She had to know what was going on up there, what was happening to those poor women. They all knew and they didn't report it. I'd like to level the whole damned hotel!"

"I think it is only recently started. The Major, he would know it was too dangerous to abuse them, if the words were to escape out. There is only so much wrath he could fend away. I expect it is something the guards had only started when the reports of the Major's death came to being."

"Well, that's at least a tiny shred of light in this mess."

Tanya shrugged. "This is not your United States. Who would they report it to? The *policía*? When you removed Major Gonzalez, they suffered a drastic loss of paycheck." She rose from the bed and dug a *tequeño* deep through the lethal sauce and took a large bite of it.

Carla tested the other green sauce tentatively: smooth, mild, avocado. Guacamole. She dipped the now-cooling fried cheese into it and bit carefully. Even though her mouth had calmed down, it still stung on the potentially permanent scorch marks that had been seared across her palate.

"The government?" Tanya continued, uncovering a plate of empanadas. "They are held aloft by the cartel income, at every level just trying to keep afloat. This country has the biggest oil reserves of any nation and is rapidly bankrupting. They can't pay their bills. Even cars and basic foodstuffs are almost impossible for purchasing."

The turnovers had elegantly twisted edges. Carla tried one tentatively. Not spicy hot, just a warm and luscious ground beef filling that was as strong in flavor as the sauce had been in heat.

"The Venezuelan military? That is the home of the many factions of the Cartel de los Soles. Perhaps you could have reported it to another faction, but they wouldn't have taken action for fear of the death of the hostages. Bolívar Estevan knew exactly where his daughter was held, but he could not rescue her without causing her death, or the death of the daughters of allies who would become very bad enemies. That is how I arranged the meeting for you so easily. You not only freed his daughter, but also did it without massive political problems he could not afford."

"Which leaves us with what?"

Tanya continued to eat heartily, which was good advice. Who knew when or what their next meal would be.

"Which leaves us with two more hours to take a nap before I can make the call."

Also good advice. However tonight turned out, it was going to be a long one.

"Want to share a bed?" Tanya's tone was suddenly dark and sultry as she looked at Carla with half-lidded eyes, arcing her chest forward to emphasize her already impressive breasts.

Then Tanya burst out with a belly laugh. "Oh, 'sister'! You really ought to see your face!"

Carla was rather glad she couldn't. She hoped that its burning heat was due to the strong spices, not at how gullible she was.

Chapter 26

KYLE WAS ON THE VERGE OF SLEEP DESPITE HIS SITTING-up position. He tumbled out the container door when it was opened and landed hard on a rough wooden surface.

The sun was blinding, painful beyond belief, punching straight through his skull and cranking up the headache that was no better after his almost nap.

Immediate action? If he was capable of any, which he wasn't sure of.

The soft clicks of two weapons coming off safety made him squint before he leaped. One close enough to be reachable, but his partner offered covering fire and was well back and to the side.

"It is too pretty an afternoon to be shot." Bolívar Estevan also stood well back, beyond his two guards.

Pretty? The only thing higher than the temperature was the humidity. Kyle had always hated the idiots who were behind you "110 percent," as if there was such a thing. But wherever "here" was, he could almost believe in 110 percent humidity. The mere act of breathing had his shirt clinging to him.

"Let us sit under the trees and speak." Estevan's fluid Spanish reminded him to watch his choice of language. Thankfully, he'd learned gutter Spanish from a Mexican migrant worker who'd spent time at his father's dojo. Carla's Spanish had softened it, but even a trained linguist would tag him as authentically Mexican.

No one approached close enough to help him to his feet, but the gestures of the men with the rifles left no doubt of his best course of action.

It took no acting to look debilitated. He rested a hand on the cargo container to help prop himself up and almost burned it. The sun had shifted while he dozed. It was now late afternoon and this end of the container had been baking in the high tropical sun. He was dehydrated and partly roasted alive.

Once on his feet, he finally took in his surroundings. A small pond, perhaps a hundred meters across, definitely less than two hundred. Some palm trees standing well back from the water. Mostly flatland, barely above the water and covered in thick green growth. Bushes. In his world there were bushes and there were trees. This was mostly bushes with trees farther back serving as a screen against a wider view to the horizon. The trees were far thicker than in the city of Maracaibo, the air moister. Was Lake Maracaibo around the corner, or was he off the map and prisoner in the deep jungle?

The container sat on a dock stilted up out of the water. He was weaving, his breathing wrong.

"I'm not going anywhere." He hoped that Estevan understood. He had to lower his core body temperature.

Kyle flopped face-first off the dock and into the water. He heard a shout of alarm before he submerged. If they were going to shoot him, they could. He had no defenses, nowhere to run, no energy to do so. But no bullets had slammed into his back by the time he surfaced. The water was not much cooler than the air, but it was enough.

He stayed near the dock, ignoring the guards who still had their weapons leveled at him.

It wasn't a lake. He had to paddle idly to keep from drifting away from the dock. A current. A river.

Perhaps one of the ones that fed into Lake Maracaibo on its way to the sea. That would make sense. It would be more convenient for Estevan if he could hide his operation close to a city, for Kyle had no doubt that's where he'd been taken.

His brain was finally kicking back into gear. He ducked his head under once more to cool off as much as he could in the warm water. There was a deep thrumming—motor noise of some sort.

He brought his head up. During his brief submersion, he'd drifted out from the dock a half-dozen meters. From here he could see just around a point of the land where the lakeshore meandered in and out.

There was a conning tower visible just between two low trees.

A submarine's conning tower.

Estevan was in the submarine business. He wasn't a middleman who might lead them to the kingpin they were looking for; he was the man they wanted.

Except when Kyle's team posed as Sinaloa, who in turn was pretending to be an expanding U.S. distribution operation, they were in direct competition with Estevan.

Oh, crap! They'd accidentally challenged the dragon head-on. No wonder Estevan had risked kidnapping him.

He swam back to the dock.

If anyone else on his team was still alive, they were so screwed.

—⁓—

Carla used her encrypted satellite phone for the first time on the mission. It took her a few minutes to find her way to Fred Smith aboard the USS *Freedom* from the hotel room.

"Hi, Carla. How are you do—"

"Are you in position?"

He harrumphed at her slicing through the niceties.

A gregarious CIA… Who knew such a thing was possible?

"Yes, we have a ScanEagle drone aloft over the lake with an ELINT package aboard."

"Just one?"

There was a silence that she hoped meant there were other electronic intelligence assets in the air besides a small two-meter-long drone.

"Our only other asset in the area is the helicopters. We've been holding those back at the ship in case you need emergency exfil."

If they needed an emergency extraction, it was going to be in the middle of the goddamn storm, but Carla didn't see any mileage in pointing that out.

"Most likely position is at the south end of the lake," she told Smith when she could be sure of her voice control.

"We can only tap radio waves, cell or satellite. If he's using a landline, then—" Smith didn't sound happy. Like Carla cared.

"We're screwed, I get that. But there aren't a lot of services down there. Cell or satellite is far more likely."

At her nod, Tanya dialed and left her message.

"We're calling out now." Carla monitored the line.

"The number is a cell phone somewhere in

Maracaibo," Fred Smith reported back. "Because you have us flying at the south end of the lake, we can't locate it any more accurately than that."

Carla didn't bother answering. For ten agonizing minutes, they sat and waited. Neither she nor Tanya could think of a thing to say, so they just sat, Tanya's hand hovering near the hotel's room phone and Carla clutching the satellite phone so hard that her fingers hurt.

Even the constantly voluble CIA agent didn't buzz in her ear.

She actually cried out when the hotel room phone rang, causing Fred Smith to curse in pain. It rang with a harsh bell, the likes of which she hadn't heard since she was a girl, except as a retro ringtone.

Tanya snatched at the phone, stopped, took a breath, and answered it. She listened for a moment and nodded.

Carla whispered, "Go," into the satellite phone and could hear Fred Smith relay the order to trace the call. It was hard to do while sitting on a ship a hundred miles offshore, but that was a problem for the signal intelligence folks. She just needed Estevan to stay on the line long enough for them to do whatever they did.

Tanya handed her the hotel phone, then leaned over until their shoulders were touching and she could tip her head close so that they could both listen.

The bodily contact reminded her of Kyle's shoulder against hers and she drew strength from the memory.

"This is Carla."

"Is it? Not Claudia?" Bolívar Estevan's voice was still as pleasant and jovial as ever.

"No." Would the real Empress of Antrax break her cover over the phone? Carla thought not.

"Not Claudia Ochoa Felix, who I see by her social media post is presently in a Guadalajaran nightclub?"

Had he seen a photo of the real Claudia? The woman was a Kim Kardashian look-alike; built like a brick shithouse. Far more so than even Tanya. If Estevan hadn't seen her photo, Carla could claim the woman in Guadalajara was a body double that she'd hired while out on a business expedition.

Too risky.

She could continue to deny her link with Sinaloa and Antrax. Or—

"That bitch!" Carla practically shouted for reasons she didn't yet understand. "One of these days the real Empress of Antrax is going to bury her ass. I swear it on my father's grave or my name isn't—"

"Marisol," Tanya mouthed at her.

"—Marisol Torres." Which it wasn't, so that made the swear safe.

Most intelligence reports indicated that the real power behind Sinaloa was in the hands of two quieter, far less photographed, and extremely intelligent sisters. Marisol was a good choice; she was even less visible than Luisa Marie. It was these sisters with business degrees and their father's lethal training that Estevan would have to reckon with.

Estevan tried to interrupt, but Carla continued her tirade, layering every foul phrase of gutter Mexican that Kyle had taught her on Claudia Ochoa Felix's head. She went on until Tanya pinched her sharply. Okay, maybe she needed to stop soon, so she made one final slur about the woman only getting off when she went down on her hot-pink AK-47 in a dark closet, and then shut up.

After a lengthy pause, perhaps to make sure she was done ranting, Estevan finally spoke once more.

"As I observed earlier, *señora,* you are a very passionate woman. I too am passionate about what I do. Perhaps we can meet tomorrow under less, shall I say, mutually distrustful circumstances."

"And why should I do that after today's events?"

"Because otherwise your husband will be, how do you say, rubbing shoulders with the fishes."

The threat meant to strike fear into her heart instead coursed through her body like an adrenal shot of relief. Kyle and Estevan had been speaking, and Kyle had found a way to communicate to her that he was alive by using that odd turn of phrase until Estevan had repeated it.

Rubbing shoulders.

He was still alive. Still, hopefully, in one piece.

Tanya pinched her again hard.

Estevan had been speaking and she hadn't heard a word.

"I'm sorry," Carla cut him off, "I was having trouble catching my breath. What were you saying?"

"Tomorrow at nine a.m., be at this number." His tone had not the slightest hint of friendly. Then he was gone.

By tomorrow at 0900, Bolívar Estevan was going to be sliced, diced, minced, peeled, and fed to wild piranhas. And if Venezuela didn't have piranhas, she'd fly them in from Brazil or wherever they came from. Then—

She picked up the forgotten satellite phone. "Tell me you got him."

"We have him, and it's ugly."

She was Delta.

Ugly didn't bother her for a moment.

————*————

Kyle watched Estevan walk back from the office container that he'd been called to. Unlike the one that had been his prison, this one had windows cut into the steel sides. Through the open door he could see several desks and chairs.

He'd sat quietly and nursed a glass of iced coconut milk and tea sweetened with guava. His two guards were well trained and vigilant. They sat at two different points that would allow them to fire at him without hitting either Estevan or each other.

Estevan sat back down with a contented sigh.

"Is your wife so passionate in bed? You must be a very lucky man. It is a pity I must kill both of you tomorrow."

Alive! roared into his brain.

"A pity," Kyle agreed, trying to buy time to control his emotions.

Alive, and she'd be on her way long before tomorrow. With any of their team still able to walk or crawl.

"Especially because the answer to your question is yes. She is beyond incredible." He did his best to remain in the state of poised readiness that his father had worked so hard to teach him. No tension must show. No strong emotion. No exposed thoughts that the enemy could capitalize on.

But it was hard. It was his first hint that Carla was alive. He wanted to kiss the man who had just told him they both were going to die.

And if she lived, that probably meant that at least

Chad and Tanya—who had left the church with her—did as well. And yet he'd been worried for her when she left the safety of the church. There was a laugh.

"I like you, Mister Javits, or whatever your name may be." Estevan sipped his drink as if they were discussing the latest James Bond film. "I knew I had to be cautious if your 'Carla' was indeed Claudia Ochoa Felix, because I know who is the power behind the Sinaloa curtain. Incurring the wrath of Marisol Torres is not something I would do lightly. Murdering her is an entirely different matter."

Kyle tried not to groan. No matter how they played this, it just kept getting worse. Estevan's next comment proved that he hadn't hidden his thoughts as well as he'd intended.

"I see you understand waiting and futility both. I will miss you. I thank you for rescuing my daughter. Even though I have sent her to a hospital, under very heavy guard I assure you, I know that what was done to her is not your doing. As a reward, I will give both of you easy deaths."

Chapter 27

THE SATELLITE PHONE RANG AS CARLA AND TANYA were racing toward the agreed-upon meeting point well south of Maracaibo. Chad, Duane, and Richie should have long since secured a speedboat and transferred their gear over from the sailboat.

In the last few hours, while they'd been awaiting the phone call, the wind had increased sharply and any hint of sunlight had retreated to ride out the storm somewhere happier. And less wet. The first sprinkles had suppressed the dust; the building rain was now turning it all into mud.

Getting out of the city had been tortuous. Vendors were clogging the roads. They had shuttered their stalls against the rising storm and were now trying to drag them to places of safety. Carla almost killed a spice merchant and hit three different wheeled food stalls before she managed to sling the car out beyond the core market area.

Then they'd gotten lost in the snarl of city streets: narrow, winding, and poorly lit at the best of times. The storm had chosen the moment of the quick equatorial sunset to kill off Maracaibo's dodgy power grid.

It was as much luck as skill that finally freed them from the city's vile clutches and allowed Carla to rocket south, winding around pedestrians and bicyclists who had waited too long to seek cover.

Tanya answered the phone and handed it to Carla as

she spun the wheel to avoid a group of three men. They had apparently thought the dusty front yard she had veered through to get around a truck and donkey jam was a good place to play cards and drink.

"What?" she shouted into the phone.

"We have bad news and worse," Fred Smith announced.

"Don't you dare ask me which I want first." The man was a goddamn cliché. She jumped off the curb back onto the street and drove through the middle of a soccer game. The kids scattered, but the ball was toast with a loud bang that for a moment she feared was a tire. It wasn't.

"Okay, bad news first. We're not the only drone aloft."

"And you're calling me on the goddamn phone to make me easier to trace?" How dumb was the man?

"They're out over the lake. We estimate their machine is visual, not ELINT, as it wasn't involved in the call he placed to your hotel room. Their patrol line will pick you up within miles of the dock south of Maracaibo. Worse news: we also don't have decent imagery of Estevan's operations to know what assets he has there. We never inspected it before."

"So look now."

"The bird we sent out was ELINT only; if the intelligence isn't electronic, this craft can't see it. We pinpointed his signal, but we didn't have enough payload capacity to send up any cameras."

She spotted an open stretch of road and hammered down on the Toyota's accelerator. She could see Tanya bracing her feet in the foot well as if they were about to crash.

Carla flicked on the high beams and looked into the gathering darkness. They'd driven out of the rain—at least they were moving faster than the storm—so she killed the windshield wipers. Houses down either side of the road were no longer crammed together. Still a strange jumble of pleasant and shanty, but with more space. This must be suburbs.

Nope, not toast yet. She kept the accelerator down.

"Well, get me something before the storm lands on Kyle's head and you can't see anything. And get Estevan's drone out of the sky."

"How? Our bird's a ScanEagle, not a Global Hawk or Predator. It doesn't carry any weapons."

"Ram it, Smith. Take the ScanEagle and ram it into his drone. I need a clear path. If I have to go in blind, I'll go in blind. But if I'm going in blind while he can see me, that isn't going to work."

He sputtered for a moment. "You want me to destroy a half-million-dollar UAV by using it like a battering ram?"

"*Smith!*" she shouted loud enough to hurt her own ears. "Get that goddamn drone out of my sky, or I'll come back as a ghost and haunt your ass!"

She beat the phone on the dashboard several times for good measure before hanging up and tossing it to Tanya. Then she hammered the Toyota's horn, scattering a flock of chickens feeding in the middle of her lane moments before she turned them into cutlets.

She was on her way to save Kyle, and anything or anyone who stood in her way was going down—and going down harsh.

Chad idled the boat out on Lake Maracaibo beyond the end of the assigned dock. They were meeting Carla and Tanya at the south end of the city where the eight-kilometer-wide sea access opened up into the massive, near-circular lake.

The chop on the lake was at two feet and building rapidly. He'd bet that by the end of this night, he'd wish he'd stolen something bigger. The ten-meter aluminum boat had a wraparound rubber fender like a Zodiac on serious steroids, but even so, the ride was going to be a rough one before they were done.

The towering clouds to the north were filled with lightning as they rolled over the city. The weird thing was that there was lightning to the south as well—quick flashes, high up—though the sky directly above still showed the first stars.

"Catatumbo lightning," Richie said. "That type has its own name, after the Catatumbo River. This is the only place in the world that it occurs. Very cool." He started into one of his too-much-information things that Chad had long since learned were safest to just let roll over him.

"Wait, what?"

"I know," Richie answered. "Isn't it amazing? Half the nights of the year, eight to ten hours a night, three hundred lightning strikes per hour. That's like three thousand a night."

"You dropped a digit, buddy." Duane handed around energy bars.

"You mean I picked up a digit." Richie was a nut about precision. "And, no, I didn't."

"Shit!" Chad spotted a distant set of headlights approaching their pier and kept an eye on them. "People live down there? Are they psycho?"

"It's all cloud to cloud. A couple miles up. Unless there's a storm. That brings the show down to sea level."

"Oh man!" Duane had also spotted the approaching headlights and unslung his weapon, though they were safely a hundred meters offshore with their running lights doused. "Please tell me we aren't going anywhere near that lightning craziness. I almost got hit once on a training mission in Japan. No three thousand strikes a night for this boy."

"No, we aren't going near it." Richie had something up his sleeve as he waited out Duane's exclamation of relief.

Chad kept quiet.

The car pulled right up to the end of the pier and honked its horn three times before shutting off its lights. If Carla had seen the pier in the daylight, there's no way she would have driven onto it.

"We're going right *into* that craziness." Richie sounded totally pleased. "Estevan is right up the delta of the Catatumbo River itself. Can't wait to see it firsthand."

"Fucking geek," Chad offered in a friendly fashion.

"Geeks rule," Richie agreed happily.

Chad ran them forward, fighting the chop and trying not to look at the growing storm ahead.

"A police boat?" Carla looked down at the long, powerful craft. "Don't you think that's a bit obvious?"

Chad smiled up at her from beneath the small headlamp he wore. They each wore one. They dragged the bundles of weapons they'd taken from their raid on the Hotel Castillo out of the Toyota and loaded them aboard.

"You said fast, lady. This boat has the prettiest little trio of three-hundred-horse outboards. It's rough and ready."

"Where's the rented sailboat?"

"What sailboat?"

Carla shook her head. She didn't even know why she asked.

"Oh, you mean the one we bribed the police with to look the other way while we took this one? The cash that was left wasn't enough, so we tossed in the sailboat. They're probably filing off serial numbers and repainting the hull even as we speak."

"So you basically gave the cops a brand-new drug-smuggling sailboat."

"Well…" Chad drawled at her and nodded toward Duane who was releasing the last line.

"I might have left a breaching charge down in the bilge somewhere. It should cut a pretty disastrous hole in the hull about four hours from now. Storm should be peaking over Maracaibo about then. She'll go down fast and ugly. Really hope old Freddie Smith selected 'yes' on the insurance form when he rented it for us."

Carla grinned at them. She was last to jump down off the dock into the pitching boat. As an afterthought, she tossed the keys back toward the car. Maybe at least one of the vehicles they had rented would get back to the agency.

"You guys are nasty. I like that in a team."

She high-fived each one and then she and Tanya started arming up as Chad turned the police boat south and opened up the engines with a bone-shuddering roar. In moments, they were slamming wave top to wave top on their way south.

—–∿∿–—

A guard rushed up to Bolívar where he sat with Kyle Javits-Torres at the small table beneath the gently swaying trees. The wind was already making small waves on this side branch of the Catatumbo. The storm was coming, but it would still take another hour or so to cross Lake Maracaibo, and he was quite enjoying his talk with his prisoner.

"The drone, sir," the guard panted out. "It is gone. Not crashed. One moment we had signal, the next we didn't. Not on any channel."

Bolívar Estevan was unable to suppress his curse. He did not like revealing anything in front of this calm, cool lover of the Empress of Antrax seated beside him.

Their story had checked out.

Forty-eight hours after the eradication of that bastard Major Gonzalez, they had popped up out of nowhere in Aruba as if by magic and rented a sailboat to come to Venezuela. His own people had sighted it leaving, not suspecting then who was aboard. They had called in his shore crew to intercept it. His "acquisitions" crew had radioed that they'd located and were overtaking the sailboat, then silence. They'd never been heard from again. When the sailboat showed up with a window shot out, he knew that the five who had arrived on the boat had beaten his most experienced and ruthless crew.

Then there had been the strike at the Hotel Castillo that had freed his daughter. Four bodies and who knew how many others who simply had vanished.

He, like every other person in Venezuela, had assumed it was a battle won by one faction of the Cartel

de los Soles over another. He had believed it until his
lovely, abused daughter had arrived by taxi and told him
of the beautiful woman with long, dark hair and the men
who leaped to her commands.

This Empress of Sinaloa he met at the church had
unquestionably been the same woman.

Sinaloa was a threat past imagining. And the serious-
ness of the threat was that one of the Torres sisters was
here personally. Not an emissary, not an underling thug,
but one of the sisters in person. This wasn't her research
trip for the "export" business; this was the tip of the
spear striking at the heart of his entire enterprise.

He looked up quickly as the night was riven by the
first shocks of Catatumbo lightning. Darkness that
revealed itself to night-adapted eyes, blinding bright
light, then a black so deep in comparison that the world
might have ceased to exist.

His drone had gone down before the lightning began
in that region of the sky. If his drone had failed on every
channel simultaneously, it had been shot down. And the
operator hadn't reported anyone on the lake's surface.
No one who knew the lake was foolhardy enough to
ignore the oncoming gale. The unique geography of the
lake made for brutal chop that slapped from every direction during a storm.

That meant that his drone had been taken down from
the air. The Empress of Antrax had air assets in Venezuela
and didn't want him to see that she was coming.

Well, her power was not as great as this storm. It would
soon wash the most advanced helicopters from the sky.
The compound was lit like a strobe light by three successive flashes, his men moving in jerky stop-frame motions.

Nor was Marisol's number of forces even close to his own. He had thirty fighters here in addition to the workers. He had never counted more than the five with her, one of whom sat here beside him looking up at the lightning show as if he had all the time in the world.

Six. If that Tanya Zimmer woman arrived here, then that meant she was with them rather than an innocent dupe. They would come by air, flying before the very teeth of the gale. He would be ready for them.

One thing was certain. He no longer needed the Empress's husband. She was already on her way to rescue him. He had no idea how his signal had been tracked, but the death of his drone promised that it had been.

Well, the rescue would be the death of them all. Then perhaps he would take the fight to Sinaloa for dreaming of coming into his country uninvited.

Estevan signaled his guards. "Take him down to the end of the dock and kill him. Let him truly rub his shoulders with the fishes." He liked that phrase. It was personal and reminded him of *The Godfather*.

The man didn't protest. He simply walked, head bowed, toward the water with three guards following close behind him.

It was like a stage drama in strobe light.

A lightning flash.

The prisoner and three guards close beside him.

Darkness.

Flash.

Grouped at the head of the dock.

Darkness.

Flash.

The husband turned to face his firing squad at the dock's far end. A brave fool.

Darkness.

Then a massive double-strike close by—the first of the storm-driven Catatumbo lightning to reach the ground—rattled the empty glasses on the small table by Estevan's chair.

In the aftermath of its blinding light, the man's body tumbled into the water.

The next darkness was broken by the gunfire flashes that the guards were pouring down onto him to ensure his death.

A bright flash revealed no body, then another close behind it showed the body floating to the surface well out across the lake.

Then darkness.

Chapter 28

"NEXT...TIME, STEAL...A...BIGGER...BOAT," CARLA managed to shout, each word knocked from her by the next wave top.

Richie had taken over the wheel because he was the best sailor, other than Kyle. Bastard laughed and whooped as nine hundred horsepower launched them off the top of another wave and sent them flying.

Even with the throttle wide open, it took them over two hours to reach the Catatumbo River delta.

Carla had spent ten minutes gearing up with every weapon she could think of. Spent thirty seconds double-checking that Tanya did indeed know what she was doing with her weapons selection. Without looking, Tanya took many of the same weapons Chad had chosen. Even their armament style matched.

Were she and Kyle that sappy? She reviewed what they each carried. It was a piece-for-piece match, right down to the number of spare rounds. Of course, she and Kyle had spent months debating their selections item by item during OTC, such as why they liked a Heckler & Koch stock suppressor versus a SureFire on the HK416 beyond ninety meters.

She and Tanya both grabbed for an AK-47. The rifles had a very distinct sound, which might identify them as allies of the bad guys.

Confuse the enemy.

So she handed each person one that they'd taken from the guards at the Hotel Castillo. Then Carla dumped the rest of the arsenal they'd taken from the tenth floor over the side of the police boat.

For the remaining hour and forty-five, Carla had nothing to do except hold on to a water bottle like it meant something, watch the clock, and keep it together.

The emptiness inside her was far more barren than the night. They raced barely ahead of the storm, lightning both in front and behind—which made no sense no matter what Richie said—roaring engines completely overrunning any other sound. Only the closest lightning strikes, hammering down sometimes barely a hundred meters away, crashed thunder sufficiently loud to momentarily drown out the engine roar.

Inside her was an echoing silence so vast that nothing could fill it. It was what she had felt as she'd looked down into the barren grave moments before they lowered her brother into it. If she died tonight, it would only be an outer husk that died.

If Kyle died…

Carla looked inside herself, trying to find the second half of that thought.

If Kyle died…

There was a yawning emptiness inside her far more vast than any mere chance of death.

They slowed as they came upon Congo Mirador. The town sat astride the entrance to the Catatumbo delta that they needed to penetrate. Tonight it didn't so much sit astride it as cower in it.

Carla looked at the one- and two-room tin-roofed houses perched on stilts just a meter off the ragged waters that already lapped up onto front porches. Small boats and canoes had been hauled onto those porches. As they puttered the police boat carefully down the main street of the town, only darkness greeted them.

"Hit the lights." She kept her voice low. She could feel the eyes watching them, but needed to know if they were armed as well.

Richie flipped on running lights and the big spot. It would be easy to see that they were a police boat.

Under the glare of their bright spotlight, the houses appeared to have only two colors: blue worn to a gray, and gray worn bluish. The only structure over a single story was the church's steeple made of dark, unpainted wood.

Carla took the microphone on the PA system and flipped it on.

"The governor of the state of Zulia has asked us to perform extra patrols tonight. If anyone needs help during the storm, fly a sheet from the corner post of your deck. We will be nearby. Be safe."

Tanya looked at her oddly.

"In case Bolívar Estevan has a spotter in the town, it will help to explain our presence."

Tanya's shrug matched her own assessment. Fifty-fifty that the ploy would work.

They stayed in the main channel to the east as they left the town. That would further allay the fears of any of Estevan's watchdogs. His compound lay just a few kilometers up the west branch.

At a likely spot on the west bank of the eastern

branch, they grounded the boat where it would be protected from the worst of the storm's battering.

The team and Tanya huddled in the small cabin of the boat. At that moment, the storm unleashed a pounding rain that sounded so loudly on the aluminum roof that they had to shout at each other to be heard.

Richie turned on a map display of where they were. It cast an eerie blue light across their faces. Everyone had painted their faces with broad streaks of green-and-black camouflage paint stick. Tanya and Chad pulled dark watch caps down over their light hair. The five of them positively bristled with weapons and spare rounds.

"We cross this hundred-meter island at a bearing of two-five-oh, trying not to get mired if it's swampy. There's a channel ten meters across; sentinels will be watching it for a boat. Use a log to cross, because we have no idea of the depth or current speed. Beyond that we have a complex terrain of bush and trees that will be thick with unknown personnel, many of them armed."

"Indentured workers," Tanya informed them, "practically slaves. They will be unarmed innocents and will scatter into the jungle at the first sign of trouble. But he will have many guards."

"Oh good," Chad remarked drily.

"Makes it easier," Duane offered. "Plenty of distractions for the bad guys."

"Our one surveillance photo"—Richie brought it up on the screen—"is off a mapping satellite pass from three months ago. It shows very little, a few indeterminate structures. There is a house, and Estevan will assume that to be our primary point of attack. Watch it, but avoid it. Questions?"

There was a pregnant pause from the guys that she interpreted easily. Delta had a very specific form of action when a combat situation went dynamic. A stranger, if they moved differently, might inadvertently become a target.

They were waiting for her to solve it diplomatically.

"Tanya, you stick close by Chad. You don't know our methods. If you stay by him, you'll be safe."

"Relatively," she commented.

"Relatively," Carla agreed. "One friendly is out there"—at least she hoped to God he still was—"though we can bet he's unarmed. Anyone else with a weapon simply goes down with extreme prejudice."

Chapter 29

THE NIGHT-VISION SCOPES WERE USELESS. THE Catatumbo lightning flashed and flared. Each unpredictable flash of light maxed out the sensors, and the scopes automatically shut down to protect users' eyes. The recycle recovery time was too long and would leave them even more blind than the lightning's aftermath.

Worse, visible heat signatures through the goggles could be either lightning reflected off a wet tree or an enemy poised to fire.

Movie theater. They'd practiced doing a terrorist takedown in a large theater while a movie was running. Light, dark, light, constantly changing visibility with the images on the screen.

Carla let that training roll over her and tuned her actions to match the moment.

Light: freeze, shoot.

Dark: move, pre-aim.

They crossed the stream and moved forward in a wide line.

Something blocked out the sky. The Catatumbo flashes were now dimmed beneath the forest canopy, except there weren't enough tree trunks for it to be a jungle.

Camouflage netting. Estevan's entire compound was covered with it. That's why there'd been nothing to see on the photo. Even if they'd had a bird to overfly it, there wouldn't have been anything to see except the house.

Under the netting, cargo containers, work sheds, and piled-up equipment were spread over an acre or more. It was going to be hell to secure with just five people.

Unless...

Hell, if someone was going to be nice enough to set a trap for them, why *not* walk right into it?

Carla trotted along the edge of the netting line and swept up Richie and Duane as she did so.

A brief burst from an AK-47 off to the south said that Chad and Tanya were probably occupied at the moment.

Quick signals had them in position, prone and ready to fire. They each unslung their AK-47s. They'd sound like friendlies, adding to the confusion.

In a dark moment between bursts of lightning, she popped a flash-bang and heaved it through the front window of the house. For an instant the house was brilliantly illuminated from within. Outlines of men were at every window looking out.

Richie had been right. Estevan had set it up as a trap. Kyle would be stashed somewhere else.

Time for Delta to get to work.

In moments, there were six less of the enemy.

Four more ran out into the night clutching weapons and were dropped in their tracks.

This time she tossed in an incendiary.

At the first flash of fire, three more emerged and were mowed down.

Duane sprinted up to the house and did a quick circuit, popping up to check briefly through each window while she and Richie provided cover. Twice he fired a double tap at someone inside. No point in counting how many when they didn't know the total. Fewer than they started with.

Duane finished his circuit and made a sweeping upward signal with his left hand. "Come." No more danger. Also, no Kyle about to be caught in the fire.

The AK-47 was spent. Rather than reloading, Carla dumped it and swept her first HK416 forward.

They split up as they moved. Carla chose the northernmost path and shifted five meters off-path into the lush bushes to follow it. Three combatants came running down the trail from the opposite direction as she worked her way along beside it. She dropped each one as they passed by, shooting during the flash of lightning to hide her suppressed muzzle flash and be certain of her aim.

They were all rushing from somewhere back toward the beacon of the now actively burning house. It spat up a tower of flames despite the deluge.

The rain was so thick that it was getting hard to breathe. Each intake of air included the need to suppress a cough.

Carla trotted through the brush and arrived at a wide-open area. The camouflage netting overhead muted the flashes, but not enough to make the night-vision viable. The net extended out over the water but couldn't hide the unmistakable shapes.

Conning towers rising from bulbous cylindrical decks.

She'd been right, submarines.

Three of them.

Two were still on land, one in the water.

She dumped a magazine and reloaded. A dozen men stood on or around the subs. All armed. Any workers had long since gone for cover.

Multiple rounds of gunfire and cut-off cries sounded south of her, so she was probably on her own for the

moment. Her radio remained quiet, so no calls for immediate Delta backup.

She chose a line of three stout trees and lay down
beside the first one. She pulled off her second rifle and
tossed it toward the third tree.

Deep breath. Next time she'd wear a hat with a brim
to keep the rain out of her eyes.

The wind gusts were so strong that even at a mere
twenty meters from the men guarding the submarines,
she was going to have to compensate.

Another deep breath.

Lightning flash…and go!

She fired four shots, choosing two men standing well
apart so that the fire would appear to come from several
directions. She didn't wait to see the two men drop.

Rolled to the other side of the first tree.

Dropped two more.

Rolled to the far side of the second tree and fired
from there. Then back to the leading edge of the second
tree and dropped another.

She did the same at the third tree. It would look like
there were six shooters in the trees rather than one.

In a panic, those remaining began to fire wildly.

When she rolled over her second rifle, she dropped
the first one nearing empty and began shooting with the
second one.

She worked her way back to the first tree, shoot-
roll-shoot until she'd swept the line of guards who had
frozen in place assuming they were surrounded.

With a final crash-bang of lightning—it landed so close
that the hair stood up on the back of her neck—she took
out the last visible guard before he could discover the ruse.

She waited.

She kicked out the empty magazine, the bolt having rung empty on the last shot.

Then she reached for a fresh magazine.

There was a soft click from close behind her, a safety coming off. It echoed in the sudden silence between crashing lightning bolts.

"Welcome, Señora Torres." Bolívar Estevan's voice was soft and as grim as death from close behind her.

His voice was just far enough away that there was nothing she could do before he'd shoot her. A cautious man.

Carla's Lesson Number One: *You're on your own, girl!* had just toasted her ass.

"You are a most impressive shooter. I understand why you are known as the Empress of Antrax. I regret that you must now join your husband who I had to dispose of earlier. Now you will both be rubbing shoulders with the fishes."

Carla put her head down against her gun.

Kyle.

The hard edges of the rifle's top rail and scope cut into her cheek.

Dead.

No longer an "if" statement.

She'd been too slow. Not good enough. Not fast enough.

Without Kyle…what was the point?

Was that what he'd meant when he said he loved her? That his world would be empty without her?

Maybe yes.

In which case, it was a good final thought to have in

her head when she died. Perhaps she could carry into the grave the memory of how much she loved him.

There was a flash of lightning.

Estevan gasped in surprise behind her.

Then a quiet double-spit from an HK rifle before it rang open on an empty chamber.

She was…alive.

She felt the ground by her feet shudder with the impact as Bolívar Estevan collapsed.

The shots had come from her own rifle, the one she'd left nearly empty by the third tree.

A flash of lightning revealed Kyle kneeling by the tree with the empty rifle in his hands.

A very alive Kyle Reeves.

Her training had taught her never to hesitate.

So she didn't.

She threw herself at him.

Chapter 30

KYLE REALLY HAD TO REMEMBER TO COME BACK FROM the dead more often. The perks were great.

Carla's kisses and throttlehold by both of her arms around the back of his neck were almost as powerful as the full-body impact of her flying into his arms and driving him backward into the mud.

By the time he'd untangled himself from Carla, the battle was finished. The others filtered into the clearing until they stood staring at the submarines.

The worst of the storm had blown through and only the higher-elevation lightning, now rippling and rumbling benignly across the heavens, lit the subs in successive flashes.

"I am so damn proud of you, guys." He hugged the sopping wet Carla who was still clinging to his side. She hadn't spoken yet, but she hadn't let go either, so he wasn't complaining.

"Thought you'd be dead, bro." Chad slapped him on the shoulder away from Carla.

"I was. At least Estevan thought so. I was about to try to tackle my personal firing squad barehanded when a ground-strike lightning bolt had them blinded for a moment. So I tumbled into the water and curled right back under the dock while they shot up the empty river. Then I swam well out and let myself drift to the surface. Good thing these guys didn't know to do an extra shot to make sure I was dead. Would've stung like hell."

He said it with bravado, but he'd been far more terrified when he'd spotted Estevan with a pistol aimed at the back of Carla's head as she lay helpless before him.

"You, by the way"—he kissed her temple—"were magnificent. We definitely need to add that to our training. I started swimming over from the opposite shore of this piece of the river when the mayhem began. I thought the entire team was here, not just you."

Carla squeezed him a little tighter around the ribs but didn't look at him.

Richie came over from where he'd been inspecting the subs. "You know, I think these things would actually work. And all three are already loaded."

"Loaded?" Chad looked at him in surprise. "With what?"

"Large bales of very expensive drugs. Fred Smith said around ten metric tons in each boat. So figure thirty tons total or about twenty percent of what enters the U.S. each year is sitting right here. We found their main submarine guy." He gave Estevan's expensive, Italian leather boot a kick.

"Dude." Chad high-fived Richie. "If I was still on the street, I'd be rich."

"Yeah, too bad we can't get it out of here. Only one of the subs looks finished, at least I think so. The other two don't have fuel or their electronics suite yet."

"The one in the water works," Kyle agreed. "When I was swimming in the lake, I could hear them testing the engines."

"Too bad we can't tow the others outta here and get rid of them somewhere deep."

"Richie, my man." Chad wrapped an arm around his shoulder. "You just said the magic word. C'mon, babe."

Tanya fell in beside him and they disappeared back into the woods.

Carla was still having trouble speaking. She did manage to stop clinging, but she'd be damned if she let Kyle out of her sight. She was far from over the miracle of his resurrection.

They prowled through containers and sheds, marking several for destruction.

When Chad and Tanya had pulled the *policía* boat into the backwater of Estevan's compound, they returned to the subs. Duane loaded up on charges and moved off to blow shit up. In a matter of moments, Chad had pulled the other two subs into the water where they rode comfortably, tied so that they could be towed in a line off the powerboat's stern. They wouldn't be able to go fast or far, but it would be enough to get the subs out into the lake and sink them deep.

"Too bad we won't have anything to show for it." Richie was looking at them sadly. "They're actually impressively well-thought-out craft."

"You know…" Carla knew her voice was rough, and she could still only speak facing away from Kyle. Each time she looked at him, her heart was too full to allow words to escape. She tried again. "You know, Q…" She drawled the moniker. "I'll bet that you could pilot a submarine."

It only took a moment before he latched on to the idea and was racing to the finished sub still tied to the dock to study it in more detail.

"That was cruel." Kyle came up close beside her and slid an arm around her waist.

Carla nodded. Richie would never tire of telling stories about the day he'd captained a narco-sub. They'd be living with that for a long time to come.

She turned into Kyle's arms and looked up at his eyes for the first time since he'd miraculously come back to life. By the flickering light of the now-distant Catatumbo lightning she could see how he looked at her.

That too was something she could live with for a long time.

But the words were still locked up, so she merely tucked her face into his collarbone and breathed him in. He smelled damp, muddy, and one hundred percent Kyle.

—∿∿—

They gathered for a moment around Bolívar Estevan's corpse.

Kyle felt as if he deserved a moment of silence. Another drug lord would rise up in his place, and he too would have to be beaten down, but the bastard had been a good and worthy opponent and a major kingpin.

Tanya was last to join them and wore a wicked smile. "What?"

"Found these in your kit bag." She held up an Antrax black kerchief with the silver jaw of a fanged skeleton on half of it. And, by the next fading flash of lightning, he saw that she held aloft one of the shoulder boards from his Venezuelan general's military uniform. On it was the round "Sun" pin of his pretended rank.

"Shall we confuse them out of the living daylights?"

"Timothy Dalton's first Bond film," Richie intoned. "Bond girl was Maryam d'Abo."

They turned to stare at him.

"What? *The Living Daylights*. Opium wars, bad generals dealing drugs. Maryam is pretty hot. It all works."

They turned to stare back down as Tanya tied the kerchief over Estevan's face as a declaration of who had done the deed. And then attached the sun pin right between the fangs on the kerchief.

Kyle had to smile. He wasn't sure he had a laugh in him, but it was very good.

It was an invitation to a war. Drug cartel against drug cartel right across international boundaries. The bloodbath at Estevan's compound by the hands of a supposed alliance between Sinaloa and an unknown faction of the Cartel de los Soles would change the entire landscape of the Latin American drug trade.

For the worse, if you were in it.

Chad swept Tanya into his arms to plant his approval squarely on her lips.

Kyle nodded his thanks.

"Now let's get out of this place."

There wasn't a single complaint.

Chapter 31

CHAD AND TANYA TOWED THE TWO NONFUNCTIONING subs out to the deepest point of the lake with the rest of them following in the sub that Richie was driving.

Kyle really hoped that Richie got the hang of it soon. He was improving, but they tended to yaw side to side unexpectedly, once doing a full circle before continuing forward and then nearly diving with the hatch still open.

Once they were out over the deepest part of the lake, Duane spent time aboard each of the derelicts before joining them on the operational sub. The unfinished boats were already sinking out of sight.

"I opened the ballast tanks to the lake. I rigged a thermite charge in the cabin to go first. That should burn up the cocaine or at least most of it. If someone had told me I was going to be incinerating twenty metric tons of the stuff, I'd have come better prepared."

"Twenty billion delivered, six or seven times that on the street." Chad sighed. "Now that's some walkin'-around money."

"Yep," Duane agreed, "but then you'd have assholes like us after your sorry ass. See, crime doesn't pay, bro. Anyway, after that burns for a while, around when the sub reaches the lake bottom, the small charges I set will slice each sub into about eight parts. Shouldn't see anything up here but bubbles."

"Like a giant fart." Chad sounded as pleased by that as by the idea of twenty billion cash in his pocket.

"A sweet one." Duane had to have the last word.

Tanya had been at the controls of the police boat, shuttling Duane where he needed to be with Chad as his assistant. In between, they'd moved their gear and finally all boarded the functioning sub.

She pulled up close alongside.

"Come on over." Chad held out a hand. "We can just let that boat drift. No one will care."

She didn't bring it any closer.

Carla tucked her hand in Kyle's and clamped on hard.

He turned to look at her, but she was watching Tanya with a look of pain on her face.

Oh shit! And Chad didn't see it coming.

Kyle didn't know what to do to help him.

"You are so sweet," Tanya said in that teasing tone of hers from across the watery gap between their craft. "I think you have something wonderful started here. I have many contacts other than the General and Estevan. No one still alive except you knows which side I'm on. With the right misinformation, we might really get something done here."

"No wait!" Chad was edging out as far as he dared on the curved deck of the sub, but Tanya expertly idled the boat a few meters farther away.

"Maybe next time, cutie."

She waved at Chad.

Then, after slamming down the throttle but before the engines really took hold, she blew a very sincere-looking kiss to Carla.

An instant later she was gone.

Duane moved in to console his friend and to keep him from tipping off the side of the sub into the lake.

Kyle looked down at Carla's smile as she watched Tanya shoot away across the now-quiet lake. "Any explaining you want to do?"

Damn woman only smiled and shook her head before moving over to console Chad.

Once they were below, Richie insisted on being the tour guide for "his" sub. It was broken into several compartments, none of them meant for comfort. Most of the central area was taken up by bales of cocaine. They were stacked everywhere, barely leaving slither space between them.

Richie sat on a high chair that reached up inside the conning tower. He had a dashboard of controls, wheel, foot pedals, radio, sonar. Carla had to admit that she was impressed, but she didn't look beyond that.

"Imagine their faces on the *Freedom* when we surface beside them with ten tons of cocaine." Richie was crowing, but Carla barely heard him.

There were words forming inside her. They'd be coming, and coming soon. Though she still wasn't sure what they were or what they meant, they were slowly filling the aching void inside her. Except the void no longer ached as badly as she'd grown used to.

The sub's rear compartment was filled with diesel engines and the big battery packs for when they had to run submerged, like through the channel across from Maracaibo. Chad and Duane took over engine operations right away.

The forward compartment was mostly food and two very narrow bunks to stretch out on. Hot-bunking. One person would roll out and another would roll in, sleeping in shifts.

All she cared about was that the others were soon busy with their own tasks.

The sound of the engines thrumming through the hull smoothed out as Chad and Duane worked their magic. Richie had finally gotten control of the ballast and trim tanks. The soft light of the breaking dawn, muted by the thick fiberglass of the hull, shifted as the sub sank to a lower profile until only the engine's air snorkel and a short periscope showed above the surface.

She pulled the curtain on the cramped forward area.

Finally, it was just her and Kyle.

He dragged her down beside him onto the lower bunk. They leaned back against the curved hull and propped their feet up on packs of foodstuffs. It couldn't have been more like the end of the Forty-Miler unless there was a campfire. The pressure of his shoulder against hers reassured her that it was safe to continue.

No, it was safe. Full stop.

"There was a cavern inside me."

"Guessed that."

"Shut up."

Damn man just grinned at her, cocky bastard. So full of himself and every bit of it deserved.

She thought about trying to explain the emptiness that had been the last four years of her life since Clay's death—a cavern so vast and wide that she'd become lost in it.

But now, sitting beside Kyle's quiet strength, she

understood that the only thing that mattered was how full her heart was, not how empty she'd been.

"Sergeant Kyle Reeves."

"Yes, Sergeant Carla Anderson?" Having found herself, she could happily get lost again in his voice. Every single time, even on that first day, she had trouble hearing him because she so enjoyed listening to that deep, warm voice.

She could make a life's plan out of doing just that.

What the hell, why not? She knew for a fact she would never find a better place to be than beside Kyle Reeves. Never find anywhere else that she wanted to be. If she didn't know what that meant, then she was impossibly stupid. And as she'd told Colonel Brighton, *I ain't stupid*.

Carla finally understood what had been building inside her over the seven months since she'd first rolled into The Unit's compound. And like Delta training, it made perfect sense once you'd gotten through it and could look back. Typical Kyle, he'd seen it long before she had, but she'd gotten there.

She raised her right hand.

"Kyle Reeves. I, Carla Anderson, do solemnly swear that while I may be a wild woman, I am completely and desperately in love with you and that I will, from this day forth, bear true faith and allegiance to you."

Hey, if she was going to mangle the Oath of Enlistment of the U.S. Armed Forces, she might as well do it the whole way.

"So help me God."

Kyle burst out laughing—a sound that filled the sub's chamber and filled her heart. He pulled her into his lap and held her tight in the circle of his powerful arms.

She buried her face against his neck and breathed him in, could feel his chest rumble when he spoke.

"May he help us both."

Carla breathed him in again. "It's she."

By Break of Day
Night Stalkers Book 7
by M. L. Buchman

—⁓—

NAME: Kara Moretti
RANK: Captain of the army's stealthiest remote piloted aircraft
(*don't* call it a drone)
MISSION: To be the eyes of the team

NAME: Justin "The Cowboy" Roberts
RANK: Captain of the army's most powerful helicopter
MISSION: To redeem the past, at any cost

They put life, limb, and heart on the line

Two new captains join the Night Stalkers with two different
strategies in life, love, and combat. When Brooklyn-raised
Kara joins the crew, she knows one thing as an absolute truth:
to stay safe, keep everything and everyone at a distance. Born
in Texas, Justin flies with all his heart. When Kara and Justin
collide on a secret mission deep in the Israeli desert, then the
battle truly begins.

—⁓—

Praise for M.L. Buchman:

"Like Suzanne Brockmann and Catherine Mann,
Buchman's work has catapulted him to the top of the
military romance genre pack." —*RT Book Reviews*

For more M. L. Buchman, visit:

www.sourcebooks.com

About the Author

M. L. Buchman has over thirty-five novels in print. His military romantic suspense books have been named Barnes & Noble and NPR "Top 5 of the Year," *Booklist* "Top 10 of the Year," and RT Book Reviews "Top 10 Romantic Suspense of the Year." In addition to romance, he also writes thrillers, fantasy, and science fiction.

In among his career as a corporate project manager he has: rebuilt and single-handed a fifty-foot sailboat, both flown and jumped out of airplanes, designed and built two houses, and bicycled solo around the world. He is now making his living as a full-time writer on the Oregon Coast with his beloved wife. He is constantly amazed at what you can do with a degree in geophysics. You may keep up with his writing by subscribing to his newsletter at www.mlbuchman.com.